Grasping Hope

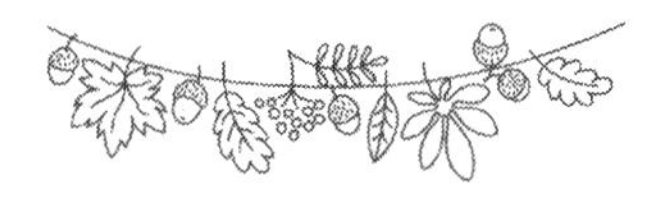

HEATHER GREER

MantleRockPublishingLLC.com

Published by Mantle Rock Publishing LLC
2879 Palma Road
Benton, KY 42025
http://mantlerockpublishingllc.com

Printed in the United States of America

ISBN 978-1-945094-76-7

Cover by Diane Turpin at dianeturpindesigns.com

For everyone who has found themselves in the fire. God sees, God cares, and God can work through this time. Don't give up. You are never alone. I pray you know where hope is found.

"This hope we have as an anchor of the soul, a hope both sure and steadfast" Hebrews 6:19a

Praying you know the hope only God can give!
Heather Greer

Chapter One

Katie McGowan set the brown paper bag on the elevator floor and reached into the outer pocket of her monogrammed purse. Her slender fingers moved aside her car keys and fished through the odds and ends inside to find her cell phone. A quick glance at the time and Katie slipped it back into the purse. She ran through her plan one last time to make sure nothing was left to chance. Nine-thirty. He had called to say he was working late, but expected to be home by ten thirty. That would give her enough time to tidy up his apartment and set the table. Hopefully, he would be on time. She didn't want the food getting cold.

As the elevator settled into place on the top floor, the doors slid open. Katie carefully picked up the bag, balancing it on both hands to keep from jostling the contents. Realizing she would need one hand to open the apartment door, Katie hoisted the bag onto her hip feeling the warmth of the takeout containers through her fitted cotton blouse. She slipped the key from her pocket and frowned as she turned it in the lock. Why was the door already unlocked? Jacob wasn't that careless.

He must have gotten off earlier than expected, because he would never leave without checking the door. Oh well, so much for a surprise. She wouldn't be able to have it all set up for him, but they could still enjoy dinner from his favorite Chinese restaurant.

Trying to keep from completely losing the element of surprise, Katie quietly opened the door and stepped into the apartment. She gasped as her hand flew to her mouth. The bag fell from her grasp, splattering lo mien noodles, egg rolls, and sweet and sour sauce on the beige carpet.

The couple, entangled in a passionate embrace, halted their forbidden activity. They hadn't expected an audience any more than she had expected the show. A raven haired woman looked over the naked shoulders of the man sharing the couch with her. Katie recognized the haughtiness in those eyes. Fury warred with disbelief in Katie's mind as she saw the woman's eyes light with victory over being found with her lover. Maybe she'd expected or at least hoped for an audience after all.

"Wha, um, what? Why?" Katie's ability to think and speak betrayed her as well. She closed her mouth realizing the futility of trying.

The man scrambled to right himself on the sofa, no easy task considering two were occupying the same narrow space. As she watched his clumsy movements, Katie fought against the tears that burned behind her eye lids. She refused to let her hurt add to the woman's pleasure over the situation. She'd taken enough from Katie already. Instead, she kept her attention on the man who had hastily grabbed his pants from the floor, turning to face her as he finished zipping them. Katie wanted to scream. How could Jacob let this happen?

A wave of nausea swelled up inside Katie as their eyes locked. Those eyes. Those beautiful grey-green eyes didn't belong to Jacob.

Katie forced her eyes open. Every muscle in her body trembled, as if overtaken with the deep chill of winter. But that couldn't be. The real cold of winter hadn't descended on them yet. Besides, sweat coated her body under her light cotton sheet making her sticky. An invisible vise held her chest in a merciless grip as Katie furiously tried to suck air into her lungs with quick, shallow breaths. Each passing minute left her feeling more light-headed. Katie's heart beat against her ribs in a frantic attempt to escape her chest. She stared into the inky blackness surrounding her, but instead of seeing nothing, the phantom images from her dream played on an endless loop in her mind.

Desperate to find comfort, Katie tried to focus on her hand and the ring that circled her finger. Though the lack of light in the room kept her from seeing it, she could feel the cool metal and weight of the solitaire against her finger. With her right hand, she twisted the ring around and around, reassuring herself that it had only been a dream.

Oh, Lord, Katie cried to the only one who could hear her at this hour, the one who could calm her frantic mind and tame her runaway emotions. *Not Austin. Please, God. Not Austin.*

The tears she refused in her dream now soaked her pillow. Austin's shame filled eyes haunted her. Why couldn't she force those eyes from her mind? Austin and Mariah. Only it wasn't supposed to be Austin.

"It wasn't Austin," Katie scolded herself between panting breaths. "Austin is not Jacob. Austin would not ever. He couldn't. Oh, please, God, don't let it be Austin too."

The pain of catching her first fiancé in his infidelity rushed back in on Katie with ferocious intensity. Even when she had gone back to him, believing him sincere when he promised he had changed, the sting of his betrayal would still sneak up on her when she least expected it. When she realized Jacob's changes were only superficial, Katie had been devastated. God had used her helplessness and the pain Jacob had inflicted to bring her back into His loving arms and eventually her home town. Secure in her renewed relationship with God and His love for her, Katie's heart healed enough to accept the friendship Austin offered her and later his love.

A little less than three months later, while she and Austin enjoyed the cool fall air and a picnic on the cliff that served as his own private sanctuary and the backdrop for so many of their "moments", Austin proposed. The princess cut solitaire had sparkled with the fire of the sunset as he held out the tiny black velvet box, waiting for her answer. Not even the radiant fall colors could compete with the token of his love. The yes had slipped from her lips with ease. No shadow of doubt marred the beautiful moment. No hesitation in her answer. Katie knew only joy and peace and love as Austin took the ring from the box and slid it onto her finger.

No, the specters that haunted her dreams hadn't materialized immediately. When they had appeared, they weren't as they were now, visceral images reducing Katie to uncontrollable panic. There was an occasional shimmer of fear or a tiny whisper of doubt that could easily be pushed away. Now, a month into their year-long engagement and with wedding planning well underway, Katie found the fears crippling. Instead of growing quiet, the doubts were screaming in her ear.

At first, Katie simply ignored their plaintive cries for attention. They tended to come out at night, and sleep would close their mouths. Daylight hours brought much needed clarity. Time with Austin reassured her of his faithfulness. The doubts fled in the face of his love, leaving Katie in peace for a moment. As they demanded more time, Katie would pose questions and make comments to Austin designed to elicit calming responses without cluing him in to the battle going on inside her. Now, she could do nothing but clench her fists as she willed herself not to sob. Her doubts were ruthless in their invasion of her sleep, taking her body captive to their whims. How did one fight their unconscious mind? There was no way to guarantee her dreams would be free from the nightmare they had become. And if her dreams weren't content to show the nightmare as it really happened, if they insisted on twisting reality to induce even more doubt and fear, how could she deal with the resulting panic?

"God, help." Even that phrase was enough to steal what was left of the air in her lungs.

Austin and Mariah. Together. The images were vivid in her mind. But it was a dream. It was only a dream. Austin would never. He didn't even know Mariah. But he did know other women. No. No, Austin wouldn't. But if a woman needed help, pastoral help? It could start innocently. He could have gotten in over his head. Maybe Austin . . . no. Austin didn't cheat. It was Jacob. Jacob and Mariah. Jacob cheated.

"Oh, God." Fragments of thoughts whipped through her mind, and she couldn't grab hold of one long enough to deal with it once and for all. In tandem with her emotions, the resulting onslaught felt like the fury of a hurricane she couldn't protect herself against. "I can't do it, God. Lord, help me, please."

Austin's guilty eyes. Mariah's hateful brown ones.

"I will lift up my eyes to the mountains."

Two bodies with nothing between them. A new wave of nausea.

"From where shall my help come?"

Ragged breaths. But were they her breaths or theirs? No. No, it wasn't true.

"My help comes from the LORD, who made heaven and earth."

But it wasn't him.

"I will lift up my eyes to the mountains. From where shall my help come? My help comes from the LORD, who made heaven and earth. I will lift up my eyes to the mountains. From where shall my help come? My help comes from the LORD, who made heaven and earth."

Katie couldn't have told anyone why that particular verse came to mind, but she had no doubt as to Who put it there. Her panicked heart had cried out to her Father, and He had answered in His mercy. Katie whispered it into the dark room. Her pulse started to slow down. Again she whispered the verse. Her breathing returned to normal. With each repetition her mind closed the door on her tortured thoughts a little more until all the remnants of her nightmare were contained. Emotionally and physically spent, Katie should have been susceptible to her panic returning, but peace took root in her heart instead. As she continued to meditate on that single verse, her fatigue took its rightful place causing her to drift off to sleep, undisturbed, for the rest of the night.

Chapter Two

"Why didn't you tell me he was coming?"

Katie blinked at the high-pitched hysteria and pulled the phone away from her ear. With her free hand, she rubbed the sleep from her dry eyes. Her mouth stretched open in an unfeminine way as a yawn forced her to suck in more air than her lungs could hold. After blowing out the excess to return her lungs to normal capacity, she spoke. "Would you mind telling me what you're talking about, Erin?"

"What in the world is wrong with you? Are you sick or something? You sound awful."

Blunt as usual. "Tired. A phone call from a maniac spouting gibberish into the other end of my phone woke me up."

"Woke you up? It's ten o'clock in the morning. Are you feeling ok?"

Katie grinned at the concern in her best friend's voice. Katie had never been a morning person, but she rarely slept the morning away. "I'm fine. A dream woke me up in the middle of the night, and I couldn't get back to sleep last night."

Erin laughed. "Oh please spare me the sickeningly sweet details of your romantic dream starring your knight in shining armor. I don't need to hear about how even dreaming up your love left you too excited about your wedding to get back to sleep. If only I had the problems of the happily engaged."

Katie's voice was dry. "It wasn't exactly rainbows and sunshine that woke me up. More like a horribly realistic nightmare."

"Wanna talk about it?"

Katie considered the offer. It could help, but the idea of dredging it all up again after successfully containing it was too much. "No. I don't want to think about it, much less talk about it."

"Sure?"

"Positive. Now what am I supposed to have forgotten to tell you?"

Katie cringed as Erin squealed. "You, my supposed best friend, failed to warn me that your hunky store manager is coming to town."

"If I failed to tell you, how did you find out?"

"He messaged me to see if I wanted to go for coffee or something this weekend while he's here."

Katie finger combed the bed-head tangles out of her auburn curls. "Where's the problem? Paul told you he's coming. So, why am I in trouble again?"

Katie shook her head as Erin growled dramatically. "The problem is that he's going to be here today. To-Day. And I only found out last night."

"Still not seeing the problem."

"Katie! Really? In your engaged bliss have you forgotten how hard the dating game can be? I have to go get my nails done AND find a new outfit for our date."

Katie bit the inside of her cheek to rein in the sarcastic retort trying to escape. She had learned early on that Erin's friendship came with a "handle with care" warning in regards to snarky remarks. There were times and places when she could handle it, but letting loose in times like this would only hurt Erin's feelings.

"It's going to be ok, Erin. Paul's coming to go over some work stuff, and it will take a chunk of his time this weekend. Besides, he's not supposed to be here until this evening. You've got time . . ."

"Oh, that's perfect, Katie! I'll be there in thirty minutes."

Confused, Katie was not sure what she had just suggested. "Umm . . . okay. But, why are you coming over?"

Erin giggled. "To pick you up, silly. You and I are going to Nail Bliss to get our nails done, and then we'll stop by Kohl's to see if I can find a new outfit. I want something cute and trendy, but not too much. It's just coffee, and besides, it will be our first date. I don't want to overdo it."

"Of course not." Katie rolled her eyes. "I'll see you in thirty minutes. Don't bother knocking. Just come on in."

Katie hung up the phone and moved to her bathroom for a quick shower. The grit in her eyes convinced her that cool was the way to go, and she shivered as she turned off the water minutes later. "There is never a good time for taking cold showers," she muttered, her teeth chattering as she wrapped a fluffy towel around her for the dual purpose of drying and warming herself. "Erin better appreciate my sacrifice for her perfect date."

Moving to the kitchen, Katie put a pod into her coffee maker and slid a clean mug into position to catch the steaming liquid. Glancing at the numbers glowing on her microwave, Katie realized Erin would arrive in less than ten minutes. Momentarily forgetting her coffee, Katie hurried to her room to change. She threw on the closest pair of boot-cut blue jeans before sniffing the fitted t-shirt hanging on the back of the chair by her desk. Good enough. Katie pulled it over her head and snatched the comb from her dresser grimacing as it snagged on the tangles in her wet hair. She dabbed on a light lip gloss before giving herself a brief once-over in the mirror.

As she headed to the kitchen, her sleepless night caught up with her. The cap sleeves on her shirt rubbed the skin under her arms, irritating her. Katie tugged at the sleeves to no avail. She huffed as she headed back to her room. She had experienced this too many times to ignore it. Stress or fatigue always seemed to make her intolerant of little physical annoyances with her clothing. Her next two choices were equally unacceptable with one collar feeling tight around her neck and the other shirt sitting too snugly on her hips. Realizing her only option was throwing out any desire to dress stylishly in favor of complete comfort, Katie pulled a hunter green V-neck men's t-shirt out of her closet.

Katie inhaled its scent as she slid it over her head. It was Austin's shirt, and the smell of his cologne clung to the fabric despite its having been run through the washing machine. She took comfort in the familiar scent. She had almost refused when Austin had insisted she change into it after she had dropped a huge forkful of his homemade lasagna on her own shirt during a recent candlelit dinner at his house. She was glad she hadn't. The scent calmed, and the loose cut didn't offend her frayed nerves. It would be perfect after her rough night. Katie finger combed her curls then went to retrieve her coffee from the kitchen. She doctored it to her liking and took a sip. Before she could take another the front door opened.

"In the kitchen," Katie called to her friend.

Erin frowned. "I can't believe you. Here I am feeling guilty for dragging you out for a girls' day after your rough night, and I come in to find you looking like this." Her hand waved up and down the height of Katie. "I need to know your secret, girl. It doesn't matter what you do or what you wear, you're always tall, thin, and gorgeous. My stumpy self can't even hope to compete."

Katie smiled behind her mug before taking a sip. As she set her drink on the counter, Katie shook her head at Erin's theatric compliment. "You're not that short, and you have the perfect figure for it. Besides, Paul doesn't seem to mind your stumpy self."

Katie watched Erin's cheeks turn pink above the dimples creasing her cheeks. "Do you really think so?"

"I know so."

Katie learned early that Erin's exuberant personality was like makeup to cover doubts about herself. It had been difficult for Erin when she realized Austin only had eyes for Katie. But God protected their friendship during that time, and she would always be thankful for that. The situation had, however, reinforced Erin's unfounded ideas that she was the lesser one in their relationship. Katie prayed the budding romance between Paul and Erin would help her see herself as the perfectly put together person God created her to be.

Erin still looked doubtful. "Paul wouldn't have called and asked you out if he didn't really want to. He's not like that."

Katie watched as Erin brought her hand up to her mouth and toyed with her lip. "You're right. I think Paul just might give Austin a run for his money in snagging the Mr. Perfect title. Anyway, are we going to get our nails done, or are we going to stand here gabbing all day?"

Katie glanced into her coffee cup. The amber liquid rested half-way up the side. Resigned, Katie took one last long swig before pouring the rest down the sink. "Let's get going then."

She grabbed her purse hanging on the coat rack by the door and turned the lock on her way out. A day spent with Erin was always a whirlwind of activity and girl talk. Hopefully it was what she needed to pull herself out of the funk her dream had put her in.

Two hours later, Katie realized the futility of her thinking. On the drive to the nail salon, Erin talked incessantly about how Katie and Austin needed to double date with her and Paul while he was in town. At Nail Bliss, Erin didn't stop with simply trying to guess Paul's favorite color for her nails. Nope. She insisted on knowing Austin's favorite color so she could help Katie find the perfect polish for her nails as well. After spending forty-five minutes in Kohl's trying on what seemed like an endless collection of clothes to find the perfect outfit for Erin's date, Katie was nearing her limits.

"I'm serious. You should really try to find something new to wear for Austin."

Katie crossed her arms over her chest. "My clothes are fine."

"Of course they're fine. But that doesn't mean they couldn't be better. Something new is always nice."

"Aren't we here shopping for your date? Let's just concentrate on that."

Erin rolled her eyes and pouted. "Come on. You're no fun. Your nails look awesome. And what about that double date? You could really wow Austin with a new blouse or sweater."

"The ones I have are fine."

"What about this?" Erin suggested as she held a fitted, royal blue button up blouse in front of Katie for inspection. "I think it would look great with your red hair and green eyes. Oh, and we could pair it with a simple black pencil skirt and some black heels. Austin won't be able to take his eyes off you. Why don't you try it on while I look for the skirt?"

Katie blew out a frustrated breath as the last vestiges of her patience fled. "No, Erin. I don't want to try it on. I didn't want to try on the last one you suggested, and I'm not going to want to try on the next one you find, no matter how perfect it is or how much Austin would love to see me in it. We're here to shop for your date with Paul, and I wish you would just find what you want and leave me out of it."

A twinge of guilt pricked at her conscience at Erin's crestfallen look. She opened her mouth to apologize but promptly shut it. She pushed the conviction from her mind. She had nothing to feel badly about.

"Whatever," she muttered. "I'll be waiting in the car when you find what you want."

Refusing to make eye contact, Katie spun around and headed towards the door. Pride kept her shoulders straight and head up as she made her way through the parking lot to Erin's VW bug. Only when Katie dropped into the passenger seat did the storm of emotions finally erupt. Guilt, fear, and exhaustion joined forces to crumble her defenses. Her tears, once started, would not be stemmed. Caught in her own tumultuous emotions, Katie didn't register Erin joining her in the driver's seat.

"Katie," Erin's quiet voice broke through. "What's going on? Did you and Austin have a fight or something? Talk to me, please."

Katie's sniff filled the small car's interior. Without raising her head from her hands, she answered. "No. We didn't fight."

The warmth of Erin's hand seeped through the material covering her shoulder. "Come on, Katie. Don't tell me nothing is wrong. I have eyes. Something is most definitely wrong. You're my best friend, and I don't like seeing you like this. You know you can trust me."

Katie nodded, still refusing to look up. "Yeah, I know. It's just . . . I'm not exactly sure what's going on. It was a stupid dream, but I can't shake it."

"Your nightmare? The one that kept you awake last night?"

"Erin, I know it's crazy. But it was so real. It doesn't feel like a dream, but I know that's exactly what it is."

"Why not share it with me? I'm not trying to push or pry, but you need to get it out in the open where you can deal with it."

Katie raised her head, leaning it against the headrest. She stared at the gray felt stretched across the roof of the car. It wasn't surprising to find the images playing across this new screen as clear as they played in her dreams. Katie took a deep, shuddering breath.

"Do you remember what I told you about me and Jacob? I mean why we broke up the first time?"

"Sure. He was cheating on you." The words, spoken matter-of-factly, sunk like a knife into Katie's chest.

She turned her head to look at Erin. "Yeah. That's what happened, and I was devastated when I found out."

"How did you find out? Did he suddenly grow a conscience

and confess or did the other woman tell you to get you out of the way?"

"I found out when I went to his apartment to surprise him with dinner. I caught him and Mariah on his couch. It's an image that is burned into my memory whether I want it there or not."

"I can see why it would be. But you're not with Jacob any more. I don't understand why dreaming about him would cause this kind of reaction."

Katie sighed. "Because it wasn't Jacob. It was Austin."

Erin's brows knit together. "Austin? I'm not following. Austin cheated on you? When did this happen? Why are you still with him?"

"No, Austin didn't cheat, not really. It was the dream. It happened just like it did with Jacob. Visiting his apartment. Catching them on the couch." Katie shut her eyes, but it did nothing to hide her mind from the memories. "I can still see Mariah's face looking at me over his shoulder. The dream felt as real as when I caught Jacob. But when the guy looked at me, it wasn't Jacob. It was Austin."

Katie looked at Erin who sat beside her shaking her head. Something akin to pity was reflected in her blue eyes. "I'm so sorry, but you know it was only a dream. Other than God himself, you're the most important thing in Austin's life. He would never do that to you. He's not another Jacob. He loves you."

Katie gave a tight-lipped smile as she nodded her head. "That's the hard part." Erin frowned. Katie took a breath and started again. "I know Austin is nothing like Jacob. Austin has never given me any reason to question his faithfulness to our relationship. He's a good, godly man. I KNOW these things. But it didn't stop the panic when I woke up in the middle of the night. Erin, I couldn't think. I could barely breathe."

"How often has this happened?"

Katie shrugged. "It didn't start this way. When we first got engaged, little things I heard or saw on TV or whatever would remind me of Jacob. I'd wonder how he could do it. I'd wonder why I never saw it coming. Then, I'd find myself doubting whether I had any discernment at all. And if I don't have discernment, where does that leave me now? If I wasn't equipped to see it then, how can I believe that I would see it now?"

Erin's hand covered hers. "Oh, Katie. I can't imagine what that feels like. I mean, I think everyone has doubts about the person they're with at times. Or I guess more about their ability to be what the other person is looking for. But to have gone through something like Jacob put you through and then try to move on with someone else only to have the past haunting you. It's awful. But you're not the same person you were then."

Katie used her free hand to brush away a tear. "My relationship with God is the only thing that's different. And that has nothing to do with whether or not I'm going to be enough for Austin."

Erin sat back in her seat. "Of course it does. Trust me. It's not easy when you struggle with self-doubt, but you belong to God now. Your worth doesn't come from anyone but Him. You don't have to measure up in the eyes of other people. It's not your job to be enough for anyone but God. And He says because of Jesus' blood, you are enough."

"But what if Austin doesn't see it?"

Erin bit her lip while considering her next words. "I can't promise you that he always will. I wish I could, but no one can ever promise that. All we can do is be the kind of girlfriends or wives that God calls us to be in scripture. If we are who God wants us to be, we have nothing to be ashamed of."

"That's easier said than done."

"I think you'd be hard pressed to find a woman who didn't agree with that. And I'm not sure it isn't harder for us than for the men in our lives. Personally, I think it's part of the battle of the sexes that was started in the garden of Eden."

Katie considered her friend's words. She loved her bubbly, carefree friend. This was a side she'd not seen before, and it made

Katie realize how special their friendship was. "Have I ever told you how awesome and wise you are?"

Erin glared at her from across the seats.

"I mean it. I know what you're saying is true. I'm just not sure how I can get my heart to believe what my head knows."

Erin turned to look out the windshield as she put the key in the ignition and brought the small car to life. "I don't have an answer for you on that one. And don't think I have it all figured out either. If you'll remember, we just spent the day preparing me to be the woman of Paul's dreams. I'm not sure exactly where that falls on the 'don't try to measure up to other people' scale."

Katie chuckled. "I guess we all have a ways to go, huh?"

Erin nodded. "Just promise me you won't try to do it alone. Keep talking. To me. To Austin. To anyone. I don't care what time it is or how stupid it feels, just call. Promise me, Katie."

She swallowed. Erin wouldn't be content until she'd gotten that promise, but Katie wondered if she was making a deal she couldn't keep. "I promise."

"Good. Now, let's get you home so you can get some rest before you meet with Paul."

"I THINK we're just about done here," Katie said as she stretched her hand across the desk towards Paul.

Paul took his boss' hand and shook it. "You can't imagine what this means to me. Thank you. You've been more than fair."

Katie couldn't help smiling. "You deserve it, and I hope it's everything you're hoping it will be. Besides, you're kind of doing me a favor. Don't ya think?"

"Maybe it goes both directions?"

"I can agree to that." Katie was careful to keep her expression bland as she continued. Now that their business was completed, a little teasing never hurt anyone. "So, you want to do something tonight? I mean, you're not from the area, and you don't know many people. I would hate for you to be stuck in your hotel room without anything to do or anyone to talk to tonight."

Paul ran a hand through his sandy blonde hair. "I would, but, well, I mean, I guess we can. Sure."

Katie laughed at his unease. A look of confusion crossed his face before realization took its place. He groaned. "You've been talking to Erin?"

"I'm sorry, Paul. I just couldn't pass up the opportunity. Yeah, Erin told me you're going out for coffee. But I want to hear from you. Is there anything I should know?"

Paul looked like a school boy caught passing notes to the cute girl across the aisle. "Erin and I have talked a few times since you moved back down here. When I knew I was coming down, I asked her if she might like to meet me for coffee or something. No biggie."

"Hmm. I'm sure you're right. It's not a big deal. That's why I spent the better part of my day shopping for a new date outfit and getting a manicure."

Katie had Paul's full attention. "Did you really? So, she's looking forward to it? Do you think coffee's ok or should we do dinner or something? I mean, I really enjoyed getting to know her when I helped you move, but I wasn't sure if she felt the same way. Do you think she does? Feel the same way, I mean?"

"Here's a novel idea. Why don't you ask Erin how she feels and leave me out of it? You two are worse than high school crushes." Her tone was full of pleasure at the thought of her two closest friends hitting it off. Of course, she wasn't about to admit it to either one of them.

Katie stood from her desk. Paul followed suit before Katie continued. "Now, I don't want to keep you from this all important coffee date. We'd better get out of here, or I won't hear the end of it."

As he held the door open for Katie, he turned to her with a wink. "You're the boss."

"Not anymore. You just signed on the dotted line. No take backs."

Paul laughed. "I wouldn't dream of it. I know a sweet deal when I see it."

She slid past him and into the parking lot. "Are you going to tell Erin today?"

He shut the door and moved out of the way so she could lock it behind him. "I would love to, but I don't want to step on your toes. It's my business, but it's also yours. If you don't want me to, I'm fine with that. It can be your news."

Katie shook her head. "Absolutely not. It will give you guys something extra to celebrate." She walked across the asphalt covered ground to her Jeep. Her hand paused on the door handle. She turned to face the parking spot next to hers. "Hey, Paul?"

He stopped with one leg in his little Versa and looked at her. "Yeah?"

"Do you think it means anything that I'm completely ok with this? That I don't even feel like it's a bittersweet situation?"

Paul rubbed his chin as he considered her question. "No." His hand slid across his chin to the hair at the nape of his neck. "I'd actually be surprised if you didn't feel some relief. You've gone through a lot the last couple of years, and you're in a good place now. Other than me, this is the last thing tethering you to Bloomington." He lowered his head to duck into his car before raising it back up with a smile. "And don't even think there's a chance that you're going to get rid of me. I'm not going anywhere."

Katie smiled. The reminder of their growing friendship encouraged her. "You may not have a choice. I know a feisty little blonde that may end your life completely if you don't get out of here and go pick her up."

One eyebrow raised in mock concern for the situation. "You're probably right. I'll see you later."

Katie watched him slide into his car and start it up before getting into her own. As she backed out of the space and headed home, she couldn't help feeling free. "Thank you, Father," she prayed in the otherwise empty car. "I know your hand is in this, and I thank you for the opportunity." Her thoughts traveled to the surprise Erin would have on her date. Imagining the over-the-top squeal of excitement that would threaten Paul with deafness, Katie couldn't contain a happy giggle of her own. "God, you are so good. Bless my friends and this new beginning."

Chapter Three

"You look beautiful tonight."

While driving separately to the small fifties themed cafe had not been Erin's idea, Paul's look of adoration as she approached the table made it worth it. She flashed a sweet smile as he stood and pulled out her chair. "Thank you."

Erin pushed a straight strand of hair behind her ear, her eyes never straying from Paul as he reseated himself across from her. "How did things go with Katie today? Did you get all your business taken care of or is this going to be all I see of you this weekend?"

"If you think unfinished business would keep me from seeing you again, then you have seriously underestimated how much I've been looking forward to getting to know you."

Erin looked away from the seriousness in his gaze. The table top was a safer place to focus her attention. She hoped he missed the flame that covered her cheeks. After taking a brief moment to try to cool the heat, she raised her eyes to meet his. The boy-next-door grin on his handsome baby-face convinced Erin she hadn't hidden her embarrassment at all. "I've been looking forward to it too." Her reply was barely above a whisper.

Erin noticed a twinkle in his brown eyes. "Have you now? Let me guess." He pointed to the hand she rested on the table, but before he could continue their waitress approached.

"Hi there. I'm Kendra, and I'll be your server tonight. Can I start you off with something to drink?" She held a well-used order pad over the white apron protecting her uniform. The red and white striped shirt-style dress with its white sleeve cuffs and lapel could have been plucked from a long-gone era, right down to the scarf tied to the side around her neck. It matched the décor creating an experience of nostalgia mixed with quirkiness, making it one of Erin's favorite places. She did wonder whether or not Paul would enjoy it though.

Erin watched Paul smile politely at the woman before looking to Erin. "I know we came for coffee, but I have to admit, I'm thinking an old-fashioned chocolate malt might be more fitting. How about you, Erin?"

Erin glanced back at the waitress. She kept glancing from her to Paul and back again, making her long blond ponytail swing furiously behind her. "Make it two chocolate malts, please."

She nodded. "Be right back with those malts."

Once the waitress was a safe distance away, Paul turned his attention back to Erin. Lips pressed tightly together did nothing to hide his desire to laugh. His obvious struggle caused Erin to widen her eyes in false innocence. "What's the matter?"

He shook his head. "How does she do it? I thought for sure that pony tail bobbing back and forth was going to swing around and smack me in the face. I can't imagine how she goes all night with it doing that."

Erin giggled at the picture he created. She shouldn't have. His smile grew wider and took on an impish quality.

"That's got to be a health hazard. I can't imagine how many waitresses get whiplash from their hair swinging back and forth like that every night. The worker's comp claims have to be astounding. Honestly, it makes me wonder if that's where the guy came up with the idea for bobble heads."

The combination of his dramatic voice and picturing their waitress as a bobble head was too much for Erin. She didn't even try to stop the laughter that burst out. She had barely made headway towards controlling it when the server in question brought their malts. Erin mumbled a quick thank you and turned her head to look out the window, avoiding the eye contact she knew would make her loose the modicum of control she had managed.

The waitress set paper wrapped straws on the table beside the frozen treats before heading back to her spot behind the Formica covered counter. Erin worked to calm her giggles before looking back at Paul. He sat sipping his malt with wide eyes. She wasn't fooled. His picture of innocence was contrived. She flashed what she hoped was a disapproving look.

"You may as well drop the act. You've given yourself away already. You are going to be a bad influence."

He brought a hand to his chest in disbelief. "Your words hurt me, Erin. I have done nothing but show concern over the well-being of bobble headed waitresses everywhere. I'm a crusader."

Erin rolled her eyes. "Whatever you say. You're a regular hero. But we have gotten completely off topic. You were telling me how you think my day went before we were interrupted."

Paul sat back from his malt. "It doesn't matter. I was just going to tease you about how you and Katie spent your day shopping and such. But this discourse on the dangerous hairstyles of the fifties has been so much more enlightening and worthy of our time. Don't you think?"

"It has definitely been something. Not sure I would jump straight to enlightening. Entertaining, yes. Worthy? Maybe not so much." Erin took a sip of her malt before continuing. "But since we don't have to cover the subject of my shopping habits now, how about you tell me how your meeting with Katie went. I assume you were telling her what an awesome and capable manager you are in the Bloomington store while she's living hours away in Carbondale?"

"Well, while it is true that I'm an awesome manager, I'm way too humble to make a point of it. In fact, that's part of what makes me so great. But that wasn't the reason we met. It was a little more exciting than that. At least, I think it's exciting. I guess, it might not be to you. Then again, maybe it will be. I don't know."

"Would you just tell me already?" Erin reached across the table and shoved his arm.

"You are looking at the new owner of Pages Book Store in Bloomington, Illinois."

Erin squealed. "Oh my goodness! I can't believe it. Are you serious? Katie sold you her store? Is that what you two were meeting about today? This is so exciting. How could you keep this quiet the whole time we've been here? Weren't you just ready to explode with excitement?" Another squeal punctuated the end of Erin's breathless verbal expression of joy.

Paul laughed. "If you'll slow down a minute, I might be able to answer at least one of your questions. Let's start with, yes, I am serious. And as a bonus, yes, I'm beyond excited. I've been praying for an opportunity like this, and God has given it to me in the last way I expected."

"What do you mean?"

Paul shrugged. "Pages is all Katie. Sure, Jacob helped her market and grow it, but the idea, the dream is all Katie. I was shocked when she called me up asking if I would be interested in buying it. I never dreamed she'd sell."

Erin tucked a lip between her teeth. "I hadn't thought about Katie's part in it. I wonder what prompted her desire to sell the store she always dreamed of owning?" Erin's eyes slid shut as her earlier conversation with Katie came to mind. "Oh, no."

She opened her eyes to find Paul looking at her with open curiosity. "Oh, no, what?"

Erin looked down at the table top as she fidgeted with the napkin in front of her. "It's nothing. Don't worry about it."

"That's not going to work with me, Erin. You're worried about something, and I'd like to know what that something is. Katie is my friend too. If something is wrong with this deal, I need to know." Stubborn silence. "Erin, look at me please."

Erin raised her eyes to his without really looking up. "It's fine, really. It's only, well, I can't get into it. I'm sorry, Paul. It's probably nothing. It's just happened so suddenly. I hope Katie's thought it through."

Paul frowned. "Sudden? It was far from a quick decision. Katie and I have been discussing the sale for the last few months. Discussion started right after she returned to Carbondale. She wasn't completely decided then, and I didn't push it. But it's been months since she first approached me with the idea to sell me the store."

Relief spread through Erin. *Thank you, God.* The prayer was silent, but no less heartfelt. Her fear that Katie was selling as a knee-jerk reaction to the panic she'd been feeling recently was misplaced. And she didn't have to break Katie's trust to get her reassurance. "Oh, I guess I misunderstood. I get it now."

Paul was not to be put off. "That's not going to work either. Something had you worried. What's up?"

Erin shook her head firmly. "It's nothing related to the sale of the store. I see that now, and I'd appreciate you dropping it. I know Katie's your friend too, but that doesn't mean she wants all her business spread out in the open for everyone to know. Please respect that." The last words were a quiet plea.

"Is there anything I can do to help?"

"Pray. Just pray."

"Always."

Erin's smile came easily once she realized Paul wouldn't push the issue. His reassurance that the store was not being sold prematurely didn't erase the need Erin felt to check in with Katie, but for now she put her questions aside to focus on getting to know the man sitting across from her. "So, what changes do you have in mind for the store to make it yours?"

Paul rested his elbows on the table, clasping his hands in front of him before propping his chin against them. "You know something? I don't really know. I mean, I've always thought about it. From the day I was hired I would think about how I'd like to do this or that. In the last several months, the temptation to do so was even stronger. I think I fought it though."

"Why is that?" Erin sipped from her malt as she waited for his answer.

Paul pushed his own malt away from himself and toyed with the straw. "I think I was afraid to. I prayed that if it was God's will, the deal would happen. But I think I was hesitant to believe it could be His will. I didn't want to presume, and I guess trying to flesh out my plans felt a little like telling God I had his will for me all figured out."

"But you know now." Erin gave Paul what she hoped was a look that conveyed equal parts challenge and reassurance.

Paul nodded as a hesitant smile formed on his lips. "You know something? You are completely right, Erin. The store is mine now, and it's time for me to figure out what I'm going to do with it."

Chapter Four

"You're going to tell me what I want to know, and you're going to do it now before the boys show up."

Katie stared at her usually easy going friend like she'd lost her mind. She'd expected Austin when she opened her front door. Instead, Erin stood on the other side with arms spread open at her hips and her bright blue eyes radiating curiosity. "I thought Austin and I were meeting you two at the park."

Erin left Katie standing in the empty doorway as she moved into the house. Confused, Katie shut the door and turned to find her friend plopped down on the sofa. "I'm waiting. Now start talking."

"I'd be happy to, if I knew what in the world you're referring to?"

Erin flipped a lock of straight blonde hair from her eyes. One finely shaped brow rose in doubt. "Don't give me that, Katie McGowan. You know exactly what I'm talking about. Without one word to me you sold your store in Bloomington to Paul, and while I'm thrilled that he's getting the chance to do this, I'm not convinced your motives are good. I want to hear your reasoning from your mouth, and if you don't do it now, the guys are going to walk in on us talking. For that matter, does Austin even know about the sale?"

Katie joined her friend in the living room, but nervous energy kept her from sitting. Instead, she planted herself in front of a window and pushed the flimsy curtain aside for an unobstructed view of the front drive. Contrary to her friend's warnings, Katie had no intention of discussing this matter in front of the guys.

"Well?"

Katie's glance flitted to Erin before turning back to the window. "Well, nothing. When I came back home from Bloomington, Paul agreed to watch the store for me. He's been great, but almost immediately, I felt like God was moving me in a different direction. I considered opening another Pages here in Carbondale, but it didn't feel right. The hole I saw in the book industry in this town wasn't in the mainstream books. You've got a major chain store and a family owned store across the road from each other. What you don't have is a Christian store. There are others in the area, but none in Carbondale. I'm still praying about it, but I believe that's the niche God wants me to fill. A book store that is also a ministry to the families and churches in the area."

Erin crossed her arms and speared Katie with a look that dared her to mislead her. "So, this has absolutely nothing to do with the anxiety attacks?"

Katie shook her head. "No. This decision has been a long time in the making. I just didn't want to discuss it before I had finalized things with Paul. It was his business to tell, not mine. And in answer to your other question, yes, Austin does know about it. He's totally supportive of By the Book."

Erin grinned. "Buy the Book? Isn't that a little blunt?"

"By, B Y. Not B U Y. Like live your life by the book, the Bible. I thought it would be an interesting play on words."

"Oh, that's so cute! And since I know this isn't some crazy reaction to your panic attacks, I'm happy for you. This is so exciting for both you and Paul. And I want to know everything."

Katie let the curtain fall. "Everything will have to wait. The guys are here. Come on."

Katie didn't wait for Erin to catch up before heading out the door. She knew Erin would lock it as she followed her.

Katie watched Austin pause beside the hood of his Ford F-150 as he noticed her and Erin coming to meet them. His short, light brown hair was styled with a just rolled out of bed tousled look, and his grey-green eyes crinkled at the corners as he pulled a lopsided grin. Katie couldn't help the flutter in her heart. She loved that boyish look as much as she loved the man himself.

As she neared, Austin reached a hand out to pull her close. He planted a kiss on her lips in greeting. "Hey, babe. I guess you two are ready? Why the change in plans?"

Katie shrugged. "Just gave us time for a little girl talk."

"Should I be worried?" Katie looked to where Paul stood on the opposite side of the truck with Erin beside him.

Erin swatted his arm. "Of course you should be worried, silly. Shouldn't men always be worried when women get together to talk?"

Paul put his hands up in mock surrender. "I refuse to answer on grounds that it might incriminate me."

Austin laughed. "Good answer." He motioned to the row of seats in the extended cab. "Now, since Paul has already called shot gun, you ladies get the back seat. Besides, men need more room to stretch out."

Katie rolled her eyes. "Oh, please. Paul's legs are a good four inches shorter than mine, but we won't argue about that. We'll just sit in back and tell secrets all the way to the park."

Paul offered his hand for balance as Erin stepped up into the tall truck. "Well, Austin, you've done it now. Mark my words. We're going to pay for this one." He shut the door and climbed into the front seat where Austin already waited.

Austin laid a hand on his shoulder. "I'll let you in on a little secret, Paul. With these two around, there's always something to pay for. Better get used to it."

Katie was sure the open mouthed look of indignation on Erin's face mirrored her own. A quick look into the rearview mirror revealed a self-satisfied smile on Austin's face. He knew he had gotten them both in one try. She nodded her acquiescence to his trumping them, this time. He lowered his eyes and backed out of the driveway.

KATIE SAT with her back to the front window of By Sweet Design bakery. Erin and Paul sat on either side of her making flirty conversation as they waited for Austin to return with their drinks.

The hours they spent hiking at Giant City Park were definitely cold, but Katie and Austin felt good at having shared their favorite trail with Paul. Their constant movement kept the winter chill at bay, and the time was filled with friendly banter no one wanted to end. They decided to extend the good times with a drink from the coffee bar at Austin's bakery.

Katie watched as Austin skillfully mixed four iced mocha lattes for them. Lucy, the college student Austin hired several months earlier, was taking care of the paying customers, but Austin was too conscientious to ask her to make theirs as well.

Katie sighed. *God, what did I do to deserve a guy like him?* Katie watched as a young woman came up to the counter, passing right by Lucy to stand across from Austin. Her long, straight black hair resembled soft silk. Her short, shirt-style dress over leggings with boots that were more cutesy than practical, gave the impression of youth. But she wasn't too young to be able to catch Austin's attention. She couldn't hear what the woman said, but Austin turned and gave her a polite smile. As he continued mixing their lattes, he nodded in the direction of their table. The young woman turned. Katie dropped her eyes quickly as if listening to the chatter of the couple flanking her. She quickly looked back up to find the woman's attention back on Austin.

Lucy started towards them, but Austin shook his head and raised a hand to stop her. She turned her attention to the other customer at the counter while Austin listened to what Katie could only assume was the woman's order. Katie's eyes narrowed as she watched the woman comb a strand of hair behind her ear and bat her dark, full lashes.

Katie's throat tightened. Her breathing seemed to catch momentarily as her nerves put her stomach into knots. Austin seemed oblivious to the woman's wiles, but it was not for lack of trying on her part. Katie couldn't look away as the little minx's flirting came out full-force in a flirtatious giggle at something Austin said. It worked to draw his attention from the mundane task of filling her order. Or maybe it just coincided with his finishing of the task. It was difficult to tell from across the room. Whatever the reason, Katie's stomach threatened revolt as she watched Austin smile at the woman who took it as a positive signal and covered her smile with her hand in fake shyness. As she took the to-go bag from Austin, she was careful to "accidentally" brush his hand with her fingers before flashing one more smile meant to encourage him to think about her long after she left. Only she didn't leave.

Katie had to will her body to bring air in and out of her lungs at a normal rate. She could feel her insides begin to quiver and knew it was only a matter of time until the shaking reached the surface where everyone could see it. She lowered her gaze to the table. *Dear God*, she begged. *Please don't let this happen in public. Not over something as stupid as . . . that.* She lifted her eyes to the unwanted scene only to find it less than comforting.

The woman hadn't let up, and Austin seemed to be returning her attention. She chided herself. No, Austin was being a professional. It was his business, and he was taking care of a customer. She'd done it hundreds of times herself. Austin was simply being polite. That's all. He couldn't help the woman's misplaced attention.

Katie closed her eyes against the scene in front of her only to have her mind conjure her dream images with potent realness. She swallowed a lump forming in her throat as she opened her eyes to stare at the table top. She flinched as a hand covered hers.

"Katie?"

Erin's quiet voice was her undoing. Katie blinked back tears. Her own voice was barely audible. "I . . . can't. I've got to go."

Without waiting for a response, Katie fled from the table into the ladies' room.

ERIN LOOKED from Katie's retreating back to Paul. His confused eyes were wide. Erin sighed and offered a weak smile.

"What was that about?"

Erin shrugged.

"Oh no you don't." Paul shook his head, his eyes fixing Erin in her place. "I've never seen Katie like that, but you don't seem all that surprised. I think you know exactly what's happening, and I'm asking you to tell me."

Erin looked down the now empty hall leading to the restrooms as she debated her options. Katie trusted Erin with her secret, but her relationship with Paul was in its infancy. Would it hurt her chances with him if she refused to tell him what she knew? And if she told, would Katie ever be able to trust her again? Would Erin even be able to live with herself if she broke her best friend's trust?

Erin's heart did a flip in her chest as she turned back to Paul, seeing worry in his eyes. "I'm sorry, Paul. I do know, but I can't tell you right now. I can't do that to Katie. Please, try to understand."

Erin tried to look confident as Paul searched her face. Inside, she could feel herself shaking. The nervous energy transferred to her hands which she began wringing without thought. The seconds crept by before Erin felt the warmth of his hand covering hers, stilling the anxious movement she hadn't realized was happening. Worry kept her from smiling at his understanding, but she appreciated it nonetheless.

"Thank you." She looked back down the hall. "Now, if you'll excuse me, I need to go check on Katie."

KATIE HEARD the light tapping on the heavy wood door. "It's taken."

"It's Erin."

"I'm fine."

"You open this door right now, or I'm going to Austin."

Katie cracked the door open. "You wouldn't."

Erin grinned. "No, I wouldn't. But I did get you to open the door. Now, are you going to let me in there or not?"

Katie stepped back and moved toward the far wall. Erin entered, closing the door behind her. Katie rested her hands on the white porcelain sink and watched Erin watching her in the mirror that hung behind it. The silence was heavy.

Erin leaned against the wall. "You can't keep it from him forever."

"He doesn't need to know. It's getting better."

Erin snorted. "Don't lie to me. It's getting worse. You weren't asleep in there. You weren't dreaming. If I were a betting woman, I'd say this was brought on by the not so subtle hair flips and batting eyelashes. You couldn't seem to take your eyes off what was happening at the counter."

Katie thrust her arms out, fingers splayed. "So what? I've got things under control. No one else needs to know."

"Too late for that. Austin may not have seen it, but you put on quite a show for Paul."

"You told him?" Her voice sounded high, almost hysterical even to her own ears.

Erin's head cocked to one side. Her look was almost impatient. "No, I didn't tell him. I told you I wouldn't, and I keep my promises. But he saw your reaction. He has questions. He's worried about you. He's going to need some answers, and he's not the only one. You need to tell Austin. He loves you, and he deserves the truth."

Katie combed her fingers through her curls in frustration. "Why can't I just get this under control? I don't want it to be like this. But I can't stop it no matter what I do."

Katie covered her face as her tears began. She felt Erin's arms slip around her. "Have you prayed about it?"

It didn't matter that her friend's voice was soft and gentle. The words and the meaning they carried ignited sparks of irritation and futility in Katie. She pulled away. "Of course I've prayed about it." She watched Erin flinch at her harshness, but it did nothing to influence Katie's tone as she continued. "I pray about it all the time. It doesn't do any good. I've read books. I've read articles online. I've read every scripture, and focused on 'whatever is true, noble, right, pure, lovely', and everything else. I've done it all, Erin. And none of it helps. So what's the problem? I'm not doing it right? I don't have enough faith? I've failed God, so now He's not going to help me?"

Erin's brows lowered. "God doesn't work that way."

"Really? Because from my vantage point, it doesn't seem like He's working at all." The wide-eyed shock on Erin's face convicted Katie immediately. She shook her head. "I'm sorry, Erin. I didn't mean that. I know faith doesn't treat God like a genie granting my every wish. God is working, even in me, even with this mess. I'm just tired of feeling like a flunky of the faith who can't even pray with the faith of a mustard seed to get through this."

Katie leaned the back of her head against the paneled wall of the bathroom. She stared at the ceiling tiles, not really registering their existence. A sigh escaped from deep within. Her eyes slid shut, and she didn't try to open them even when she felt Erin's hand on her forearm.

"I'm so sorry you're going through this." Erin's voice told Katie she was close to tears, feeling Katie's pain as her own. "I wish you weren't. It's not fair that Jacob's cheating is still messing you up like this. But you have to believe me. I don't think any less of you because of what you're going through, and Austin won't either."

Katie frowned. "I wish I could believe that."

Erin's shoulders drooped. "Believe it about me or about Austin?"

Katie shrugged, wishing she could be honest without hurting her friend. "I know it's what you want to feel. But I've seen it too many times in Christian circles. People don't take kindly to it when prayer and time in the Word don't wrap up every problem and finish it off with a pretty bow."

"I can't speak for other people, but I don't feel that way. God is bigger than anything we face, but that doesn't mean the answers come easily. Prayer is powerful. Scripture does strengthen us and help us understand God better. But there are some struggles that just take time."

Katie knew that Erin believed what she was saying, at least in theory. Only time would tell if she could believe it once it became part of day to day life. Katie bit her lip as she considered the uncharitable direction of her thoughts. Erin was a friend, her best friend. And she deserved the benefit of the doubt.

"So what do I do to pass the time without destroying everything I have?" Katie lowered her head from the wall so she could look at her friend.

Erin shrugged. "I wish I could tell you. The only thing I know for sure is that you shouldn't keep it to yourself. It's bigger than you are, and you need to tell Austin."

Katie huffed. "Yeah. Sure. Telling him is the one thing I can't do."

Erin rubbed her palms down her face in frustration before holding them open in front of her. "Oh come on, you can't be serious. Austin needs to know."

Katie shook her head. "If Austin thinks I don't trust him, it's over. And, as strange as it sounds, I do trust him."

"Fine, don't tell him. But you can't hide it from him forever. If Paul can see there's something wrong, don't you think the man you're marrying will be able to tell too?"

Katie walked to the sink and flipped the handle up. Cupping her hands under the warm stream, she filled her palms before splashing the water on her face. She ripped a paper towel from the holder and patted her face dry before looking at Erin through her reflection in the mirror behind the sink. "Let's just hope love stays blind until I get this thing under control."

She walked to the door and grasped the handle. "Now let's get out there before the guys start wondering what's happened to us."

She opened the door and walked out with Erin following close behind. A quick look around the bakery confirmed that the chatty Cathy customer had taken her purchase and left. Austin was standing by the door, flipping the sign to closed. That meant his employee had either left or was in the back cleaning up. Paul sat at the table where they had left him. His gaze flicked between Katie and Erin as they walked up.

"Everything alright, ladies?"

Katie gave him a smile she didn't feel. "Everything's peachy."

She amped up her smile when she felt Austin's arms come around her waist. She leaned her head to one side to accept a kiss on the cheek. "Where did you two go off to for so long?"

Katie felt Erin's panic-filled eyes on her. Not one easily flustered, she patted Austin's hands where they rested on her middle. "Just a little girl talk."

Austin loosened his hold on Katie and stood back, crossing his arms in front of his chest. One eyebrow rose into a peak over amused eyes. “More girl talk, huh?” He looked at Paul before returning his attention to Katie. “I’m not buying it? What do you want to bet there wasn’t talk about any girls, Paul? I’m thinking the subject of discussion may have revolved around people with a little more testosterone.”

Paul stroked his chin in mock thought. “Are you thinking of anyone in particular? Maybe a couple of good-looking, charming fellows. Modern-day knights in shining armor, perhaps?”

“A couple of real princes, to be sure.”

Both men raised their chins in playful smugness. Erin rolled her eyes. Katie laughed, coaxed out of her funk. “We were discussing real life, gentlemen, not fairy tales.”

“I think she just besmirched our honor, good sir.” Austin touched his splayed hand to his chest.

“We shall just have to prove ourselves chivalrous with good deeds,” Paul said as he moved to the door. “Let me begin with a small act of selflessness.” He pushed the door open and waved the girls through.

Erin and Katie shook their heads as they walked through the open doorway. Katie groaned. “Wonderful. Now they’re going to spend the rest of the day trying to prove how great they are.”

Erin laughed. “If we just admit now that you’re both very chivalrous, even better than the knights at the round table, can you guys let it go and end this charade?”

The men looked at each other. Austin shrugged. Paul’s eyebrows lifted in question. They spoke in unison. “Sure.”

“Great,” Erin said. “Now we can get on with our day like normal human beings.”

Austin cleared his throat. “Not quite yet. You haven’t actually said anything at this point.”

Katie looked to Erin who nodded her agreement. “Fine. We agree that Austin and Paul are the most chivalrous people to ever act chivalrously. If you were to look up the word in the dictionary, we are sure that pictures of Austin and Paul would accompany the definition."

Erin looked to the men. "There. It has been said and agreed to. Now can we get back to normal?"

"Whatever you say," Austin agreed. "Just don't think we'll forget this any time soon."

Katie laughed as Erin rolled her eyes and commented. "We wouldn't dream of it."

Chapter Five

Austin watched as Katie walked from the front door to join him on the couch. Paul and Erin had just left, and for the first time all day it was him and Katie. She snuggled in beside him as he put his arm around her shoulders. With the push of a button, the credits to the movie they had finished watching went black. He sighed. He hated to do it with Katie so relaxed next to him, but it had to be done.

"So, are you going to tell me what was going on today?"

She stiffened but didn't move. "I don't know what you mean."

"Don't lie to me, please."

She pushed away from him, and Austin saw fire in her green eyes as she glared at him. "Are you calling me a liar?"

Careful. Austin could see fear under the surface of her reaction, though he had no idea what Katie was afraid of. It was clear, however, he had just inadvertently put her on the defensive. He had to tread carefully or lose this chance to get whatever was gnawing away at her out in the open. He cleared his throat. "No. I'm not calling you a liar. But I am saying there is something going on that you're not telling me. I could see it today at the bakery."

"We told you, girl talk."

Austin shook his head. "And I'm telling you, Paul might believe that, but I know you better than that. You were upset about something, and I'd like to know what it's about."

Katie's arms crossed in front of her chest. Austin saw it as an act of defiance and protection. It was a warning to back off, but Austin couldn't make himself do it. His brows rose in question as he waited patiently for her answer. "Well?"

"Well nothing. There isn't anything to talk about."

Austin was skeptical. "There's nothing to talk about, or there's nothing you want to talk about?"

He watched her gaze drop for a moment before she glared back at him. The accusation he saw in her eyes was evident in her voice as she responded. "Why are you pushing this? If I say it's nothing, can't you just accept that and move on?"

"Katie . . ."

Her auburn curls swung from side to side as she shook her head. "No, Austin. I think you should go."

"Katie?"

She refused to look at him. "I mean it. You need to go."

Austin waited to see if she would change her mind. *God, what is going on here? I don't know what I've done, and it doesn't seem Katie's going to fill me in.* He watched her as he prayed, but she was immovable in her decision. She wouldn't even look at him as he stood from the couch. He had strong doubts that she even glanced up as he walked away from her, grabbed his coat from the coat rack and headed out the door.

As he made his way to the truck each step was weighted with confusion. Had he been wrong to try to get her to open up? There had never been secrets between them. From the day they met, Katie had always been able to share whatever was on her mind. The amount of trust they had enjoyed as their friendship grew had been tested when Katie returned to Bloomington with Jacob, but that was behind them. God had allowed that wound to heal quickly after her return to Carbondale. Besides, that had been his wound to heal, not hers. She had never stopped trusting him, and he couldn't help wondering what was causing her to doubt him now.

He arrived at his home without really knowing how he'd gotten there. He had been consumed with his questions the whole way home. He muttered under his breath in frustration as he unlocked his door. He knew the questions, but the answers were far from him. Had he done something to cause this change? He went to his bedroom and flopped down on his bed. His mind replayed everything it could come up with over the last few months. He considered when he started noticing the changes in Katie, but for the life of him, he couldn't determine a single incident that could have caused her to stop trusting him like this.

Eventually, the questions exhausted Austin, and he fell into a restless sleep.

KATIE FOUGHT the urge to answer Austin's questions. But why should she? If she wanted to deal with this on her own, she should be able to. She let that thought fuel her decision to remain stubbornly silent and eventually to tell him to leave. It was almost too much for her. Austin loved her, and he wanted to help. But Katie knew the whole issue was silly. He would see it that way too. Besides, no matter what Erin said, Katie couldn't quite shake the feeling that Austin would be devastated to learn that after all they had been through, she didn't fully trust him. What would happen if he realized even a small part of her questioned his faithfulness?

As she heard the door click shut, Katie almost gave in and ran after him. Only the thought of seeing his eyes filled with hurt because of her doubt gave her the strength to remain in her seat. Long after she heard his truck pull away, Katie sat motionless exactly where he had left her. Afraid of what she would do if she allowed herself to cry, Katie pushed back the feeling when her eyes started to fill. She had to stay strong. It was for his good. As soon as she could figure out how to defeat this crippling doubt, things would go back to normal.

Normal? Was she lying to herself? Telling him about her doubt was unthinkable, but Katie couldn't ignore the blaringly obvious. She'd asked Austin to leave and refused to share with him. There was no escaping the knowledge that her decision would cost her. Damage had been done. She didn't have to see it to know the hurt that would be present in his eyes. She'd seen that look before. That pain and confusion was there the night of their first kiss, the night she'd decided to return to Bloomington with Jacob, leaving him behind without explanation.

The memory broke through Katie's defenses, and her tears began. Answers didn't come. Peace was elusive. Her pain and confusion robbed her of her ability to pray. Every time she tried, she found there were no words adequate to express herself to her Father. Instead, her sobs remained uninterrupted except for ragged, gasping breaths until they left her exhausted. Only one question badgered her as she drifted off to sleep. Would Austin have been better off without her?

Chapter Six

Katie rubbed her eyes and shook her head in an attempt to clear the fog from her mind. A relentless buzzing pulled her from sleep. But how had she ended up in her room? No, first things first. The buzzing had to stop. She looked toward the sound as her groggy mind finally registered that the offending noise came from her cell phone. She had set it to silent and never switched the ringer back on.

The buzzing stopped before Katie had time to reach for the phone. Not really caring who was trying to call, Katie lay back and closed her eyes. Just a few more minutes wouldn't hurt. Her breathing deepened and she felt her limbs grow heavy. She groaned as the buzzing began again.

"I might as well forget it," she muttered as she sat up, reaching for her phone. Austin's name flashed across the caller id. She tossed the phone next to her on the mattress, wishing she could as easily push aside her guilt at refusing to give him the answers he asked for. He deserved her trust. He deserved answers. But Katie didn't even understand what was going on. He wouldn't understand it any better than she did. It was better to figure it all out first. Then she could make it up to Austin. At least, that's what she kept telling herself.

A quick glance at the clock beside her bed told Katie it wasn't the right time for working it out. She and Paul were supposed to meet at the bank about the sale of the bookstore, and she was running late.

Katie had barely made it to the bank in time for their meeting, but with business concluded, Paul decided it was time to address whatever was going on. "You look horrible this morning."

Katie's glare was as sharp as her words. "Well, thank you for keeping that opinion to yourself until we finished our business."

Paul ignored her sarcastic tone. "It must be something in the southern Illinois air. Austin looked miserable this morning too. Interesting coincidence, don't ya think?"

The glare deepened. Paul waited patiently for her answer, unruffled by her prickly attitude. He was staying with Austin while he was in town, and the man had looked like death warmed over before Paul left for the bank. He hadn't had the chance to question Austin, and he wouldn't anyway. He and Austin weren't close enough for Paul to feel comfortable prying. Katie was another matter entirely.

"What did Austin say?"

Paul allowed a slight grin before he forced his expression to remain bland. He knew curiosity would get the better of her. And Katie had just handed him confirmation that there was something going on. Paul shrugged. "Nothing. I didn't ask. But he looked awful. And it sounded like he tossed and turned all night."

Paul could hear Katie's irritation in her tone. "You won't bother him for personal information, but you have no such qualms about digging into my personal life?"

"That just about sums it up. What's going on?"

"And if I tell you it's none of your business? Are you going to run to your new girlfriend and drag the answers out of her?"

Reason told Paul that Katie's reaction was self-preservation, but it still irked him. "Listen, Katie. Tell me or don't. But don't insult me. I'm not some teenage girl who needs the latest lunchroom gossip. I'm your friend, and I know something's wrong. I've seen it more and more since I got here. Whatever it is, I know you think you've got it under control, but you obviously don't. I'm offering a listening ear and maybe some help to take the weight from you. If you don't want that, it's your decision."

Katie's jaw was set as she stared silently at him. Paul waited for an answer, an acknowledgment of what he'd said. The silence was uncomfortable between them. When it became clear that Katie wasn't going to answer, Paul sighed with a barely perceptible shake of his head. "Have it your way. I'm here if you want to talk. I'll see you later."

Without waiting for a reaction, Paul turned and walked to his car. Katie was still standing like a statue on the sidewalk when he pulled out of the parking lot.

KATIE SWALLOWED hard and closed her eyes. How dare he? The ink on the contract for the sale of her store wasn't even dry, and he was stomping off in a fit. Of course, maybe she had brought it on. Then again, didn't she deserve her privacy? Why should she unload to him? Besides, he was staying with Austin. It could slip out when he least expected it. True, she knew better than to insinuate that Paul only wanted to know for knowing's sake. Paul wasn't that way. He'd supported her through some of her hardest times. He had been there when she finally found her faith, and their friendship had grown from that moment on. Maybe she should tell him.

She opened her eyes in time to see Paul's car pull out of the parking lot. First Austin. Now Paul. Neither was speaking to her at the moment, and Katie couldn't really blame them. She probably wouldn't speak to herself either under the circumstances. They were her friends, but she couldn't muster up enough trust to share what was bothering her. The weight of her secret pressed in on her chest.

She sniffed and raised her fingers to her cheek, wiping away a tear. "Oh, God, what do I do?" Silence. Maybe God wasn't talking to her either.

Fighting the hopelessness that threatened to consume her, Katie got in her jeep and drove. Tired of silence, she flipped the knob on her radio. She drove aimlessly down the main highway and out of Carbondale. She had no place to be. The noise of the radio didn't begin to drown out the hurt and questions, but she left it on. It was better than nothing.

Tears streamed down her face as she followed Highway 13 East, and they hadn't stopped when she turned right onto 148. Not as familiar with the road that would lead her to the tiny town of Goreville, Katie almost turned back. But right now, getting lost didn't seem like such a bad thing. Besides, she knew the landmarks to watch for. Turn right at the little convenience store and follow the backroads home. Home. It sounded peaceful, but Katie knew it didn't hold peace for her tonight. Every nook and cranny would serve as reminders of the tension between her and Austin.

Her phone buzzed on the seat beside her as Erin's image alerted her to the caller's identity. With her eyes on the road, Katie answered using the hands-free device Austin had gotten her shortly after they started seeing each other. A deep breath to fortify her emotions, and she was ready. "Hey, Erin."

"Don't you 'hey Erin' me like nothing is going on. I'm sitting outside your empty house after having a very interesting conversation with Paul. I don't know where you are, but you are coming straight home. It's time for a talk, whether you like it or not."

Katie harrumphed.

"Don't take that tone with me. I'm not taking no for an answer. You will come home, and we are going to get this worked out before you push everyone who loves you so far away you won't be able to find them when you come to your senses."

Usually the most laid back person she knew, Erin could be a bulldog when the mood struck her. It looked like she managed to push all the right buttons to unleash her tenacity. Even if she didn't get home until midnight, Katie knew Erin would be waiting. "Fine. I'm on the backroads between Goreville and home. I'll be there in fifteen minutes."

"Goreville? What were you doing in Goreville?"

Katie slowed to accommodate a sharp curve in the road. She came back up to speed only to slow down for another sharp curve. "I'm just driving. It's been a long day. I needed to think."

Another sharp curve before Katie's jeep popped over the top of a hill. Katie gasped as her first view of the blacktop in front of her revealed a deer standing only feet in front of her mesmerized by her headlights. Everything in her screamed to swerve, but these back roads were too narrow and edged with deep ditches or trees. Brake! No, it was too late for that.

Sirens penetrated the empty darkness that engulfed her. But in this place void of light there was also silence. Couldn't she stay in the quiet for a little while longer? It wasn't exactly peaceful. It simply was. For a brief second, the sounds seemed to win. She tried to lift her eyelids. Slivers of light sent shooting pain through her head. Never mind. She didn't need to open her eyes. Besides, each eyelid weighed a ton. It was easier to keep them shut and stay in this place of nothingness. Finally, relief from the haunting dreams and the voices incessantly pushing her for answers she didn't have.

Chapter Seven

Katie's sense of smell woke first, and she didn't like what it told her. The air was too clear, sterile, and dry. It was tinged with the unmistakable scent of facilities dedicated to medicine. Ugh. A hospital. What was she doing in a hospital? It had to be a trick of her imagination. She was . . . what was she doing? She went to the bank with Paul. They fought. She drove. But what happened after that?

Katie forced her eyes open. Their grit almost convinced her it wasn't worth it, but she had to get some answers. Being awake was the only way to make that happen. Her eyes adjusted quickly as someone had the foresight to dim the lights in the room. She saw Paul first where he leaned against the far wall, his arms across his chest. Still angry, but he was there. The worry trumped anger in his eyes. A hand sliding up his arm drew Katie's attention to Erin standing beside him. She had been so happy to get them together, but now she wondered what kind of force she'd have to deal with when they ganged up against her. And if things weren't worked out quickly, Katie had no doubt it would come to that.

Katie felt the warmth of a hand covering her own on the stiff white sheet. She turned her head only to have it swim. She shut her eyes until the motion stopped and reopened them to focus on Austin sitting beside her bed, leaning in close. His smile was relieved but tired. "Hey, Sweetheart. How're you feeling?"

Katie opened her mouth but found it feeling like someone had stuffed a bag of cotton in it while she slept. Instead of being able to ease his worry, the spasms that wracked her body as she coughed caused something near panic in Austin's eyes. Of course, it did nothing for her either. Sharp pain seized her rib cage, stealing the air she needed to take in. Trying to calm her coughs, Katie pointed to the plastic pitcher and cup on the movable table near the end of her bed. Austin quickly filled a cup and handed it to her. The tepid water felt wonderful as it forced the prickly feeling in her throat to subside.

"I'm ok." Her voice was hoarse, barely a whisper, but she had answered. She laid her head back against her pillows and closed her eyes. The coughing fit had taken more energy than she would have expected, and it left her with a headache. Or maybe the headache was already there. It was hard to tell at this point. Every part of her body ached. If she could rest for a minute, Katie was sure everything would be better.

"You've had us a little worried, Katydid."

Her dad's voice, trembling with worry and age, came from somewhere on the other side of her small room. Weight settled in her already aching chest. She knew the concern she would find in her parents' faces, but she knew she needed to reassure them. Learning from the last time, she kept her eyes closed and turned her head in the direction her dad's voice had come from. Slowly, she opened her eyes giving herself time to adjust to the light and focus. Her parents were sitting next to each other in uncomfortable looking hospital chairs. Both tried to force a smile, but neither was successful.

Katie cleared her throat. "Mom, Dad, you shouldn't be here."

A spark ignited in her mother's eyes. "And just where else would we be? We get a call from Erin that you've been in an accident. Had to wait until we got here to find out anything. And then, you're unconscious from the moment we get here. And you think we would be anywhere else but right here by your side?"

Her dad reached across and patted her mom's hand. "Now, now. Our little Katydid has been through enough. No need to get worked into a tizzy. I'm sure she's just worried about us too. She's not thinking like a parent. She doesn't understand it would be impossible for us to be anywhere other than here."

Her mother's shoulders released from their rigid line. Katie had yet to determine the extent of her injuries. Maybe she was wrong. Maybe her parents did have reason to worry.

"What's wrong with me?"

Her father answered. "That doctor said you've got a couple bruised ribs along with a lot of other bruising. But there's no broken bones. And they're treating you for a . . ."

She waited wondering what the rest of the diagnosis was, but her father struggled to think of the word. What could be so wrong that he was unfamiliar enough with it to forget the name?

Her mother leaned towards him. "It was a concussion, dear. They're treating you for a concussion."

"Oh." A concussion wasn't that bad. Why was her dad struggling to come up with that one? She'd thought maybe there was something seriously wrong with her, but doctors knew how to treat concussions.

"They said your memory might be hazy or even gone in regards to the accident. Do you remember what happened?"

Katie tried to think. Her mind felt like mush. "I met with Paul at the bank. I went for a drive. Did I wreck?"

"Yes, but don't you worry about that none. You're jeep's in the shop already. It'll be right as rain before you know it. Until then, your insurance got you a rental."

Her jeep was in the shop. Good to know, but she hadn't been worried about it. She'd have to be able to keep her thoughts in line enough to be able to worry, and right now they were a jumble. If she could only sleep a little bit more. She closed her eyes.

"I'm just going to rest for a minute." Without waiting for an answer, Katie slipped into sleep.

AUSTIN GAVE Paul the key to his apartment and accepted another comforting hug from Erin before turning to go resume his vigil beside Katie's bed. Though he wouldn't leave yet, he had encouraged the couple to head home and get some rest. He'd already convinced her parents to go home, promising he wouldn't leave Katie's side. But there was nothing to do at the hospital except wait and pray. Paul and Erin could do both from the comfort of their own beds. For him, it was different. The doctors had assured him that Katie was fine, and he believed them. But he couldn't handle the idea of Katie waking up alone. So, he sat in silent prayer that her healing would be quick and complete.

A quiet moan from Katie pulled Austin from his prayers. He looked expecting to see her beautiful green eyes looking back at him, but once she'd succumbed to sleep after her first time awake she'd not opened them again. She mumbled something unintelligible. Austin grinned as he watched her sleep.

One decipherable word erased his grin. A rock settled in Austin's gut and cold seeped through his body. It was as clear as if she'd been awake, and Austin didn't know what to make of it. She was asleep. She was dreaming, and logic told him Katie couldn't control her dreams. But it didn't matter. He rubbed his hand through his hair, sitting back in his chair. *God, what does this mean? Am I overreacting?*

Austin tried to tell himself it was nothing to worry about. But Katie had been acting so strange lately. She was distant emotionally before she even began pushing him away physically. They hadn't spoken since she told him to leave her house. And from what Paul had shared with Austin, Katie had been keeping him and Erin at arm's length too. Could this be the reason?

The desire for answers was overwhelming. Austin reached out to wake her, but drew back before touching her. Her need for rest was obvious. It was selfish to even consider waking her. Katie's body needed to heal, and Austin told himself he would just have to be patient and wait. He worked to distract his mind. He tried prayer, but it circled around to his worries. Austin reached into the bedside table and pulled a Gideon's Bible from the drawer. It took less than a page for him to realize he had no idea what he was reading. Frustrated, Austin tossed the Bible onto the bed and laid his head on the edge of the mattress. He drew in a deep breath, holding it for a moment before slowly releasing it. No good. The pressure was still there. All he could do was wait. Wait for answers. Wait to find out why, in her dreams, Katie had called out for Jacob.

KATIE WOKE FEELING MORE RESTED than she had the first time. Maybe she could manage to stay awake for a reasonable amount of time. Her body ached, but her head wasn't pounding as relentlessly as it had been. It was time to assess her injuries. Her ribs were wrapped. That was right. Her dad said she bruised them. Her muscles ached, and she noticed air bag burns on her arms. Other than that, she seemed to be in one piece. Looking at the blue sky peeking through the slats in the window blinds, Katie realized she must have slept through the night and well into the next day. She groaned as she looked at the clock on the far wall. Even sick she never slept that late. Her parents were missing from their chairs. Good. They needed their rest. Paul and Erin were no longer stationed by the door, but Katie grinned as she realized she wasn't alone. The chair next to her bed was not empty. Austin had stayed. Even after their fight, he stayed by her side.

Katie felt a new surge of the love she had for him. She reached out to comb her fingers through his short, blonde hair. Like it or not, the time had come to tell him about her fears. Being truthful was the only choice if she wanted to honor their love. Katie knew it could still end in disaster for their relationship, but there definitely wouldn't be a relationship if she remained stubbornly silent. And the fact that he was by her side despite their fight? That was reason for hope.

Austin stirred and sat up, rubbing his eyes. As he turned his attention to her, she knew she couldn't wait any longer. While her waterfall or his cliff would've been her choice for a heart to heart, she had no choice in the matter. What she needed to say couldn't wait. "Austin, I need to tell you something."

The change was immediate. His eyes narrowed, guarded against what was coming next. He straightened back against the chair. His lips were a straight, tight line. Katie frowned at the change, surprised at the abruptness. Was there reason to hope after all? Austin's current look would indicate otherwise, but she had no idea what caused the change.

"Just tell me one thing." His voice was a deep growl.

Katie nodded.

"Do you love him?"

The air left her lungs, and if bruised ribs weren't enough to cause it, Austin's words sent a sharp pain through her chest. Did he think she was cheating on him or something? Her voice was quiet, her confusion evident. "What are you talking about?"

He looked away from her, but Katie couldn't tell if it was to hide hurt or because of disgust at her over this imagined indiscretion. "You know exactly what I'm talking about. Do you love him? If you do, I'll walk out now and not bother you again."

Katie reached out to him, but Austin moved his arm just out of reach. "If I knew, I wouldn't ask. Who am I supposed to love, other than you?"

His snort of disbelief was insulting, but Katie refused to

respond. She waited silently for him to answer her question. When he turned to face her, there was no doubt what Austin was feeling. It was written in the set of his jaw and the anger in his eyes. "I just want the truth, Katie. As much as I'm going to hate it, I at least deserve the truth. Have you been in love with him the whole time? Did you ever stop loving him?"

"Stop loving him? Who? Jacob?" He was the only other man Katie had ever loved. And even at that, Katie had learned through her relationship with Austin how shallow and self-centered her first love had been.

"You said it."

Katie shook her head. "Just because I can guess who you're talking about doesn't make it true. I don't love Jacob, and I don't understand where this is coming from."

One eyebrow raised as Austin cocked his head to the side. "Really? You don't have any idea? Did you really think I wouldn't find out? Do you think I'm that stupid?"

His voice may have been quiet in respect of the public place they were in, but each word was laced with ice. It was worse than yelling. Katie bit her lip to try to keep from crying. "I've never thought you were stupid, but I do think you're misinformed. Why do you think I'm in love with Jacob?"

The chair nearly toppled as Austin stood up and began pacing at the edge of the bed. Katie's own frustration grew, but her injuries made doing anything about it impossible. "Well? Are you going to answer me?"

He stopped at the foot of her bed and speared her with a condemning look. "Fine. You want to know why I think that? Let's start with the way you've been pushing me and everyone else away. You're keeping secrets and getting angry if anyone even tries to bring up what's going on. That didn't tell me what was happening, but you did just a few hours ago."

"A few hours ago? A few hours ago I was sleeping."

"Yeah, you were. But you also called out in your sleep, and it wasn't for me. You were calling out for Jacob. Now tell me the truth. Do you still love him?"

Katie felt a wave of nausea. She had brought this on herself with her insistence on handling her fears on her own. "I can explain."

"I'm counting on it. But I want the truth, Katie, all of it."

She motioned for him to sit. He ignored her gesture. "Please. I don't love Jacob. That's the something I wanted to talk to you about."

"You woke up after your accident wanting to tell me about how you don't love Jacob?"

"No. I mean, yes. I mean, just listen for a minute." Smacking her open palm onto the bed emphasized her words and aggravation. She tried to take a deep, calming breath only to be stopped by a sharp pain in her lungs. Once it subsided, she continued. "I've been having dreams."

"Dreams about Jacob?" His voice was laced with jealousy.

Katie shook her head. "Not really. They started that way, or at least they seemed to. It was the night I found Jacob with Mariah. Everything was exactly the same. It was like an unwanted instant replay of that night, and it felt more visceral than any dream I've ever had. But it wasn't Jacob with Mariah." Katie stopped knowing what she was going to say would hurt Austin. She chewed on her bottom lip and turned away from him to face the window. Tears filled her eyes, and she forced herself to continue. "It wasn't Jacob. It was you. You were the one I found wrapped around Mariah on the sofa. I . . ."

Katie couldn't continue as retelling the dream brought on a new panic attack. Her hands shook, and her heart pounded in her chest. Her breathing, already strained, became nearly non-existent. She wanted to gasp for breath, but the tightness around her lungs prevented it. Her head spun. She looked back to Austin in time to see regret replaced with concern.

"Katie? Katie, what's wrong? Do you need the nurse? Are you in pain?"

She shook her head and closed her eyes. Focus. I will lift up my eyes to the mountains, where does my help come from? My help comes from the Lord, the maker of heaven and earth. I will lift up my eyes to the mountains, where does my help come from? My help comes from the Lord, the maker of heaven and earth.

As she repeated the verses, Katie felt herself calming once again. Minutes later, after her breathing had evened out, she knew she needed to continue. She had been so distracted by her thoughts, she hadn't noticed Austin clutching her hand like a lifeline. She managed a small smile. "I'm ok. But now you see my problem. These dreams cause panic attacks. The idea that you could . . . anyway, I know it isn't true. But knowing doesn't erase this irrational fear. I tell myself over and over that it's nothing more than a crazy dream. The panic comes anyway. At first it was only after my dreams. Then, it changed."

"At the bakery?"

Katie nodded. It was embarrassing to admit, but it had to be done. "It was that customer."

Austin frowned. "Why would one of my customers cause you a panic attack? Did you know them?"

"I don't have to know them. It's not logical. I know that, but I can't stop it. When that woman came in and was obviously flirting with you it caused an attack." Katie shrugged.

Austin leaned back in his chair. "I don't even know who you're talking about, but I can assure you I wasn't flirting with any woman, whoever it was. I love you. You're the only one I want to flirt with."

"I'm not accusing you of anything. That's why I didn't want to say anything. I know it's hard to understand, but it's true. This isn't about you. This, whatever this is, it doesn't follow any rhyme or reason. I can tell myself you're not flirting. I can tell myself it was

Jacob who cheated. My brain knows all these things, but my body doesn't get the message."

"How do you fix it?"

Austin's quiet words were too much. The tears Katie had successfully fought to this point won the battle, streaming down her face. She swiped them away with the back of her hand. "I don't fix it. I don't even know for sure what starts it. I pray and try to focus on scripture. That seems to help, but I never know when it's going to happen or why."

His eyes held a mixture of hurt and something Katie thought looked dangerously close to betrayal. She watched, helpless to go to him, as he stood from his chair and walked to the window. With his back to her, Austin lifted the slats of the blinds to peer out. His shoulders rose and fell with a quiet sigh.

"Austin? Please talk to me."

He attempted to school his features, but he wasn't quick enough to keep Katie from seeing the smirk on his face as he turned to her. Her stomach tied in knots.

"Me talk to you? I've never had a problem talking to you. I talk to you all the time, about everything. I don't keep secrets. Do you even remember the other night at your place? I wanted to know what was going on with you. I wanted to help or at least be there to support you. You told me to get out."

Katie didn't bother trying to wipe away the tears now flowing freely down her face. Her ragged breathing caused pain to slice through her ribcage, but it was nothing compared to the pain of knowing Austin was completely right in his accusations against her.

"I know, I . . ."

"No you don't know. I love you. I want to spend the rest of my life with you, and you told me to get out. When Erin called to tell me you were here, I came immediately. It didn't matter that we'd been fighting. It didn't matter that you weren't even speaking to me. I had to be here. I've not left your side or stopped caring about you and your family. I'm the one who encouraged your parents to go home when I saw it was wearing them out to see you banged up like this, and I'm the one who's given them regular updates. I promised I'd stay with you. I would've done it anyway just so you don't have to be alone. But you pushed me out and didn't think twice about it."

Katie swallowed the lump in her throat. How could she have been so wrong? She didn't mean to create this mess. She was trying to keep him from feeling like she didn't trust him by refusing to tell him about her attacks. By not telling him, she had convinced him of that very thing. Was there going to be room for forgiveness? When she'd needed him, he'd come. Austin was hurt, but he loved her. Would it be enough to restore their relationship?

Katie dropped her head back on the pillows, looking up to the tiled ceiling. *God, how do I fix this? I've messed up, and I don't know how to make it right.*

She started when Austin's hand came to rest on her shoulder. She looked up at him. The past few weeks had put her in a world that ran on illogical fear. The fear that wound its way through her insides now was different. There was nothing illogical about it. Austin's eyes had reflected his love for her long before they should have. Those same eyes seemed empty now. That was a very real reason to fear.

She licked her lips. She didn't want to push. She was certain she wouldn't like the answers. But she had to know. "I'm sorry. You're right. I should have trusted you with it. I don't know why I didn't. It doesn't make sense now that I'm looking at it from this side of things. But you know now, and we can get past this, right?"

His hand fell from her shoulder, as he returned to the window. Katie knew she needed to give him time, but his silence was more than she could take. "Austin? You do want to get past this?"

Though none fell, Katie could see tears in his eyes when he faced her again. His voice was hoarse with emotion. "I'm not sure what I think or what I want right now. I'm sorry, Katie, but I've got to go."

Without another word, Austin left the room. Watching him leave without the promise of returning was too much. Katie fell back onto her pillow and didn't even try to stop her tears.

Chapter Eight

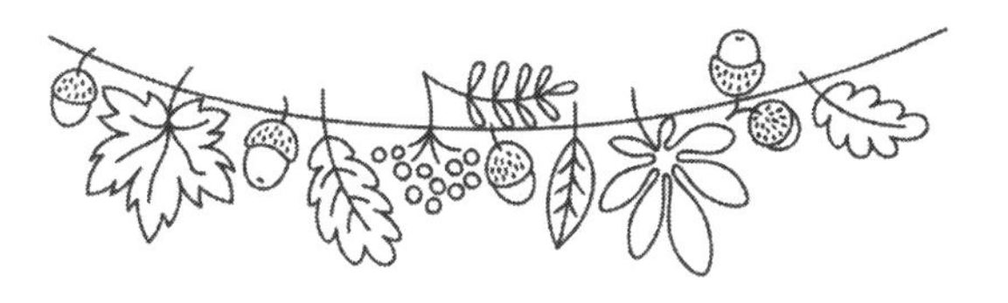

Even though current circumstances left Paul and Katie's friendship strained, Austin hadn't been surprised Paul extended his stay in Carbondale after Katie's wreck. What did surprise him was seeing Paul's car outside his apartment without Erin's yellow bug parked beside it.

"I figured you'd be out to lunch or something with Erin."

Paul turned from loading the dishwasher and looked to Austin standing in the kitchen doorway. "And I figured you might need some guy time today. It's been a rough couple of days."

Austin ran his hand through his hair, blowing out a frustrated breath as he did. "You have no idea."

Paul nodded to him. "It's settled then. I've got an order of wings waiting to be picked up. I'll get them and pick up some drinks too."

In spite of his fatigue, being with someone sounded a lot better than being alone with his thoughts. "I think I'll grab a hot shower while you're out. Maybe I can wash off that antiseptic hospital smell."

"Back in a flash."

"WANT THE LAST ONE?"

Austin shook his head. "Uh, no thank you. It's all yours." He licked teriyaki sauce off his fingers before finishing the job with one of the take out wet wipes.

"Suit yourself, but you don't know what you're missing."

"I'm missing having my face burned off? Somehow I think I can go through life without that particular experience." He couldn't believe the levels of heat Paul could not only handle but seemed to enjoy.

"You're just a wimp. Can't take a little hot sauce."

"Yeah, well at least my insides won't be burning the rest of the night."

With empty wing containers littering the coffee table, Austin and Paul turned their attention to scrolling through the cable listing on the tv. Neither had an interest in sports, so they grabbed a bag of chips, refilled their sodas, and stretched out in their chairs to watch a Lord of the Rings marathon instead.

"Can I ask you something?" Austin's mind had been wandering throughout the movie, and when it went to a commercial, he took his chance.

Paul shrugged. "Sure."

"You've known Katie a lot longer than I have. Has she always been a worrier?"

Austin watched Paul mull over his question. "I'm not sure what you mean. What's she worried about?"

Austin hesitated. It was Katie's issue, but now that she'd opened up, it was his issue too. He needed perspective, but he wanted to respect her privacy. How much could he share with Paul and still do that? "I don't know. I mean, does she get scared of stuff?"

"Stuff like spiders or stuff like losing you? You're painting with pretty broad strokes, and I'm not sure how to answer." Paul picked up the remote and pressed the mute button.

Austin kneaded his forehead. "I think it's over with us."

"That's a bold statement. Do you want it to be over or does she?"

"I don't think either one of us really wants it, but I don't know if this is going to be fixed. Katie walked away from me once. I swore I'd never do that to her, but today that's exactly what I did."

Paul scratched his chin as he considered Austin's predicament. "Well, the obvious question is, if you don't want it to be over and she doesn't want it to be over, why'd you walk away?"

"I don't know, man. We were talking, and it wasn't going anywhere. Did you know she's been having panic attacks?"

"Seriously?"

Austin nodded. "She was having nightmares about Jacob and Mariah. Then, it morphed into me and Mariah. The panic attacks started happening when I replaced Jacob in her dreams."

"Ouch."

"I'm not talking about a little bit of worry either. I'm talking about incapacitating, illogical fear driven panic attacks. It's crazy."

Paul looked doubtful. "It's not as crazy as you might think. You didn't see her back then. I don't know exactly what she's told you, but I pieced together a lot of it before she left Bloomington the first time. What I didn't figure out myself, Katie told me after she'd come back to God. She needed to talk things out and find reassurance in her new found faith. Jacob's betrayal was enough to break her, and Katie's a tough one to break."

Austin's jaw tightened. "If he really did that kind of number on her, why'd she go back to him?"

"Have you asked her?"

"Sure."

"What'd she say?"

"She wanted it to work so it wouldn't be a mistake anymore."

Paul raised and dropped one shoulder as he picked up his glass for a drink. "Then, that's your answer. Guilt is a powerful motivator. Pair it with love, and it's almost an impossible force."

Austin bristled at Paul's use of the word love in reference to Katie and Jacob's relationship. A knowing look from Paul told Austin that his feelings were showing whether he wanted them to or not.

"You've got to let it go if you're going to go forward. Face it, Katie loved Jacob. It may not have been exactly what love should be, but at the time, it was love. They were each other's world for years. Not to mention, he was her only family in Bloomington. Her friends weren't there. Her mom and dad were here. He was her best friend. Like it or not, you've got to accept it and move on."

"He was a jerk!"

"I'm not arguing that he wasn't, but it doesn't make the rest untrue. Her heart is yours now and there isn't room for jealousy in your relationship. As skewed as her dreams may be, they're based in reality. She's lived it. Jacob ripped away the world he introduced her to, and it left her with nothing, no anchor to hold onto. You're an entirely different matter. What's got you so afraid? Broken heart in your past not quite healed up?"

Austin's temper flared. "What gives you the right? You don't know me, and you don't know what I've dealt with!"

Paul's jaw set. His voice was firm but calm. "You're right. I don't. That's why I'm asking."

"You were with Katie when she went back to Jacob. You saw what he did to her. You got a front row seat to the damage he caused, but she wasn't the only one hurt in the situation. And Jacob wasn't the only one doing the hurting."

Paul softened. "Go on."

Austin sucked in a deep breath and stood. Crossing to the window, he pulled aside the curtain and stared out at nothing in particular. It was easier than looking Paul in the face. "I loved her." He let the curtain fall back into place, but remained rooted to the floor. "I was the one with her when he called and her pain came to the surface. I was with her as she tried to process it all while dealing with her tempestuous relationship with her mom."

Austin stepped away from the window and dropped into the recliner in the corner, his head cradled in his hands. When he raised it again to look at Paul, he knew he couldn't stop the man from seeing everything he felt. "I loved her, and that night she chose Jacob. I couldn't understand why. I still don't understand why. I don't think I ever will. Why would she choose the man who'd hurt her so deeply over one who only wanted to love her the way she deserved?"

"I know you don't understand it, but have you come up with any answers?"

Austin looked at the hands clasped together over his knees as he considered the question. He shook his head. "No, and I felt deserted. By Katie. By God. It wasn't a good time. I walked away from my church and pretty much reduced God to a habit. In my anger, I told God it was because He took Katie away before I had the chance to help her come back to her faith. She needed me to come back to Him. Truthfully, I was angry He took her away before we had a chance for our relationship to grow."

Paul ran a hand over his mouth. "So, when she came back, everything fell into place?"

"God didn't wait. God dealt with me before Katie returned. I knew He was asking me to give her up, and at the same time, He was asking me to pray for her without anything in it for me. It was the hardest thing I'd ever done. The night we met at Denny's, I have to admit watching her with you tested every place of surrender God had worked in me."

"Watching her with me? Why?"

"You guys looked so close. I was sure she had come back and brought a new guy to torture me with."

"Listen, I never. We never . . ."

"I know. Now. Then, I wasn't so sure. But God worked it out and brought her back to me."

Paul frowned. "Then why are you so determined to give her up? What are you afraid of?"

As much as it had irked him earlier in the conversation, Austin felt like he could finally answer. "I'm afraid of watching her leave again. She's been so worried about whether or not I'll be faithful that she's pushed me away. What if she decides I'm not worth the worry? If she walks out on me again, I don't know what I'd do."

"You'd survive like you did last time. It would be hard, but you'd make it. Is it really better to lose her because of your own choice? To push her out before she possibly pushes you out? You don't know that you'd lose her if you stay. There's no chance of keeping her if you walk away."

Austin dropped his head into his hands. Paul was right. He didn't want to lose Katie, but if he walked away now, that's exactly what would happen. As long as she would still see him, there was hope for their relationship. There was no guarantee it would work out, but at least there was a chance.

He looked up to find Paul had left the room. Scanning the apartment, he found him in the kitchen emptying the dishwasher so he could refill it. "I'll be back soon. I need to see Katie before it's too late."

"I'll be praying then." Paul grinned at him before going back to the dishes. "Oh, by the way. Erin texted earlier. Katie was released from the hospital this afternoon. Erin's staying with her until she's moving around a little better."

Chapter Nine

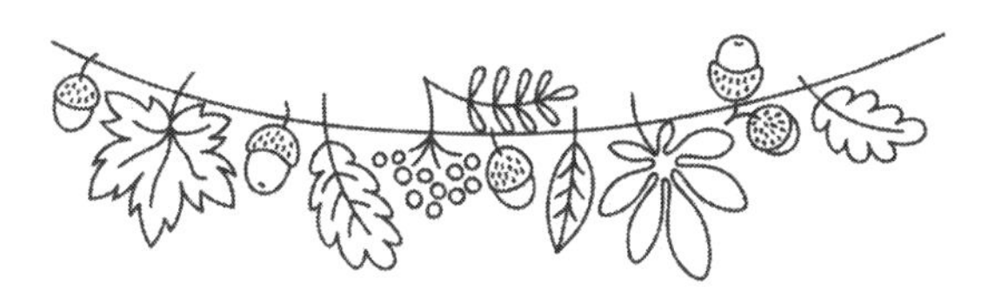

Katie felt the presence in her bedroom before she opened her eyes. Groggy from interrupted sleep, it took a minute for her eyes to focus. When they did, she questioned whether or not she was really conscious. She had to be dreaming because Austin sat in the rocking chair Erin had moved into her room when they'd arrived from the hospital.

"Don't try to stay awake. No worries. I'll be here when you wake up."

Dream or reality, it didn't matter. Just hearing his voice put Katie at ease. As much as her mind begged to stay awake, her aching body had other ideas. Her eyes drifted closed, and she slept peacefully through the evening and until morning.

The smell of coffee tempted Katie awake. "Mmm. That smells wonderful."

"Great. Austin just made it. I'll have him bring you a cup. If you don't mind, I'm going to run home for a bit. I need a nap and a shower."

Austin. So she wasn't dreaming. He'd come back. Was that good or bad? Erin watched her with raised eyebrows and arms folded across her chest. She was waiting for an answer.

"That sounds good. Take your time. I'm really feeling much better."

Erin left the room, and within moments Austin took her place carrying two mugs of hot coffee. "I fixed it the way you like it. Do you want it or do you want it on the nightstand?"

She grinned at Austin. He looked relaxed, but was that a good sign? Did that mean he was there to put their relationship back on solid ground or that he was moving on and making the decision brought him peace? She looked at his outstretched hand and accepted the mug from him.

"Thank you." She blew into the steaming liquid before taking a small sip. Still too hot. "Hazelnut. My favorite." With a little difficulty she twisted in the bed to place the mug on the nightstand to cool.

"I'm sorry it's not a frozen hazelnut mocha, but I wanted to be here when you woke up. I told you I would be. Besides, we need to talk."

Katie averted her eyes and toyed with a loose thread on her embroidered quilt. Austin's words caused her chest to tighten. She was glad she'd set her coffee aside. She wasn't sure she could get it down, much less keep it down.

"Katie, look at me please."

She raised her eyes to his, as half her bottom lip tucked between her teeth. Without realizing it, she twisted a stray curl around her finger. His eyes were full of regret, adding to her discomfort.

"I'm sorry."

Oh, no. She wasn't at all prepared for this. She could feel the burn of salty tears welling up in her eyes. She dropped her eyes to the quilt once again. She had to keep control. She had to be strong. It was Austin's right to leave after what she'd done, and she refused to guilt him into staying.

He reached out and captured her hand in his. It was warm and soft on hers but did little to ease her nervous shaking. Though she tried to will it away, her breaths were shallow. The cold sweats began, and Katie could only hope Austin couldn't feel the clamminess of her palm. This was not the time for a panic attack. She closed her eyes in an attempt to calm herself and missed his next words.

"What?"

"I said I'm sorry. I should never have walked out on you like that. You needed me, and I let you down. I can't explain how much I regret that now."

Katie swallowed as her relief brought the tears she'd been fighting. "There's nothing to apologize for."

Austin cradled her chin in his palm and wiped a tear from her cheek with his thumb. "Yes, there is. I can't pretend I understand what it's like to have a panic attack or to get why it happens in the first place. But I do understand you were hurt. Jacob broke your trust, and it left scars in your life. I don't agree with you trying to hide what you were going through, but you weren't thinking clearly. And then, when you told me, I was less than understanding. For that, I am deeply sorry."

The heaviness of fear was replaced with the weight of her own poor choices. Austin wasn't the only one in the wrong. "I played a part in this too. I shouldn't have tried to hide my struggle. I should've come to you. I couldn't see through my fear, but I should have. You would never do that to me, and I'm sorry I couldn't see that."

As Austin stood and walked to look out the window, Katie glimpsed hesitation in his eyes. Had she said something to upset him? Could he not see her regret was genuine? Was she holding onto misplaced hope? Maybe he wasn't trying to apologize and heal their relationship but apologize and leave. Had she misread him?

He turned to face her, keeping his distance. "I want this to work."

The vise around her heart loosened. "So do I."

"Then, we have to be realistic. I'd like to say I wouldn't ever do anything to hurt you, to jeopardize our relationship, but I can't. Face it, I did just last night."

"That's not the same thing. You could never betray me like Jacob."

His raised hand stopped her. "It doesn't have to be. There are a million ways we could hurt and betray each other. And as much as we love each other, any one of those could be the straw that breaks the camel's back. Any one of them could tear our relationship apart."

"But we won't let that happen, right?"

Austin smiled. "No. We won't let that happen, but we have to understand something going forward. My dad used to tell me something, and I never really understood it until now. Never say never about sin and temptation. I would argue with him. I'd tell him I could never do this thing or that thing that I knew was wrong. I was stronger than that. He would reiterate, never say never about sin and temptation. I'm beginning to see what he meant. Being cocky enough to say I would never do something is like giving the devil a challenge. That's where he's going to try to hit you again and again."

"There's no hope then?"

Austin shook his head. "There's hope. It's just where we place our hope. If I go into this expecting you to never do anything to hurt or betray me, I could very well be disappointed. Same for you. I intend to do everything I can to protect our relationship, but as much as I don't like to admit it, I'm not infallible. As unthinkable as it is right now, hurt and betrayal are possible for either of us. People fail. Our hope comes from God working in whatever circumstance we face."

The idea of moving forward in their relationship without a guarantee seemed less than desirable. If Austin could one day betray her like Jacob had, what was the point? How could she vow to love and honor him "till death do us part" if he could shatter their relationship in a moment of weakness? Their future was nothing more than a gamble, and for all his words of God working through the circumstances, Katie wondered if her bruised heart was strong enough to take that bet.

Katie realized she had gotten lost in her thoughts when Austin cleared his throat, bringing her back to the present. He smiled, but it didn't reach his eyes. He was hurt by her silence. How could she give him what he wanted?

She licked her suddenly dry lips, but the emotional strain of the conversation had robbed her mouth of all moisture. "I love you. Can you forgive me for not trusting you? Can we move on from this?"

Austin sighed. "I forgive you, and I ask that you forgive me too, for the way I acted last night. I was hurt and scared, to be honest. The way I reacted didn't help anything, and I'm sorry."

Katie held out her hand to him. He crossed back to her bed and took it in his own, as he lowered himself into the chair. "It's forgiven. But that leaves my other question. Can we move on from this?"

"I can't make that decision on my own. I want to. I want to watch you walk down that aisle. I want to vow in front of God and all our friends to honor and cherish you forever. I want to know what it's like to hold you and not have to let you go at the end of the night. But do you? Can you promise yourself to our relationship, knowing there are no guarantees that we won't mess up? Knowing we'll have times when we irritate or disappoint each other like no one else can?"

"I want that too. Well, not the messing up part, but the rest. I love you, and I want to spend the rest of our lives proving it."

Austin's grin was infectious as he leaned in to kiss her. Carefully, he pulled her into his embrace, and the fear that had snaked itself around her heart fled until only a niggling doubt remained telling her the man she loved had not been able to guarantee there would be no betrayals in their future. She forced the pestering thought out of her mind. He couldn't guarantee it, but she knew it wouldn't happen. Austin was too good for that. Wasn't he?

He wanted to tighten his arms around her but knew it would cause pain to her bruised ribs. Instead, he let go and planted his palms on the mattress on either side of her. He couldn't hold her, but he could still show her his love. He deepened the kiss, knowing he'd accomplished his goal when he heard her soft sigh. The hurts of the past few weeks, the secrets, the lack of trust, had nearly cost him the woman he loved. But now that everything was out in the open, Austin knew they could meet it head on and conquer it. He had Katie back, and he wasn't going to let anything jeopardize their relationship again. Fear might creep back into her mind, but he would confront it showing her they could make it through anything.

Austin lifted one hand from the mattress to weave his fingers through the silky waves of her hair. When he finally pulled away from the kiss, the emotional turmoil of the previous twenty-four hours left his voice raw. "Let's just do it. We don't need a fancy wedding. We'll call Paul and Erin to witness. We can go to the courthouse, and we can become husband and wife today."

He watched her brows lower. "Austin, I love you . . ."

"Don't. Don't say but. I know it seems rash. It isn't. I love you. You love me. I've spent the last few weeks watching you get farther and farther from me. I've spent the last couple days wondering if you were leaving me forever. Now, I have you back. I don't want to let you go, even for a little while. We've been planning it. Why not make it now? There's no reason to wait."

He felt her pull away emotionally, stiffening as she did so. She didn't have to answer for him to get the message, but she did anyway. "You're not serious. We can't do that."

"Why not?"

She crossed her arms in front of her chest and looked up at him as her chin lowered clearly stating he knew the reasons, and she did not need to humor him with the answer. "I'm not reacting out of fear."

Her chin lifted as she rolled her eyes.

"I'm not. I just don't see why we should wait."

A slight curve raised her lips. She gently shook her head. "Yes, you do. We want our family and friends to share that day with us. And you can tell me you're not reacting out of fear, but I think we both know you are. We've lost each other before. Coming this close to that happening again is unnerving. You said you don't want to let me go again without us being husband and wife. That's fear."

Austin tried to examine her words without giving in to the defensiveness they brought. Running his hand through his hair, he focused on the wall behind her while he considered her reasoning. Where did the truth line up with what Katie was saying? She pushed him away because of fear. Was he pulling her closer for the same reason?

"Can we at least discuss the fact that we are only two months into what we decided would be a twelve month engagement?"

"Sure. What do you want to discuss?"

Austin reached for her, carefully pulling her into his arms. "That ten more months is entirely too long to wait to make you my wife."

Warmth poured through Austin as she nuzzled against him, placing a brief kiss in the curve of his neck. "Is this fear talking again?"

"It most definitely is not fear."

"Then what is it?"

Austin softly caressed her back as he continued the embrace. "It's knowing that you feel this good in my arms and not wanting to wait for everything else that goes along with making you my wife. I'm ready to begin our lives together."

He could feel a slight tension between her shoulder blades and knew if he were to look, her cheeks would have a warm, rosy glow. He couldn't stop the grin that came with knowing the adorable woman he held would soon be his to hold for the rest of his life. "So, what do you think? Can we move the wedding?"

"What were you hoping for?"

Her voice was soft. He moved away, needing to see her face to know what her words might not tell him. While he knew lifetime commitment was a serious subject, Austin also realized it didn't need to be a heavy discussion. Everything about the morning's topics had been hard, and he knew they needed to lighten up the mood. He schooled his features into the most innocent look he could. "I was thinking we could revisit getting married today, at the courthouse."

Katie frowned. When one brow lifted, the expression told him all he needed to know. He'd seen that look before. She was not amused. "If you're going to be that way, we'll just keep it at ten months. And you can deal with it."

His hands flew up in a gesture of mock surrender. "Okay, okay. No need to be snippy. How about three months?"

Austin couldn't help his smile as her beautiful green eyes grew round, and her mouth dropped open in surprise. He chuckled at his gorgeous fiancé looking like she was trying to imitate a fish. She stared at him for several moments, as if to judge whether or not he was still playing. "Do not laugh at me. Are you even serious? Three months?"

He schooled his feature and shrugged. "Why not?"

"Oh, I don't know. How about the flowers, the dresses, the venue, the cake, the invitations?"

He captured the fingers that had counted out each item as she spoke and drew them to his lips for a soft kiss. Turning her hand over, he did the same to her palm. Without raising his head, he looked up at her. "Neither of us wants a royal wedding. We want something simple. I think we can do it. Besides, I can think of one great reason for the wedding to happen in three months instead of ten."

He watched her head tilt to one side as she considered his words. Her lips were pursed into a questioning pout. She was trying to figure out his reasoning without asking. He decided to mercifully answer her unasked question. "If the wedding is in three months, then our life together as husband and wife is just twelve short weeks away."

Her wry smile told him she wasn't buying his answer, at least not completely. But she hadn't said no outright. That was good, right? He waited patiently for the answer, unsure of what it would be. He fought to keep his body still and his expression open as her silent consideration made him as squirmy as a disobedient pupil under his teacher's scrutiny. She had to feel that he would be okay with her choice, whatever the answer was going to be.

He watched her head dip into a slight nod. He held his breath, hoping that meant the answer he longed to hear was coming.

"YES." Katie fought the butterflies created by a sliver of doubt as she agreed to Austin's plan. He had all the answers he needed. But did she? "We can pick a date three months from now for our wedding."

Austin's eyes lit with pleasure at her answer. She fought her own grin as she watched a smile stretch across his face, boyish dimples and all. It took so little to make him light up like a kid at Christmas. Of course, as her anxiety kicked up a notch, Katie wondered if it was such a little thing after all. She still hadn't gotten a handle on her attacks, and the stress of a quickly approaching wedding date could make things worse.

Austin pulled her into a bear hug, until she moaned in pain. He let her go as quickly as he'd grabbed her. His face was pale as he apologized. "I am so sorry. I wasn't even thinking about your ribs.

I didn't hurt you did I? I mean, I know I hurt you, but I didn't really hurt you, did I?"

She shook her head. "No. I'm fine."

She was glad for the pain that made it understandable for her grin to fade. She didn't want to admit the thoughts that really caused it. What did she have to worry about? Austin knew about the panic attacks now. She wouldn't have to hide it anymore, and they would work through them together. In three months, she would be his wife. Everything would work out just fine. Wouldn't it? Of course it would. Austin would never be able to hurt her like Jacob did under any circumstances, even if he wasn't sure of that himself.

Chapter Ten

"I figured you'd be on cloud nine. What's up?"

Erin turned from the window to Paul sitting in the booth across from her. She dragged a fry through the ketchup on her plate. "What do you mean? Nothing's up."

The right side of Paul's mouth raised in a doubting half grin. "We're on a date at your favorite restaurant. Your best friends have worked out their issues. And if that wasn't enough, they're getting married in three months, but you haven't said a word to me for the last five minutes. Instead, you've been staring out the window at the cars in the parking lot."

Erin shrugged. "I'm not staring at the cars in the parking lot, Mr. Smarty-Pants."

"Oh really? Then what are you staring at?"

"I was staring at the lamppost, if you must know."

Paul flattened a hand across his chest. "I stand corrected. It makes so much sense for you to stare at a light instead of the cars. Nothing's the matter, after all. How could I have been so wrong?"

She chuckled. "I guess it's a gift. I wouldn't know because I'm never wrong."

"So if your gift isn't being wrong, what is it?" His eyes narrowed. "It could be being beautiful."

She couldn't stop the smile or the blush she felt along with it. Such blatant, over-the-top flattery would be false with anyone else, but Erin knew Paul meant every word. She lowered her eyes to the glass of ice water in front of her. She plucked the lemon wedge from the rim and squeezed it into the water. Maybe if she acted nonchalant, Paul wouldn't see how much his words affected her.

"Of course," he continued, "that's only one of your gifts. You have at least one more, I think."

She couldn't help meeting his gaze. Where was he going with this? The tone had been playful, but all teasing was gone from his face. Did she really want to know? She softly cleared her throat. "What gift is that?"

"You have great skill in avoiding topics you don't want to talk about. But you underestimate my gifts. I can always bring it right back. Do we keep this up, or are you going to tell me what has you distracted tonight?"

Erin sighed. "I guess I'm worried about Katie."

"But she and Austin worked things out. You're going dress shopping with her tomorrow. Has something happened? Is there anything making you think things aren't on the up and up?"

Erin toyed with her straw, using it to repeatedly harpoon the lemon wedge she'd discarded into her cup. "I'm not sure. It just seems too easy. You didn't see Katie when she had a meltdown. It was bad. Then, they talk and not only is everything fine, but they're getting married in three months instead of ten?"

Paul reached across the table and stilled her hand, sparing what was left of the chunk of fruit. He waited until Erin met his eyes. "Are you borrowing trouble where there is none?"

She stared at the hand covering her own. "I just don't know. How has Austin been at home? Has he given you any indication on how things have gone in the last few days?"

"He's been great. More at ease now than the rest of my time

here. If there's a problem, I don't think he knows it. What about Katie?"

Erin shook her head. "I wish I knew. On the outside, she's fine. But I don't think she's as settled in the decision as she wants everyone to believe. I mean, I know she wants to marry Austin, but I don't think the trust issue is completely out of the way. I have a feeling, now that the panic attacks are out in the open, she'll find it easier to deal with them. But an absence of episodes doesn't mean the underlying problem is gone."

Paul grinned. "Look at you being all psychological and everything."

Erin huffed and pushed her empty plate aside. "I may be blonde, but contrary to what everyone seems to think, that doesn't make me a dumb blonde. Just because I enjoy having fun and joking around doesn't mean all my thoughts are as shallow as a kiddie pool. It might surprise you to know I was actually the valedictorian of my high school class and kept a 4.0 grade point average in college."

Knowing if she gave him a chance Paul would see how deeply his careless words affected her, Erin lowered her eyes to her hands where she twisted her napkin to shreds. She refused to look up when his hand reached across the table to still hers. Even when he spoke, she kept her eyes focused on their hands.

His voice was full of regret. "I'm so sorry. I was just playing. I didn't realize it would bother you, or I wouldn't have done it. I've never thought you dumb or shallow. You are insightful and smart. You are a beautiful woman, and a wonderful and loyal friend. Katie told me how you befriended her when she came home to help her mom recover. You helped her let loose when she was under an immense amount of stress. And I've seen that same giving and caring heart in a hundred different ways just since I've been here. I never meant to hurt you."

Without lifting her head, Erin looked up at him. As easily as his smile lit his eyes, his frown dimmed their shine. His apology was sincere, and though she didn't believe every word he said, she knew he did. Erin chewed the inside of her cheek. She'd been rough on him, and he couldn't have known what his innocent words would do. She knew he was trying to be playful. She owed him an explanation.

She raised her chin to give him her full attention. "I'm sorry too. I overreacted." She turned away from his probing eyes to look out the window. "I guess I've always made friends easily. Everyone likes to have fun with the girl with the bubbly personality. I never thought anything of it, until my junior year in high school. I'd been dating a guy for almost the entire year. He'd graduated and was in his first semester at SIU when he broke up with me. I reminded him that he wasn't as grown up as he thought. We were only a year apart in age, and that year didn't make that much of a difference. He said age didn't have anything to do with it."

Erin rubbed her lips together. It was so long ago. It shouldn't still matter, but it did. "He said high school was for having fun, but it was time for him to be serious about his choices. I was great for a good time, but he needed to find someone with some substance. Something real to offer. It was then I set out to prove him wrong. I'd always had good grades, but I put everything into school. If it wasn't studying or working, I didn't do it. I joined the debate team and scholar bowl. I stopped with the drama club which I loved because it wasn't serious enough. I stopped being on every event planning committee. I changed who I was, and I was miserable. It took God until my second year of college to get it through my thick head that I could be me and be a person of substance at the same time. But, as you can see, I still struggle."

She flinched as Paul's thumb grazed her cheek as his hand cradled her chin, turning her to face him. He waited until she looked him in the eyes to speak. "Thank you. You are the most real person I've ever met, and I've loved every minute I've gotten to spend with you. You've just given me another look into exactly who you are. I love to have fun with you. You remind me it's okay to be a goofy little kid sometimes. But I also love that we can be serious. Honestly, I just love you."

His words took her breath. She was sure he could hear her heart pounding from across the table. Their initial attraction had led them to keep in touch after Paul returned to Bloomington to run Pages Bookstore for Katie. Their phone calls and emails had cemented their friendship. His visit the last two weeks had proven to Erin what she felt for him was much deeper than friendship, but she only hoped he felt the same way.

"It's okay." His voice was quiet, reassuring. "Please, there's no pressure to feel the same way. I just didn't want you doubting exactly how I feel about you when I go back home tomorrow. This isn't me trying to pass the time while I'm here in Carbondale. You aren't just someone I can have fun with. You're the one I want to share everything with, good and bad. And I wanted you to know it before I leave."

A shadow of a smile played across his features as Erin searched for what to say. Rather than waiting for her answer, he grabbed the check off the corner of the table. When had the waitress brought that by? He stood and took his wallet from his back pocket.

"I'm going to go pay this, and we'll get out of here."

Erin considered the possibility that she'd hurt him with her silence. But then, he didn't sound hurt. He sounded like Paul. She didn't want to rush into returning his endearment and leave him thinking she didn't mean it. But what did one say after an admission of love if it wasn't a reassurance that you loved the person back? Thank you? That would be insulting. Besides, she did love him. She'd figured that out after their first date with the bobble headed waitress. And he was leaving in less than twelve hours. She couldn't share something like this with him over the phone. That would just be cruel.

She stood and pulled on her coat as he walked back to the table.

"All set?"

"Yep."

He held the door open for her. Then, he took her hand in his. With snow flurries in the air and a freezing early January breeze, they hurried across the parking lot to Paul's little Honda CR-V. Rather than escaping the arctic cold like any other sane person would, he came to her side of the car and opened her door, waving her in with his free hand.

Erin started to get in the car, but turned instead to face him. "I love you too, Paul."

Without a word he stepped toward her, took her face in his gloved hands, and kissed her, chasing away all thoughts of being cold. When he broke their kiss, he rested his forehead on hers. His arms were wrapped around her, holding her snuggly. His breath came out in frosty swirls as he spoke. "Not exactly what I planned for our first kiss."

"It was perfect." An involuntary chattering of her teeth punctuated her sentence.

Paul laughed and stepped away. "Let's get inside the car and get you warm."

Chapter Eleven

"He kissed you?" Katie's excited squeal drew the attention of other shoppers.

Erin glanced around the bridal shop. "Shhh. You don't have to be so loud about it."

Katie returned a wry smile. She was schooling Katie on keeping her voice down in public? The girl who danced her way across a parking lot on their first outing together? Katie knew her best friend was trying to suppress her own excitement, but she lowered her voice anyway. "So, what was it like?"

"Cold."

Katie couldn't help the full blown laugh at her friend's choice of descriptions. Who cared if everyone in the store was staring at them? Her best friends were in love. "Cold? The man you love, who's perfect for you, I might add, kisses you for the first time after admitting he loves you and all you can say is that it was cold?"

Erin rolled her eyes. "We were standing in a parking lot with snow flurries all around us. Of course, it was cold."

Katie placed her crossed hands over her heart and mustered up the deepest sigh she could manage. She made her voice as breathless as she could in a full octave above her normal speaking range. "It was soooo romantic. I was there. He was there. Snow flurries swirled around us. It was like a scene in a movie."

Erin swatted Katie's shoulder and giggled. "Knock it off. Really, it was perfect and romantic."

Katie pushed aside a hanger draped with a fluffy white gown. "I'm just teasing. It's sweet, and it's one you'll always remember. I couldn't be happier for my two best friends."

Erin's attention was diverted by one of the gowns Katie had absentmindedly pushed to the side. "What about this one? It's so pretty."

Erin pulled a tea length gown off the rack and held it out for Katie's inspection. Polka dotted tulle created the hint of a top above a modest sweetheart neckline. The tulle continued down the length of the full skirt. A narrow satin ribbon belted the waistline. It was reminiscent of the fifties and very feminine. With her outgoing, quirky personality, it was exactly the type of dress Katie knew would pique Erin's interest. But it was a little too much for her own taste.

"I was thinking of something a little simpler." Maybe her delicate phrasing would spare her friend's feelings. It really was a gorgeous dress, but Katie feared her more reserved personality couldn't quite pull off the retro glam look.

Erin quirked her mouth to the side and slid the dress back onto the rack. "Your loss. That dress is gorgeous."

"Save it for you and Paul. It would look much better on you anyway."

Erin's hand stilled on the hanger in front of her. "No one said anything about getting married. He only just said he loves me. Besides, today is about you and Austin, not me and Paul." She glanced at the dress again. "Maybe someday."

Katie left her to finish daydreaming about her someday as she went to the other side of the rack to look. Both girls slid hanger after hanger across the bar. Katie was beginning to lose hope of finding her perfect dress when Erin pulled one from the rack.

"What about this one? It's very traditional."

Katie looked from the dress to her friend whose eyelashes were fluttering in false innocence. Katie groaned. Traditional was one word for the satin monstrosity. Slender sleeves gave way to puffed shoulders that fell sharply into a deep scalloped V-neck. The entirety of the bodice, full ruffled skirt, and flowing train was highlighted with sequins and pearls. As if the look on her face at seeing the front wasn't enough to make her opinion known, Erin turned the dress around revealing a huge bow that spanned from one side of the skirt to the other and hung down several inches from where it began at the waist.

"Absolutely not."

A devious smile joined the fluttering eyelashes. "But why ever not? I think it's perfect for you."

Katie reached out a hand to touch the pearls on the bodice. "One, I don't do a plethora of pearls and sequins. Less is more. Two, ruffles and lace are a no go. And the most important rule to remember, I don't do big butt bows." Katie looked to Erin whose smile had turned impish. Katie raised an eyebrow, hands on hips. "And if you try to saddle me with something like this again, you as my maid of honor will pay dearly for it. I will find you the most hideous satin and lace creation that will rival any prom dress from the 80s teen movies."

Erin hung the dress back on the rack and threw her hands up in surrender. "Okay, okay. No more jokes. Let's get looking for your perfect dress."

An hour and several try-ons later, Katie and Erin left the boutique with an appointment to come back and speak with the seamstress about the alterations needed on not only Katie's wedding dress but also Erin's dress as maid of honor.

Katie waited by the passenger door to Erin's VW bug while Erin rummaged through her purse for her keys. While she still had some reservations about what her future with Austin would hold, the rapidly approaching date of their wedding kept her mind focused on her checklist of wedding day needs instead of her worries. And she and Erin had just checked off two very big items. "I can't believe how easy that was. We found both dresses, in budget, without a lot of hassle."

Erin held up her keys in victory. "Yes, here they are. Sorry, about that." She unlocked the door and waited until they were both buckled in before continuing. "It was a lot of fun. I'm so glad I get to be your maid of honor and do all this with you."

"I wouldn't have it any other way. You're my best friend. Besides, who else could have made dress shopping as entertaining?"

Erin grinned, pulling out of the parking lot. "I can't help it. Those designers make it too easy. Wow. To each their own, but some of those dresses were horrible. I can't imagine a woman that would look good in them."

"Tell me about it. Did you notice the one that was all cut-out lace from top to bottom? It looked like lingerie. I could never wear something like that."

Erin nodded. "Oh, and the one with the slit almost all the way up to the waist. In its defense, the skirt was so fitted, if it didn't have that slit, the poor bride wouldn't be able to move her legs enough to walk down the aisle. I just can't see what those designers were thinking."

"At least we found what we were looking for. Why don't we take a break and regroup? It wouldn't hurt us to figure out what we still need to do. Besides, I can only handle so much shopping without reinforcements."

Erin's joyful laugh was expected. "I don't get you sometimes, Katie McGowan. There is nothing better than shopping. The thrill of the hunt for that perfect item. The success of finding it at a great price. What's not to love?"

Katie rolled her eyes. "How about the crowds? Or the endless racks of everything that's wrong before you manage to find that perfect thing? Or how that perfect thing isn't so perfect once you get it home? Or the lines or rude sales people or how even sale prices can break the bank?"

"How is it that we're such good friends when you have such a poor opinion of my favorite sport?"

Katie's tone was dry. "Shopping is not a sport. But as for us being friends? I think God knew we needed each other. You're good for me, Erin Davis. You push me outside my comfort zone."

"And you rein me in and calm me down."

Katie couldn't help the snort that escaped. "Erin, there is nothing I could do to dampen your enthusiasm. I wouldn't even know where to start."

Katie didn't have to ask where they were headed. It was a given, if she and Erin were in town, they would be stopping at By Sweet Design. She'd say it was because Austin wouldn't make them pay for their orders, but they stopped there long before her relationship with Austin earned them free food. The atmosphere was bright and comfortable, and Austin made the best baked goods in town. It was the perfect place to take their shopping break.

"MISS KATIE!"

"Miss Katie! You're here!"

Setting her cup on the table, Katie turned to the excited, young voices calling her name. Her smile was immediate. She spread her arms wide as two, identical young boys raced across the room, launching themselves into her hug. She held the boys close. "What are you two up to today? Shopping with Mom?" She nodded a greeting to the twins' mother where she stood with Austin at the counter placing their order.

One blonde head nodded with enthusiasm. "Momma said we could have a treat if we didn't fight during shoe shopping."

The other took on a serious look. “I was good, but Jakey tried fighting with me once. We almost lost our treat.”

Eyebrows lowered over blue eyes. “Uh uh! You know that’s not true, Tommy. You were fighting with me.”

Tommy squared his slender shoulders. “Was not!”

“Was too!”

Katie saw their mother glance in their direction and roll her eyes with an exasperated sigh. She fought a giggle at the seriousness of their disagreement. “Okay, boys. It doesn’t matter who started it. If your mom is getting you a treat, you must have stopped quickly and behaved after that.”

Jake nodded emphatically. “Yeah, we were real good after that. I don’t wanna miss getting Pastor Austin’s chocolate chip cookies. He makes them special for me.”

Not to be outdone, Tommy chimed in. “But he makes sprinkle brownies just for me.”

This time Katie did giggle. The twins were a handful, but of all the children she taught in Sunday School each week, they had a special place in her heart. “Were you two good helpers for Miss Tammy last Sunday?”

Two heads bounced up and down in unison before Tommy stopped with a frown. “Miss Tammy said you couldn’t come cause you were at the doctor.”

“Miss Tammy was right. But I’m fine now, and I can come back to church on Sunday. What story did Miss Tammy tell you?”

Jake scratched his head. “I think. I think it was about a fire and some guys, but I can’t member their names. They were funny names. But the king was bad and didn’t like God. But the guys liked God and didn’t want to say the king was more important. So they wouldn’t bow to his statue.”

“And that made the king super mad,” Tommy interjected. “But he liked the guys so he gave them another chance. But he told them if they didn’t do what he said, they’d be thrown in the fire.”

Katie watched their eyes widen on this announcement. "So did they bow?"

They shook their heads. Tommy continued. "No. Miss Tammy said they didn't bow cause they had hearts."

Katie frowned, unsure of what Tommy meant. Before she could ask Jake smacked Tommy's arm. "That's not it."

"Uh huh."

"Nuh uh. It wasn't either hearts."

"Was too."

"That don't make sense. Everybody's got hearts, Jakey."

"Well, then, what did Miss Tammy say if you're so smart."

Tommy's little mouth puckered as he glared at Jake. Katie glanced at Erin out of the corner of her eye. Her friend's mouth was hidden behind her hand. Katie knew she'd find a huge grin if her hand moved. She couldn't say she wasn't struggling herself. The twins were adorable, even shooting daggers at each other.

"Do you remember the word, Tommy?" Katie attempted to draw his attention back to the story they were telling her.

"Course I do, Miss Katie. They had hoke."

Katie did a quick mental inventory of every possibility for the correct word. "Hope?"

"Yeah, hope. They had hope."

"You mean they knew God wouldn't let them get hurt, right?"

Both blonde heads shook. Jake took over the explanation. "Uh uh. Miss Tammy says they didn't know what would happen." He began counting off on his pudgy fingers. "The king can let them stand. The king can throw 'em in the fire. They can live. They can die."

"Yeah, Miss Katie. Them three didn't know." Tommy lifted his shoulders until they met his ears. "But God loved them. They told that king it didn't matter if they lived or died. They loved God. God loved them."

Jake's eyes were wide and his voice rose in volume as he joined in. "And God always does what's best."

The twins looked at each other before exclaiming in unison the final thrust of the lesson. "No matter what happens!"

Katie guessed the fervent exclamation was an echo of their teacher's, and she couldn't have been more proud of the twins as she pulled them into a bear hug, kissing them on top of their heads. "That's right. No matter what happens, God always does what's best. You two were very good listeners."

"Boys, let's leave Miss Katie and Miss Erin alone now. I've got a fresh cookie and brownie waiting on our table. I wouldn't want to have to eat them myself."

The boys shot out of Katie's hold and ran to the table their mother pointed to. She turned her attention to Katie. "We missed you at church, but I'm glad to see you're doing much better. The boys have prayed for you every night before bed."

"I appreciate that. I'm feeling much better and look forward to taking my class back on Sunday. You don't know how much I enjoy those kids, your boys especially. They're the sweetest."

Their mother looked over to the table where the boys were inhaling their sweets, mouths open as they tried to talk around their special treats. "They're something all right, but I wouldn't have it any other way. I'd better get over there before they destroy our table. See you two later."

As she joined her sons, Erin stood and gathered their trash from the table top. "We'd better get a move on too. We've got a lot of wedding to shop for."

Chapter Twelve

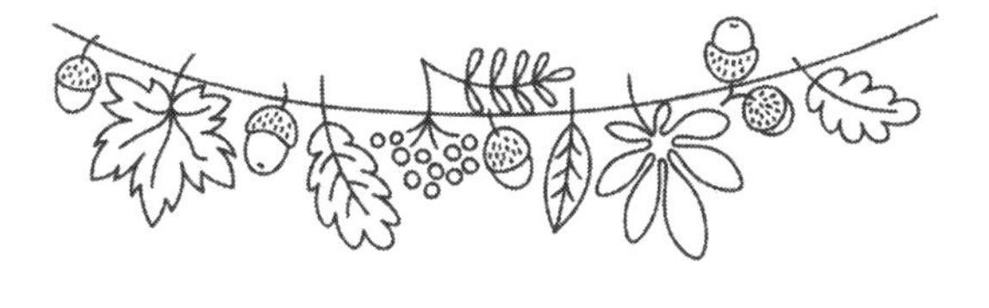

Katie tossed her purse and the plastic shopping bag containing printable wedding invitations onto a small table inside her front door. Erin had kept her out shopping much later than she had planned, but they had accomplished a lot. The dresses were bought, the flowers ordered, and the cake chosen. With their church serving as the venue for their wedding, Austin and Katie only had a few of the smaller details to nail down. They had yet to discuss who would officiate, the order of the service, or the music they would include. But those items would wait for another day. Katie's mind was elsewhere.

Though decisions were made and items were checked off her to-do list, Katie hadn't been able to get her conversation with the twins from her mind. The simple way they believed what her heart was struggling to accept was humbling. And the direction the substitute had taken the story was different than she'd ever heard.

Katie crossed the living room to the bookshelf and pulled one of her extra Bibles from the shelf. Sitting in her overstuffed recliner, Katie got comfortable and turned to the third chapter of Daniel. The twins may not have been able to recount the names of the Hebrew boys, but the story of Shadrach, Meshach, and Abednego was very familiar to her. She'd heard it from the time she was the twins' age, and it had always been the same. Katie didn't want that to dull her to anything God might want to show her. *Lord, open my heart to what You want me to know. Don't allow familiarity to keep me from hearing You.*

As Katie read, the themes she'd always heard applied to the story stood out as much as they ever had, but as she got to the trio's defense of their actions, a new phrase stood out. She went back and read it again, out loud to make certain she had read it correctly. "'If it be so, our God whom we serve is able to deliver us from the furnace of blazing fire; and He will deliver us out of your hand, O king. But even if He does not, let it be known to you, O king, that we are not going to serve your gods or worship the golden image that you have set up.' But even if He does not."

Even if He does not. The Hebrew boys believed God fully capable of changing the king's actions and saving them from certain death. But even if God chose not to intercede and keep them from the fire, they would still choose to serve Him. They would be delivered either physically or by entering into God's presence for eternity. In the end, God didn't intervene to keep them out of the fire. But He did keep them while in the fire.

Wasn't there another verse about that? Something about fire and rivers? Katie flipped to her concordance hoping she knew enough of the verse to be able to find it. After several less than successful tries, Katie finally flipped the pages open to the first two and a half verses of Isaiah 43. "Do not fear, for I have redeemed you; I have called you by name; you are Mine! When you pass through the waters, I will be with you; And through the rivers, they will not overflow you. When you walk through the fire, you will not be scorched, Nor will the flame burn you, For I am the LORD your God."

Katie set the Bible in her lap and leaned her head back against the chair. How many times had she heard messages promising only good things coming to believers if they only had enough faith?

She'd dismissed them, knowing that idea didn't hold up when examined up against countless examples like Job, Paul, or Stephen. God didn't promise her that if she followed Him, she wouldn't have to go through the fire or flood. He promised He would be there with her when she did.

God hadn't stopped the king from throwing the Hebrew boys into the fire. The boys' hope wasn't in the king having a change of heart. It wasn't even in God intervening and keeping them from the fire. Their hope was in the character of God and His promise to be with them in the fire.

"God, I'm so sorry. I've been putting my trust in Austin to do the right thing. I think that's why I've struggled so much with these fears. And I've used you like my back up plan. I've lived like if I just trust You enough, You won't let Austin betray me the way Jacob did. But Lord, You never promised me that. Austin is a person, and people fail every day. Lord, help me trust in Your love and plan for me no matter what I face. If my worst fears do come true, help me see You going through the fire with me. Take my fears and let me face whatever the future holds with real hope that I can only find in knowing You."

For the first time in weeks, Katie knew peace that was further reaching than the realm of her limited control. The ghosts of fear that had whispered unwanted doubts and kept her from fully embracing her future with unfettered joy were finally silenced. Katie knew better than to believe they would not try to whisper their poisonous opinions into her mind again, but now her heart was armed with the truth. No matter how many times it took, Katie would cling to that truth and find peace for her soul until the voices ceased their assault.

AUSTIN LOCKED up the bakery and decided what his next move should be in light of Katie and Erin's shopping trip. He shook his head at the thought of the two women being such close friends. Erin was like a tornado. She moved with speed and intensity through life, and no one that came in contact with her was left unchanged. At least unlike a tornado, Erin's change on a person was in the addition of whimsy and spontaneity, not destruction and pain. Katie was more like one of the cliffs they liked to hike up at Giant City State Park. They changed over time, but for the most part, they were steady and constant. Of course, what better friend is there for a tornado than the cliff that can retain its own identity in the middle of the whirlwind?

There were times, however, the friendship came with a price. Austin had texted Katie from his office a couple hours after the duo had left the bakery to see how the wedding shopping was going. The answer he received said little, but it told him all he needed to know.

Six more stores. Things checked off the list I didn't know were on it. Finally heading home.

Erin loved to shop. Katie hated it. All that interaction with no downtime would definitely wear Katie out. Austin could imagine her flopping down on her living room sofa and falling asleep. Food would be the last thing she'd want to take care of but something she'd need. He checked his watch. Five o'clock. The paperwork he'd had to finish after closing up shop had worked out in his favor. It was the perfect time to stop by Katie's favorite restaurant and then surprise her with dinner. Or maybe lunch, since the girls had stopped at the bakery before noon. Austin doubted they'd taken a second break in their shopping spree for something as mundane as food.

In less than an hour, he rang the doorbell of Katie's duplex while trying to balance two take-out containers of pad thai on his other hand. He knew he could walk in. If Katie was home, the door was unlocked. But making her come to the door added to the surprise. As he waited, he double checked that her car was under the carport. It was. The text he'd received from her had been sent two hours ago, more than enough time for Erin to get her home. He rang the bell again. Maybe he was the one in for the surprise.

As he turned from the door, Austin heard muffled movement from inside. He barely got turned around again before the door opened. Katie stood looking fuzzy from sleep. Her downturned mouth and the crease between her brows telegraphed her confusion, but Austin couldn't help finding her completely adorable. He grinned and held up the take-out containers.

"Hungry?"

Her eyes widened. "Is that pad thai? I hope you didn't get me above a level one. You know I'm not good with the heat. Well, what are you doing? Get in here?"

Austin laughed. She was most definitely hungry. She was also blocking the doorway. "Yes, it's pad thai. Yes, it's a one. And I'd love to bring it in if you'd kindly remove yourself from the middle of the doorway."

Her full lips formed a tiny "o" before she turned from the door and headed straight into the kitchen. By the time Austin shut the door and followed, Katie had forks and two cups of ice tea sitting on the small, round kitchen table. "I take it you're hungry?"

Katie blew out an exasperated breath that ruffled her wispy bangs and rolled her eyes. "Of course I'm hungry. For some reason, one tiny pastry and a coffee drink is supposed to sustain me through a shopping trip to umpteen jillion stores. Well, that might work for Erin, but I'm starving."

With that announcement, Katie plopped into the seat on the far side of the table and reached for one of the foam boxes. She opened it and inhaled deeply. "This is exactly what I needed. How did you know?"

Austin swaggered over to his own chair and sat down. He gave the cockiest look he could muster before speaking. "I just know my woman that's how."

With one eyebrow cocked impossibly high, Katie looked at

him. "Really? That's how you're going to play this? Your woman?"

Austin forced a serious look. "Well, of course. I mean, you aren't my woman yet, but it won't be long." When her unamused look remained, Austin decided a change of subject might be in order. "Seriously though, speaking of that wonderful day when you and I become one, how did the shopping go?"

Katie nodded toward the food. "Pray first. Talk second."

Austin bowed his head and offered a simple prayer of thanks for the meal. When he raised it again, Katie was digging into her food with gusto. Austin took pity on her, letting her finish a few bites before bringing up the subject again. "Did you get a lot done today?"

Katie nodded as she swallowed the bite of food she'd just taken. "Yeah, we did. We found dresses for me, Erin, and the flower girl. We found the tuxes. So, all you need to do is get yourself, Paul, and your nephew measured for them. We set things up with the bakery and the flower shop. Erin knows a guy who does photography, and he's reasonable. So, we're going to go with him for the pictures. And we have the invitation paper purchased and ready to print up."

Austin had stopped with his fork halfway to his mouth as she ran through the list. "Is it ready then? Is there anything left to do?"

"Of course, we have to print and mail the invitations and come up with any other decorations for the church. There are little things like shoes, jewelry, and getting the things we need to serve the cake and punch. But it's mostly done. You don't go out with Erin and come back without accomplishing all you set out to do."

Austin waved his hand over the meal. "That, my dear, is why we're having thai tonight. I figured the social butterfly would have worn out the wall flower."

"You don't know how right you are."

Austin nodded. "Oh, no, I think I do. I can imagine you are ready for a nice, long hiatus from shopping."

Katie sighed as she finished her meal, deposited the container in the trash, and dropped her fork and cup in the sink. "I really am. But no such luck. Erin's grandma Barb is coming to the wedding and asked Erin to help her pick out a dress. Since today was so much fun, I've gotten asked to come along. While we're at it, my mom is going to meet us at the mall to find her dress."

Austin choked on the drink of iced tea he'd just taken. Once his coughing fit was over, he looked over at Katie. "Erin's grandma? Gigi B?"

Katie shrugged. "I think that's what she called her. So tomorrow, I get to go dress shopping with my mother and another woman just like her. This should be a great time."

Austin chuckled. "I've met Gigi B, and shopping for someone like your mother is probably the last thing you should be worrying about."

Chapter Thirteen

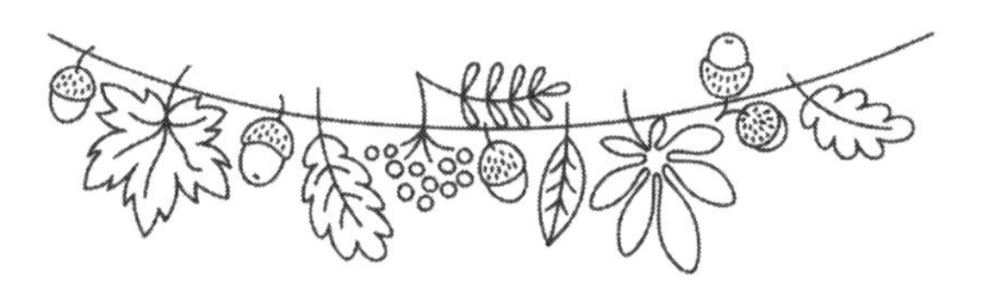

Katie and Erin arrived at the mall early for their meeting with her mother. Gigi B would join them in about an hour and a half, giving them time to find her mother's dress before going through the whole process a second time with Erin's grandma. Rather than waste time they headed for the dress section of the department store and began scouring the racks.

Before they'd managed to find anything suitable, Katie's mother joined them. "I'm so glad you girls are here to help me. I absolutely hate clothes shopping. It's a nerve-wracking experience."

Erin popped her head over the rack she was looking through. "At least now I know where Katie gets her sunny attitude about it."

"I learned from the best."

Katie's mom wasted no time sorting through the racks. "Let's get to it girls. I don't have all day to find this thing. Cal will be back to pick me up in half an hour."

Katie looked down at the rack to hide her surprise. Even she wouldn't be silly enough to think she could find a dress in half an hour. And her mom was picky. Katie only hoped she wouldn't be too disappointed if her timeline didn't work out.

Erin's voice was full of her usual optimism. "Well, then, we better get going. This dress isn't going to find itself."

Twenty minutes later, Katie was glad she hadn't said anything about her mom's crazy deadline. She would've had to eat her words. As soon as Erin lifted the modest navy blue dress from the rack, her mother insisted she try it on. The simple brocade dress fell straight to mid-calf length. While her mother didn't like the sleeveless top, it was made palatable by the short, matching dress jacket that went over it. The sleeves were the only sheer part of the design, and they were a modest navy blue tulle. It wasn't a style Katie would have enjoyed, but her mother liked it and looked nice in it.

As they walked to the checkout counter, Erin put a hand to Sharon's arm. "Oh, what about shoes? They have a nice selection here."

Her mother brushed Erin's hand away. "I don't need any shoes. I've got perfectly good shoes to wear at home. No sense in spending the money when I don't really need them."

Erin looked at Katie. She simply shrugged. If her mother didn't want new shoes, there would be no convincing her she did. The trio walked to the checkout counter and paid for the dress just as they reached the thirty minute limit. They left the department store to wait for Katie's dad where the sofas were arranged outside the store for husbands and boyfriends who tired of shopping trips with their significant others.

After a few minutes, Katie's mom looked at her watch. "Where is your father? We said half an hour, and it's been nearly forty minutes. It's not like him to run late."

After ten more minutes, Katie was beginning to worry. She couldn't help wishing her parents had let her get them cell phones. If they had, they wouldn't be sitting outside the store, worry growing with each passing minute. But they had been adamant about there being no use for them. Katie refrained from pointing out to her mother that this was the exact use for cell phones. It would only cause upheaval, and the day had gone well so far.

Five more minutes passed before Katie saw her dad hurrying through the glass entrance to the mall. He rushed over to them. “Why didn’t you tell me you were going to be at the mall? I’ve been sitting outside that other store you like to go to for the past twenty minutes.”

Her mother shook her head. “Cal, what are you going on about? You dropped me off here. Why would you go to that other place?”

Her father frowned. “What? I dropped you . . . Oh, that’s right. I got confused is all. Thought I was running late and got myself turned around. But no harm done. I’m here now. Let me carry that for you.”

He took the garment bag from her mom before including Katie and Erin in the conversation. “I hope I haven’t kept you girls. I know you’ve got your own shopping to do.”

“Don’t worry about it, Dad. We’re just glad you’re here and safe. We were beginning to worry.”

“No need to worry about me. But I better get this lovely lady home. You girls have a good time.”

He took her mother’s hand, and the two headed off towards the doors he’d just come through. Katie watched them leave. When they moved out of sight, she felt Erin watching her.

“Well, that was interesting. What do you think happened with your dad?”

Katie turned from the door. “I don’t know. I guess just what he said. He got in a hurry and got flustered.”

“Doesn’t sound like him though. Oh, well, I guess we better head back in and start looking. Gigi B will be here in just a few minutes, and I have a feeling this time we won’t get off so easily.”

Katie turned to follow her, but she was right. It didn’t sound like her dad. She’d have to speak with her mother about it at some point and find out if there was something else going on. She made an effort to push the unease to the back of her mind. Erin was right. Gigi B was due any minute, and they needed to start looking.

Katie sifted through the section of the nearest rack labeled small looking for something similar in taste to what they'd gotten her mother. Of course, they didn't need anything as dressy as her mother's choice. She was the mother of the bride. Gigi B was a guest. A country blue dress caught her eye. With its belted waist, polyester fabric, and button-up blouse style bodice, it definitely wasn't Katie's style. It was, however, exactly what she imagined someone's grandma might find attractive. She pulled it from the rack and held it out for Erin's inspection. "What about this one?"

Before Erin could respond, a voice rang out from the aisle to her right. "Oh, land sakes, no. Honey, I wouldn't be caught dead in that thing. This, on the other hand, is absolutely darling. Don't you think so, Erin?"

A flurry of flowing color swept through the empty space between Erin and Katie, stopping when it reached the display of hats on the far wall. Katie suppressed a giggle as the petite form reached up and plucked a teal, cloche hat with matching flower accents from a mannequin's head. Before she could guess what was happening, Katie watched the elderly woman plop the hat on her head and strike a pose. Though it didn't match her royal purple short-sleeved tunic or matching brightly patterned leggings, the shiny, patent leather heels she wore gave Katie the impression that the hat might actually fit the woman's style better than she would have guessed.

"I love it, Gigi B!" Erin abandoned the rack she'd been perusing to wrap the newcomer in a bear hug. "It's adorable on you! Oh, and it will complement the spring colors Katie has picked out perfectly. Now, we just have to find the right dress to go with it."

Katie silently slipped the dress she'd offered back onto its rack. There was no question it wouldn't begin to hold a candle to the large personality of Erin's Gigi B. As the two flitted off to a rack of more fitting dress styles, Katie couldn't help shaking her head at the two of them. The apple certainly didn't fall far from the tree. Katie briefly entertained the question of whether or not she would survive the shopping trip before squaring her shoulders and moving to join the duo eagerly chatting away while they searched the racks.

It took close to an hour for Gigi B to pull a deep teal colored dress from the rack and hold it up to Erin for inspection. Erin oohed and aahed over it, all the while comparing it to the hat still perched atop her grandmother's head.

Gigi B pressed it against her slight form. "It may be just what we're looking for. Now I just need to go try it on for size. Where do they keep those dressing rooms?"

Katie, still feeling like the whole ordeal was a little surreal, pointed to an alcove beyond the dresses. "I believe it's over there in the corner, Barb."

Pursed lips told Katie she had done something wrong. Erin's grandmother clicked her tongue before correcting her. "Aren't you my Erin's best friend? Is she not gonna be standin' next to you at your wedding? Isn't that why we're here buying this dress?"

Katie looked to Erin who offered no help. She was unsure how she should answer. "Yes. That's right."

"Then what's with all this Barb nonsense? I haven't been Barb since before Erin was born. If you're gonna be family, and that's what you are when you're best friends with my baby girl here, then you call me Gigi B just like everyone else. Got that?"

Katie bit her lip to keep from smiling, afraid Gigi B might take offense. "Yes, ma'am. Gigi B it is."

"Good. Now that that's settled, let's try on this dress."

Gigi B turned herself around and marched straight into the fitting room, leaving Erin and Katie no choice but to follow behind. They waited in the padded chairs next to a wall made up of three angled mirrors that served as the dressing room's viewing area. Before long, Gigi B sashayed out of the changing stall like a runway model until she stood admiring all views in the wall of mirrors.

The teal wrap around dress had short sleeves and a modest V-neck. Where the delicate fabric of the dress wrapped around to the left side of the bodice, it flowed into a ruffle down the dress from a high-waisted belt of the same fabric. The color would have been rather monotonous had it not been for the hoop of silver, studded with tiny, light teal gemstones that graced the belt above the cascade of fabric.

Though its design was more youthful than Katie would have chosen, paired with the hat and Gigi B's sass, the effect was utterly feminine and perfectly fitting. "You look great." She found that she could say the words in complete sincerity.

Gigi B speared her with a sideways glance. "I believe the word you're looking for is marvelous. This is the dress. And I have the perfect pair of strappy sandals at home to go with it. Now, who's up for a manicure? My treat."

"I really don't . . ."

Another look silenced Katie before her excuse could fully form. "Come along, then. Every woman needs beautiful nails for her wedding day or any other day for that matter. We'll use this as your test run. That way when you're ready for the real deal, you'll know exactly what you want."

In a matter of minutes, Gigi B had paid for her purchases, convinced the associate behind the counter to hold onto the flimsy plastic garment bag housing the dress and hat until they returned, and led Katie and Erin at an impossible pace down the corridors of the mall until they reached the nail salon. It struck Katie that while her own mother wouldn't even know where to find the nail salon, Gigi B seemed as comfortable with the mall's layout as she would be with her own home.

It wasn't until the trio was sitting on one side of the tables while the ladies on the other side cleaned, trimmed, and painted their nails that Katie felt like she could catch her breath. She glanced at Erin with shiny coats of pale peach being added at the seat next to her. The same color was being applied to her own nails. Further down, a work of nail art was taking place at Gigi B's table. Not content with a simple paint job, she had chosen teal enamel that changed color with the temperature like the mood changing rings Katie remembered from childhood. Though not yet applied, a layer of sparkle would finish off the look.

Katie considered her own modest color choice and smiled. She wasn't a fashion slob by any stretch of the imagination. She knew the current trends but stayed comfortable and classic rather than giving in to more fad-like choices. Even in her high school days and college, she wouldn't have chosen the look Erin's septuagenarian grandmother was sporting.

"Earth to Katie." Gigi B's voice cut through her internal dialogue. "Whatcha thinking about down there that's got you so tied up you can't even hear us talking to you? I bet it's that gorgeous, sweetheart you're fixing to marry. Am I right?"

Gigi B gave Erin a knowing look before training her gaze on Katie to wait for her answer. Katie sighed. There wasn't a way to say what she was thinking about without the possibility of offending. And she didn't want to do that. Gigi B was quickly growing on her, the same way her grand-daughter did when they first met. That was the first Sunday Katie had joined her parents at church after returning home to help her mother recuperate from a fall. She'd gotten out of going to the actual service because she'd been needed to help set up for the Thanksgiving potluck. Considering that was the day she found out Austin was a pastor, it was just as well she hadn't gone into the service. She wouldn't have heard a word of what he preached.

Katie's cheeks heated as she heard giggles and realized she'd gone off into her own world while Gigi B waited for a response. Without thinking about it, Katie answered in the direction her thoughts had taken her. "I guess sometimes I wonder if I'm cut out for being a pastor's wife. The Lord knows I wasn't too understanding when I first found out Austin was a pastor. I can't imagine what everyone will say with me as his wife."

Gigi B clicked her tongue. "They'll say, 'Look how happy Katie makes Austin. I'm so glad God brought her into his life.' And if they don't they aren't worth your worries anyway."

Katie shook her head. "I don't think you understand. I haven't always lived out my faith. To be perfectly honest, for a long time I ran from it, and I went down some roads that a pastor's wife shouldn't ever go down."

Her straight, blonde bob bounced with an exaggerated nod of her head. "Oh, I see. You were a preacher's wife back then? When you were running from God and making those sinful choices?"

Katie licked her lips. "No."

"No? Okay. How about Austin's church? I'm guessing he has pew after padded pew of people who live perfect lives. Their white picket fences guard their holiness and keep sin at bay?"

Katie squirmed. "No. They sin. But what I did . . ."

"'What you did' what? What you did was so bad God couldn't forgive it? Maybe it was something so much worse than everyone else's sin that God forgave it, but He's decided to hold it against you anyway? He's deemed you unfit for His service?"

Katie sighed. "When you put it that way, it seems silly. But not everyone thinks like you."

Gigi B swatted her free hand through the air like she was trying to rid herself of a pestering fly. "You've got to learn, precious one, that it doesn't matter what everyone else says. It's what God says that counts. And He says if you're repentant, you're forgiven. Not a little bit, all the way forgiven. Now don't get me wrong. Some sins carry pretty heavy physical and emotional consequences. Being sorry you touched a hot oven and learning never to do it again doesn't make the burn disappear. But it'd be plain wrong for someone to ban you from the kitchen for the rest of your life because of a mistake you not only acknowledge but also take measures to avoid in the future."

"I've never thought about it that way."

"It's high time you did then. You're a forgiven child of God, just like everyone else filling the pews. And if God gave you a man like Austin Blake to love and be loved by, then count yourself blessed. And as far as being a pastor's wife, that's just like being anybody else's wife except your man has more demands on his time and could use a little more prayer support. There ain't nothing in the scriptures specifically about what a pastor's wife is or isn't. There's plenty in there about women and wives and believers in general and believers in leadership. What God wants of a pastor's wife is what He wants of everyone else. Love Him with all your heart, soul, and strength. Seek Him first. The rest will fall into place. No need to worry."

The same words from anyone else might have felt like chastisement. Instead, she felt peace. Gigi B was in her corner after only having just met her. More than that, God was in her corner. Her gratitude was enough to bring tightness to her throat. "Thank you."

"It ain't nothing but speaking the truth. Own it, and you'll do just fine."

With that Gigi B surrendered her loose hand to the manicurist to add her sparkle. The conversation turned to the less serious matters of flower colors and cake flavors. The three chatted easily through the remainder of their time in the salon. And as Katie waved good-bye to Erin and her grandma after their nails were done and their purchases picked up, she couldn't help feeling like God had put Gigi B into her day to give Katie a dose of encouragement she hadn't realized she needed. She only hoped it wasn't going to be the last time He chose to bring the elderly woman into her circle.

Chapter Fourteen

Austin captured one of Katie's hands in his own and held it up for inspection. "What is this? A perfect manicure. Who are you and what have you done with my fiancé?"

Katie yanked it from his grasp. Austin reached for it immediately, threading his fingers through hers. The playfully indignant pout on her face softened into a slight smile as she looked at him. She quirked her eyebrow. "It's just one example of what happens when you spend the day with Gigi B."

Austin pulled her into his chest and wrapped his arms around her. He gently rubbed one hand up and down her back. Though the parking lot where they stood was less than private, Austin held her until she relaxed against him, laying her head on his shoulder. "I'm sorry you had a rough day. Gigi B can be intense. Maybe Bread of Life wasn't such a great idea for tonight."

He felt her head shake against his shoulder. Her voice was muffled when she spoke with her face still pressed against him. "It wasn't rough."

"What did you say?"

Katie lifted her head to look at him. One shoulder lifted in a shrug. Still hand in hand they walked from the car around the church toward the entrance leading into the fellowship hall. "I said it wasn't rough. Sure, I probably couldn't keep up with her for a full day, but Gigi B was great. I kind of see what Erin's going to be like in the future."

Austin laughed. "Am I going to need to fit your walker with a jet pack to keep up?"

"You might. But seriously, I really like Gigi B. I think I judge too quickly sometimes. Gigi B came in large and in charge. She's overflowing with sass and spunk. It wasn't intentional, but I think I decided then and there that she was full of fun and not a lot else. I did it with Erin too when we met. I liked being friends with her because she shook me out of my same old, same old. But it took a while to see there was more there. I realize what a great gift God gave me when He brought her into my life. It didn't take as long with Gigi B. God showed me just how special she is before we even made it out of the mall."

"How'd He do that?"

"Hey, you two! Wait up!" Erin's voice carried around the corner of the church causing them to stop.

Austin turned to see Erin pulling Paul along behind her as she tried to catch up to them. As short as her legs were, Paul still had to move quickly or get left behind. Austin and Katie waited for them, their conversation over, at least for the moment. Austin determined when the time was right, he and Katie would revisit the conversation. He didn't consider himself a nosey person, but this time the idea of what changed Katie's opinion seemed important. It would wait until their time of ministering to those in need was finished for the evening, but once they were alone, he wanted to hear the rest of the story.

Paul looked to Austin as he and Erin approached. "So what exactly is this Bread of Life thing Erin's been jabbering on about all afternoon? She wouldn't let me out of it, but she never would tell me what it was besides 'a way to give back'."

Austin looked to Erin. "I'm surprised she didn't tell you since it's her baby."

Paul swung his attention to the woman in question. "What's this?"

Austin grinned at the glare that judged him traitor before Erin softened her expression to return Paul's look. She looked away after the briefest eye contact. She toyed with the buttons on her royal blue pea coat with her one free hand. "It may have been my idea initially, but a lot of people helped put it together. And none of it could have been done if it hadn't been God's plan to begin with."

"Okay. So what is it?"

Austin watched as Erin's hands came free from Paul's hold and began moving in earnest as her excitement over the ministry became evident. "We may not be a huge city like Chicago or anything, but we are large for this area. And some parts of this town and the surrounding ones don't have a lot. Unemployment is up right now, and that puts a lot of people in a hard spot. Others have made poor choices and ended up on the streets because of them. That's where Bread of Life comes in. Every week, the ladies of our church get together and prepare a meal for anyone who needs one. Doesn't matter if they're a family going through tough times or a kid with issues that keep him from having a place to go home to, everyone can get a good, hot meal at least once a week. And other churches help too. So, our ladies don't end up doing the lion's share of the work each time."

Paul's look reflected more than love. His admiration for Erin was also evident. "What prompted the idea?"

"Benji. He was in my Sunday school class. You wouldn't have known anything was wrong. He was dressed alright. He was clean. But when it was snack time, he couldn't seem to help himself. He just shoveled it in like he hadn't had a decent amount of food in weeks. I found out later that he probably hadn't. His mom was a stay-at-home mom, and the appliance factory his dad worked at closed unexpectedly. Jobs are hard to come by. They got some help from the state, but it just covered expenses. They had food, but never enough to satisfy. It broke my heart to think theirs was one of the milder cases around."

"That's amazing. I don't know that I've ever seen a problem that life-changing for so many people and brainstormed the answer before."

Erin's cheeks pinked. "It's not an answer, but it's a start. There's a bigger plan for down the road, but right now, we need to get in there and help serve."

"Lead the way."

Erin took Paul's hand, and the two walked toward the door. Austin followed suit taking Katie's hand. He didn't even try to stifle the smile that grew as he noticed her wide eyes and the decidedly unfeminine way her mouth dropped open. She'd served by his side faithfully since her return to Carbondale, and she understood the ministry need. But he realized this was the first time she'd heard the story of how the ministry got its start. He couldn't help wondering if she was once again realizing just how much more to her friend there was than fun and fluff. "Come on, sweetheart. It's cold out here, and we've got dinner to serve."

THE KITCHEN WAS WARM, but no one complained as they served meatloaf with all the fixings to what seemed like a never-ending line. Katie heard from some of those in attendance that another church in the area was starting their own meal ministry in the coming weeks. The thought that all these people might be able to get two good meals a week was enough to bring tears to her eyes.

She looked across the room to see Austin speaking with Jamie, a regular at the dinners. He wasn't quite twenty-one, but no one would know that to look at him. A dirty, full beard and mustache covered a face drugs had aged beyond his years. Austin had a soft spot for Jamie and took every opportunity to encourage him.

Gaining his trust over time, Austin learned that the young man's home growing up was a place devoid of love. Giving in to their own addictions, his parents had modeled the kind of choices that led Jamie down this dangerous path. All he'd ever known was a life that invited a kid to turn to anything he could find to dull the pain. Austin saw more in him, and he encouraged him every chance he got.

As Austin moved from Jamie towards her, Katie inclined her head in the direction he'd come from. "Is he willing to try it again?"

Austin nodded. "I've talked to the rehab place, and they have a spot held for him. I'm going to take him over there tomorrow morning. He'll stay at the homeless shelter tonight. It's only for one night though. It's against their rules to take someone in who's using, but I got them to make an exception to keep Jamie in a safe place until I can take him to the rehab facility tomorrow. The church decided at last week's board meeting to take on the costs, and Jamie says he's ready for a change."

"I pray that's true." She looked from the table where Jamie sat shoveling in forkful after forkful of meatloaf to where Austin stood beside her. "I'm so proud of you. You've been Jamie's champion when no one else would even try."

Austin shrugged. "He needs someone in his corner. He's never had anyone."

The door across the fellowship hall opened, and Katie watched as a man wearing cowboy boots and a Stetson sauntered through. He looked familiar, and Katie studied him as he crossed the room to the counter. She dropped her eyes quickly as he caught her staring.

"Little Kate, I'd heard rumors you were back in town. How've you been doing?"

Her memory fell into place just in time to shield her from embarrassment. He was the only one who'd ever gotten away with calling her Kate. She raised her head and smiled at the man standing in front of her. He was a little more filled out than when she'd known him, and his five o'clock shadow had a hint of gray in it. The corners of his eyes held fine crow's feet when he smiled, but they were the same brilliant blue from her high school years. And there was no disguising the smooth southern twang. "I'm doing just fine. How about you, Nathan? What are you doing here tonight?"

His head dipped in the direction of the foam containers filled and waiting on the counter. "Just making deliveries. Got word that Tara Lynn couldn't bring them out to the nursing home tonight. So, I volunteered. Can't have the church's shut-ins thinking they've been forgotten, now can we? If you load me up, I can take the ones for my church and yours. Y'all don't know how much this home-cooked meal means to those who can't do for themselves anymore. Let's 'em know their church family hasn't forgotten them. Others aren't quite so fortunate."

"I wish there were more people willing to do their part for those who've been forgotten in the nursing homes." Austin's voice cut into the conversation as he moved to stand behind Katie. "They've given so much for so long. I can't imagine what it must be like for them, being treated like baggage."

Nathan nodded a greeting to Austin. "Not just baggage. A lot of times they're unwanted, forgotten baggage. It's not a bad thing to need help for an aging parent, but to put them in there and then put them out of your mind, to me, that's the height of self-centeredness. Anyway, get me off my soap box. It's time for me to head back. Those ladies will never forgive me if their mashed potatoes and gravy get cold. It was good to see you again, Little Kate. Austin, you too."

Katie felt Austin's eyes on her as she watched Nathan saunter from the room much the same way he'd entered it. She turned to find a smirk on his handsome face and groaned, knowing what was coming.

"Little Kate, huh? Well, Little Kate, how is it you know Nathan?"

If she didn't know better, Katie could swear she heard a hint of jealousy under the mocking tone of his voice. The thought to play it up entered her mind, but she dismissed it without a second thought. She'd been on the wrong end of betrayal, and she had no desire to make someone else feel even a shadow of what she'd felt. She couldn't do that to an enemy, much less the man she loved. "Nathan's little sister is Tonya Phillips. We were best friends from second grade until her family moved to Texas at the end of our junior year of high school. We promised to keep in touch, but that only lasts until one or both parties have found replacement friends. We lost touch. I didn't know any of them ever moved back to the area."

"Nathan's the only one in town. Moved back about six years ago. But the real question is, who is Little Kate?"

Katie rolled her eyes and smacked his shoulder as he laughed. "I said Nathan is Tonya's big brother. He was four years older, and we were the bane of his existence. He was constantly teasing me. He knew I couldn't stand the name Kate. And at the time I was worried I would always be the shortest girl in the class. So, Little Kate was born. Nathan was the big brother I never had."

Austin nodded slowly. "Hmm."

"Hey, you two." Erin interrupted as she and Paul made their way across the fellowship hall. "Margaret says it's time to wipe down the tables. And they have something going on in here with the kids this week. So, we need to fold them and put them in the hall storage closet."

She tossed a wet rag toward Katie. Thrusting out her hand to catch it before it hit her, she realized how wet it was. The soapy water sprinkled her face as the rag hit her hand. She swiped it away with her free hand. "Thank you for that." She looked to Austin. "I guess we're wiping the tables. You and Paul can put them away."

They made short work of the task, finishing before the leftovers had been divvied up for the families who needed them. A warmed up meal was better than what waited for them otherwise. With the tables put away, the quartet said their good-byes to the other volunteers and the few stragglers that remained.

"Cool Spoons?" Erin asked, pulling the keys to her VW bug out of her monogrammed purse.

Katie glanced to Austin. Seeing the question in his eyes, she shrugged. "Frozen yogurt sounds like a good plan to me."

Erin opened her car door. "Great. We'll meet you guys over there."

Without waiting for an answer, she and Paul got in her car and pulled out of the parking lot. Katie smiled, warmth enveloping her hand as Austin took it in his and led her around the church to his truck. Austin only dropped her hand to open the car door for her. Once he pulled out of the driveway and started down the road to the frozen yogurt shop, he reached across the seat and captured her hand once again.

Katie leaned back against the seat and sighed. Her previous relationship had given her the impression that opening doors for a woman and simply taking her hand as they walked was insulting. No, it wasn't an impression. He'd outright said it multiple times. Women didn't need coddling or protecting. They were perfectly capable of taking care of themselves. He'd said it, and she'd believed it until Austin came along.

He'd opened doors for her from the day they met, and she'd never felt insulted. She felt treasured. Austin didn't doubt her ability to take care of herself. When she'd asked him about it, he'd told her she was perfectly capable but she shouldn't have to. A woman should be treated like a precious gift. That included opening doors and all the other little ways Austin showed her he cared every day. Katie squeezed the hand holding hers in its gentle grasp.

Austin took his eyes from the road to glance at her momentarily. "What was that for?"

Katie grinned. "Just counting my blessings, I guess. Thankful that God gave me such a wonderful, caring man to be mine forever."

"Forever and then some. You're not going to get rid of me no matter how much you may want to. Dirty socks on the floor instead of in the hamper. Dishes left in the sink. And don't forget the times I'll be late to dinner without warning. You'll be ready to run in a month."

Katie giggled at his teasing. She couldn't fathom Austin doing any of those things. Neat by nature and thoughtful too, Austin's downfall wouldn't be any domestic shortcomings. Not that Katie was foolish enough to believe marriage would be all rainbows and sunshine with cute little puppies. Any time two people lived together there were adjustments and disagreements. She had no idea what theirs would be, but it definitely wouldn't be about dirty socks. "I don't think we need to worry about any of that. As long as you keep bringing me scones, I can forgive a dirty dish or two. I'm not going anywhere. It's you and me for the rest of our lives."

Austin pulled into a parking space at the tiny strip mall. As he put the truck in park, he looked at her and waited until she met his gaze. "I wouldn't have it any other way."

The warmth that spread through her at his words didn't dissipate as she stepped out of the truck into the cool March air. Austin loved her. They were getting married in a month. God had blessed her beyond her wildest dreams. Katie took Austin's hand, and together they crossed the parking lot to the yogurt shop.

If her own thoughts weren't enough to bring a smile to her face, stepping through the door was. Two small children drew crazy pictures on the chalk board walls in the corner next to the cash register. Fun orange and green accents gave energy to the small space. Katie and Austin made their way to the wall of dispensers that blended ten different individual flavors of frozen yogurt, custard, gelato, and sorbet to give patrons fifteen possible choices. Katie grabbed a cup and made a bee-line for the chocolate custard before going around the corner to the cold toppings bar. She added a dollop of whipped cream before turning toward a wall lined with plastic tubes. With every imaginable topping filling each tube, it made a colorful display. But Katie knew exactly what she wanted, and it wouldn't be found on the wall. She opened a small container on a nearby island and scooped spoonfuls of chocolate mint candy onto her custard.

Erin looked over her shoulder. "Predictable. You always get the same thing. You've got to live a little, girl."

Katie looked into her friend's cup. Orange sorbet was nearly hidden under a mound of gummy worms, pineapple chunks, coconut, peach boba, and whipped topping. The thought of all the flavors co-mingling on her tongue was almost enough to make her cringe, especially with the chewy sweet gummy worms. "No thank you. I'll stick with my simple cup."

"Suit yourself. You don't know what you're missing." With that Erin made her way to the cash register.

Katie followed, and by the time Paul and Erin were done having their cups weighed and paid for, Austin had joined her. After paying for their desserts, they made their way through the maze of round tables to the upholstered chairs in the far corner where Paul and Erin had planted themselves.

While they ate, Erin regaled them with their experience shopping with Gigi B. Her ability to start with a simple tale and end up with an epic adventure worthy of the big screen kept everyone laughing. She held up one hand to curb the laughter before she continued. "But it wasn't all fun and games."

Katie shot Erin a warning look. Erin didn't catch it. Or she didn't want to. Katie couldn't tell for sure, but she got the distinct impression that Erin was purposefully avoiding looking at her.

"We bonded with deep theological discussions over manicures. Gigi B proved herself not only witty but wise as well."

Erin looked to Katie for confirmation. As Katie's lungs released, she realized she'd held her breath waiting for Erin to delve into the reason for their discussion. Relief flooded through her knowing her doubts were not being offered up for public consumption. She nodded. "If I'm ever in charge of an important decision, she's the one I'd want in my corner."

Katie shifted her gaze from Erin to Austin. Her bite of frozen custard caught in her throat. The questioning look in Austin's eyes told Katie her relief was premature. She quickly pasted on a grin and turned to Paul. "Have you met Gigi B yet?"

Paul shook his head but before he could answer, Austin voiced the question she was trying to avoid. "What wise advice did you get from Gigi B?"

Her custard moved from her throat to settle in a pit in her stomach. Why couldn't he leave it alone? She should give a simple answer to nullify the question, but she knew she couldn't. The last time she'd kept something from Austin, it had nearly destroyed them. She wouldn't take that chance ever again. "She told me not to let my past keep me from being who God has chosen me to be for the future." She paused. If only that could be enough of an answer. A gentle nudge told her it wasn't. "And she told me it doesn't matter what others might say or think. God's forgiven my past, and you've chosen to make me part of your future. And if God's forgiven me then no one else has the right to hold it against me."

Austin frowned. "What would people say about you? And what does it have to do with me?"

Tears burned her eyes, but she refused to give in to them. First the panic attacks and now this. Why did she have to be the one with all the issues? Katie looked to Erin for support.

Erin took the cue. "Katie was worried because everyone knows her past. You're the pastor, and she didn't want people thinking less of you because of her. She was afraid people might not think she's worthy of being a pastor's wife. Gigi B just helped her see things a little differently."

Paul stood up, collecting the empty containers from everyone.

"Good. I'd say Katie needed to think a little differently about those things. Glad Gigi B could help. But I think it's time you and I got going. Don't you?"

Katie watched Erin's eyes dart between her and Austin before she stood. "Paul's right. It's been a long day. Call you tomorrow Katie?"

Katie nodded. "Sure."

Once their friends left, Austin stood. Katie let him take her hand to help her up and lead her out of the building. It was funny how silence could at one time be soft, peaceful even, and then another time weigh a thousand pounds and threaten to suffocate.

Austin pulled into traffic and headed south before lifting the weight from her chest. "Do you really have doubts about being a pastor's wife?"

Katie shrugged and looked out the window. "Not all the time, but yeah. God called you to this ministry. You heard it, and you answered the call. I've never really considered ministry life, and I've definitely never felt called to it."

"But you have. Don't you see that? Since the day you moved back home, you've been in ministry. You've served right beside me each week at Bread of Life. And you've taken on a Sunday school class. That's ministry."

True. "But it's not the same. Everyone can do that."

"Yes they can, but you saw the need. You felt God moving in you to help, and you did. Everyone can do it, but not everyone does. You are involved in ministry, and you're doing a great job at what God's given you."

Katie twisted the ring on her finger as she tried to formulate a response. She knew what Austin meant, but she didn't think he really understood where she was coming from. Austin reached across the truck stilling her nervous movement by taking her hand in his.

Katie carefully considered her words before trying to explain. "I know I serve, and no one seems to mind it. Everyone's been great, welcoming me back and treating me like I was never gone. But that's just them seeing me as a regular church member. I think I was worried that they would see the pastor's wife differently, that they would expect a pastor's wife to have been some kind of super Christian her whole life. And they definitely wouldn't want someone beside their pastor that's made the mistakes I've made."

Austin gripped her hand tighter. "But . . ."

Katie cut him off. "But after speaking with Gigi B, I've come to the realization that God has forgiven me completely. And God has brought you into my life. And if marrying you means becoming a pastor's wife, then God knew that too. If He wasn't okay with it, He wouldn't have allowed either one of us to be at peace with our decision to marry. And if anyone does have a problem with it, then it is their problem."

Austin put the truck in park but rather than getting out to open her door, he turned to her. "I'm sorry you've been dealing with these issues. And I'm especially sorry I wasn't sensitive enough to it to see your struggle. You don't have to deal with these things alone. I want to be there for you just like I've always been."

"I know, and you are. But this time, I think it would've been hard to accept from you. You do have a conflict of interests after all. But God brought me someone who could tell it like it is and do it with love. I'm not saying I won't ever have doubts again, but thanks to Gigi B I have the answers I need to combat them. And I can't wait for the day I become your wife."

He pulled her close to kiss her, and Katie knew Austin felt the same way. Only a few short weeks, and she would never have to watch him leave at the end of the night again. She kissed him back and slid across the truck seat so he could wrap his warm arms around her. As the kiss deepened, her arms encircled his waist. With more restraint than she felt like using, Katie leaned away to break the kiss without leaving the warmth of his arms.

The tinge of disappointment she saw in Austin's eyes was

almost enough to break her resolve. "Kisses like that are becoming more and more dangerous."

Austin groaned. "I keep telling myself to be patient. Our wedding day is just around the corner, and then I don't ever have to let you go again. You'll be my wife. And we'll be able to hold and kiss and touch each other all we want."

Katie pretended to be offended. "Is that really all I am to you? Someone to hold and kiss?"

Austin pulled her in to his chest. She could hear his heart beating and feel his fingers lightly tracing a path along her back. "You know that's not true. While I definitely look forward to all that marriage has to offer in that department, you are so much more to me than what we'll be able to enjoy together physically. In just a few short weeks, I'll have you by my side as my partner, my friend, my wife. And I'll be honest, I can't think of anything more perfect."

Chapter Fifteen

"Perfect. Now don't move."

Katie tried not to look too posed as she faced the full length mirror. She could easily imagine the photographer was getting some amazing shots that would show off her dress from all sides. Katie held the pose, with one hand hanging down holding her bouquet of colorful daisies and the other barely reaching above her strapless sweet-heart neckline as if she were adjusting the double strand of seed pearls entwined together around her throat.

"Can you straighten the hem of her gown?"

The photographer spoke to Erin while Katie fought the urge to try straightening it herself. The bodice was overlaid with a simple patterned lace accented with the same tiny pearls. At her slender waist, a narrow pale peach ribbon served to separate the fitted top from the layers of fine tulle that flowed from under it. The layers gave just the right amount of fullness to the skirt that cascaded down in the back to create a slight train. Simple yet elegant.

With the skirt properly arranged, Erin stood in front of Katie assessing the effect. "I think you should move a few curls over your shoulder. What do you think?"

The way she turned her head convinced Katie she was speaking with the photographer, but she didn't care. "I think we worked hard to pull the curls on the sides up and weave those tiny strings of pearls through them. I think we shouldn't mess them up."

Erin's lips pursed as she tilted her head considering Katie's concern. "No. It won't mess them up. Hold still."

Without waiting for approval, Erin maneuvered a few of Katie's auburn curls to lie on her shoulder. Looking at her reflection in the mirror, Katie had to admit it added something to the picture. But she wouldn't give Erin the satisfaction. "Are you done? Can Jessie finish taking the pictures now?"

"Humph. Can Jessie finish taking the pictures now?" Erin mimicked her in a whiny voice. "How about thank you, Erin. That looks great, Erin. What would I do without you, Erin?"

The smile on Katie's face due to Erin's antics was full and genuine. The photographer must have realized it too, because Katie could hear the click of the camera from somewhere just out of her view.

"READY?" Paul's hand landed briefly on Austin's back.

A quick look in the mirror to adjust his ocean blue tie, and he nodded to his best man. Together they walked out the door that opened directly onto the stage and stopped a few steps from the minister.

Austin grinned as Paul winked at Erin who stood opposite him. With the non-traditional song they'd chosen to play while Katie walked down the aisle, they'd also decided to forgo having the best man and maid of honor walk in. The bright blue color of Erin's tea length dress was an exact match to one of the many colors of crazy daisies in her bouquet. The sleeveless V-neck dress with its fitted top and A-line skirt was a great style for Erin. It accented her best features, and one look at Paul showed Austin his best man had definitely lost his heart to the maid of honor.

Paul and Erin were forgotten as the first strains of Louie Armstrong's voice singing of trees and roses drew his attention to the doors at the back of the sanctuary. Two young boys from the church opened the doors, and everyone in the building seemed to disappear as Austin got his first glimpse of Katie smiling demurely in the opening. Beautiful. And about to be joined to him for the rest of his life. He could feel his smile as it stretched wider than he could ever remember. Did all the couples he'd performed ceremonies for feel as blessed by God? No. There was no way they could have because God hadn't given them Katie McGowan.

As much as her walk to meet him seemed to stretch on forever, the rest of the service passed in a blur. He was sure they had included all the traditional things like unity candle lighting and exchanging rings and vows. He knew he would look back and remember all the details, but at that moment, he couldn't call one to mind. All he could see was Katie's sweet smile and tear filled eyes looking at him in love as the minister pronounced them man and wife and gave him permission to kiss his bride.

The hand that had been holding hers went around her waist and pulled her to him. The other cupped the back of her head, letting his fingers weave through her hair as his lips met hers. He tasted the tears on her soft lips, and pulled away enough to rest his forehead against hers. His fingers moved from her hair to her cheek where he brushed the tears away with his thumb.

"I love you, Mrs. Blake." He hoped she could hear his voice, hoarse with emotion above the clapping of the crowd.

She raised her head to lightly touch her lips to his once more before looking into his eyes. "And I love you, Mr. Blake, now and forever."

"May I present, for the first time, Mr. and Mrs. Austin Blake." The minister's voice cut into their tender moment.

The bouncy melody of Christina Perri's "Be My Forever" filled the sanctuary as Austin grabbed Katie's hand and they made their way back up the aisle. Once Paul and Erin followed them into the foyer, Austin and Katie went back to the front aisle to be met with congratulations and hugs as they dismissed each row personally before joining their guests in the fellowship hall for the reception.

Austin turned from thanking the minister as Paul approached. Paul gripped his hand, pulling him in to clap his other hand on his back in what only men would consider a hug. "I couldn't be happier for you two, but don't you think it's time for you and your new bride to get away?"

Austin scanned the room. "Where is the beautiful Mrs. Blake?"

Paul tilted his chin toward the stairs. "Erin said she went to change. I think they used the high school classroom."

"Then I'd better go find her."

Austin took the stairs two at a time to get to the room. He rapped his knuckles on the closed door.

"If that's you, Austin, come on in."

Austin pushed open the door. "It's me."

Katie was zipping the garment bag which held her wedding dress. The dress she'd changed into looked comfortable, casual. The only way Austin could describe it was an extra-long, country-blue button up shirt. Could a shirt even be made into a dress? Except for the wide tan leather belt around the middle and the gathers in the skirt, tiny white stripes made it look like one of the pin stripe shirts in his closet. Katie in one of his shirts. The thought created an image that pulsed heat through his body. He cleared his throat.

Katie pulled on one strappy, heeled sandal, then the other. She snatched a small tan purse off the table and moved toward him. She brushed her fingers from his fingertips up his arm and across his chest as she walked past him. Glancing back she gave him a look that turned the heat into a full blown flame. "Are you about ready to head to the hotel? We're going to have a long drive ahead of us tomorrow to get to the cabin in Gatlinburg. You'll probably want to turn in early so you can get plenty of rest."

She smiled sweetly and batted her eyes. She knew exactly what she was doing to him, and he loved the fact that they were free to flirt as brazenly as they wanted. He followed her out the door. He would get the rest he needed to get them to their honeymoon destination, after they had cooled the fire she had just stoked inside him. He wanted this night to leave his wife without any doubts about his desire to know her and love her in every way possible now that they were one.

Chapter Sixteen

Katie heard Austin's truck pull into the driveway, but she didn't move from her spot looking out the window of their guest room. She didn't even turn when she heard the front door open and close. She heard Austin's steps and knew from where they were silenced that Austin was leaning against the door frame watching her.

She took a slow breath and closed her eyes. This wasn't the first time similar scenes had played out since their wedding day three months earlier. The first time, he'd come home to find her daydreaming of making the room into a nursery. Austin and Katie had discussed all the demands on their time from simply adjusting to life as newlyweds to ministry needs that kept them busy. Recently, ministry was more demanding than usual since Jamie's counselors at the drug treatment facility had asked him to stop by a couple times a week to mentor the young man. It seemed there was no one in his life stable enough to do so, and Austin hadn't hesitated in agreeing. So, while they wouldn't sweat trying to prevent it, they decided it was better not to try to start a family right away.

"Whatcha doing?"

She turned from the window. "Thinking about whether we

would need to store or sell the bedroom furniture in here to make room for a crib."

She could hear his sigh as much as she saw it in the rise and fall of his shoulders. "I guess I haven't considered it. But I think we have plenty of time to figure it out. Don't you?"

She shrugged. "Maybe, but don't you think the next nine months might pass quicker than we think?"

"Why nine . . . wait. Are you saying we're going to have a baby?"

Katie could hear the shock in his voice, but determining whether her announcement was a cause for celebration or not was a little harder. "I know we weren't exactly trying right now, but it's not that we didn't want it to happen either. Right? I mean, yes, we're newlyweds, but a lot of people don't wait to have kids. And they do just fine. I just . . ."

Austin's approach cut off her words. He stood silently in front of her until she raised her eyes to his. His hand cupped her cheek. She had a brief moment to see the joy in his eyes before his lips claimed hers in a sweet kiss. His voice was a rough whisper. "I love you."

"So you're okay with this?"

"Honey, I'm more than okay with this. I can't think of anything I'd love more than to see you grow with our child until the day we get to hold her in our arms. And while you fill her mind with far off adventures from all the books you'll read to her, I'll teach her everything I know about baking. And one day I'll tell her the story of how my magic macadamia nut, white chocolate, and cranberry scones caused the most loving, beautiful woman in the world to fall in love with me and become my wife."

Katie shook her head. "Yep, it was all the scones. That and the frozen caramel mochas. Wait. Did you say she? What if she is a he?"

Austin shrugged. "Then I can teach him how to bake, and you can teach him how to play football."

Katie's laugh echoed off the walls. "You get to teach him baking, and I get to teach him football?"

"Well, you certainly can't teach him to bake. I've seen the disastrous aftermath of your attempts at baking."

She swatted his arm, trying to look offended but sure her laughter countered any look she gave him. "You and I both know I can hold my own in the kitchen. Just because I'm not a professional, doesn't mean I don't have skill. But if I have to teach him football, our child is in trouble. I've never played football a day in my life. The game doesn't even make sense to me."

"Then I guess you'll just have to teach him how to weave words together to create new and exciting worlds."

"Who's going to teach him football?"

"We'll leave that to the P.E. teacher. He'll be better off that way. I've always been sports challenged."

Austin pulled her into his arms once again, cutting off any further conversation with his kiss. Katie wrapped her arms around him, reveling in the love she felt for and from her husband. When he reluctantly pulled back, she could still feel the warmth of his lips on hers. It wasn't the kind of kiss that stoked their fiery passion. It was sweet, promising a lifetime of love as they raised their little one.

Austin opened his mouth but the ring of his cell phone interrupted. His eye closed in a flirtatious wink as he pulled the phone from his pocket and answered. "This is Austin."

Katie wandered the small space while he talked. She pictured a crib and changing table where the guest bed now sat. Of course, the tan walls would need painted over. Maybe a gender neutral pale yellow or pastel green. A wallpaper border could be added to bring a variety of color to the room once they found out if the baby was a girl or a boy.

She turned as Austin put his phone back in his pocket. "I hate to do this, especially right now, but I have to go."

Katie frowned. "What's wrong?"

A hand ran through his hair, leaving it tousled. It was adorable, but it also meant he was worried. "Jamie. That was his counselor at the treatment facility. He's talking about leaving. They're hoping I can calm him down."

"Go. I'll be here when you get back."

"Thank you for understanding. I hope I won't be long."

She stopped his retreating back with a few quiet words. "They're right, you know."

He turned. "What do you mean?"

"You've got a special bond with Jamie. I know it's frustrating at times, but the kid needs you. He knows you care, and it's making a difference."

Austin crossed the room to give her one last kiss before heading back through the doorway. "Thank you. Just pray that I have the right words to say."

"Always."

ERIN TOOK the glass of sweet tea from Katie's hand. "Where's Austin tonight? I didn't know we were going to have a girls' night."

"We weren't. He got called out to deal with Jamie at the rehab center. It was kind of last minute and sounded urgent."

Erin grabbed a ceramic bowl full of grapes from the fridge, popping one in her mouth before picking up her glass and following Katie into the living room. "With Jamie it's always urgent. That kid just can't seem to keep it together for long."

"True. As bad as his life's been, I don't think he's hit rock bottom yet. Until the unthinkable happens, I don't think God's going to get hold of him once and for all. But I did get to talk with Austin about something pretty important before he left. I think it's something that's going to change our lives forever."

"Life changing events, and I've been here nearly thirty minutes without you dishing? What kind of friend are you?"

"The kind that's going to make you Auntie Erin in approximately nine months."

The high pitched squeal emanating from Erin raised Katie's eyebrows. She was sure neighborhood dogs were running away in terror. Erin pulled her from her seat and hugged her as they jumped up and down in excitement. Words tumbled from her mouth at speeds that were hard to keep up with. "Oh my gosh. You're going to have a baby. I'm going to be Auntie Erin, and rightfully so. Oh, this is going to be so great. And you said that Austin knows? Of course Austin knows. You'd tell him first. You said you told him first. What did he say? Does Paul know? Oh, I love this. I have news he hasn't heard first! Can I be the one to tell him? I can't believe it. I didn't even know you were trying. It really doesn't matter. All that matters is you're having a baby! Are you feeling okay? When is the baby due?"

Katie belly laughed. "If you'll slow down for a minute, I'll tell you everything."

Erin flopped back into the recliner, seemingly spent from her outburst but eyes shining with happiness. "Well? Get on with it then."

Katie sat back on the sofa and took a drink before answering. It was amusing the way Erin was trying to be patient and failing miserably. Her foot tapped a staccato beat on the floor, and she leaned forward eyes wide urging Katie to share. As funny as it was to watch, Katie knew she needed to put her out of her misery. "We weren't trying, but we weren't trying to keep it from happening either. We were taking things as they came. Yes, you can be the one to tell Paul. Austin seemed happy enough about it, but he had to run out the door pretty quickly after I told him. I'm not sure he's had time to take it all in yet. I don't even think I got to tell him when the baby's due."

"When is the baby due?"

"As close as I can tell, it should be around March fifteenth. I called the doctor's office today, and they said I'll have an ultrasound at my first appointment that will give me a more accurate due date. But since I'm usually like clockwork in my cycles, I don't think it will be too far off."

"March. I can't believe I'm going to be Auntie Erin in March. And you're going to be a mother. A mother. Can you believe it?"

Katie plucked a grape from the bowl on the tray sitting between them. "I'm excited, but it doesn't feel real yet. I mean, I'm not sick. Which I'm not complaining about, by the way. I don't feel any different than I did a month ago. It's strange. Like in my head I know there's a baby growing inside me, but nothing feels different. I'm trusting a little piece of plastic with its pink plus sign to be accurate and tell me the truth about one of the biggest changes that can happen in my life."

Erin leaned back in her chair. "I can't say I totally get it, because I've never been pregnant. But I can see where that little bit of doubt could sneak in. Maybe it will be better after the ultrasound. When is your appointment?"

Despite what she considered a completely unreasonable nagging doubt, Katie couldn't keep the excitement from her voice when she answered. "Next Monday."

Chapter Seventeen

"We're going to be late if you don't get a move on."

Katie yanked her purse from the hook on the wall and headed to the front door where Austin waited less than patiently. "We have plenty of time. You'd think you were excited to find out about your son today."

Austin rolled his eyes at her. "Yes, I am excited to see our daughter today. That first ultrasound didn't even look like a baby, no offense. This time, not only will she look like a baby, we'll be able to tell once and for all that she is a girl."

"And if she's a boy."

"I'll be happy either way. But just so you know, she's a girl."

Katie shook her head as she followed him out the door to his truck. It shocked her how time could pass so quickly and slowly at the same time. She was twenty weeks today. Half-way through her pregnancy. But it seemed as far as they'd come, the day when they'd finally meet their baby seemed light years away.

A flutter in her abdomen drew her hand to rest there. Due to her thin frame, she'd begun feeling the first subtle movements of their baby at about eighteen weeks. She looked forward to the time their child would make his or her presence known strongly enough that

Austin could feel it too. It connected her to their child in a very real way, and she longed for Austin to experience a similar bond.

AUSTIN WATCHED the black and white monitor eager for the pictures of their child to appear. He took in a breath as the first image of their baby showed clearly on the screen. Unlike the early ultrasound which simply looked like a little ball, this one allowed him to see his baby's profile clearly. Though grainy, he could see his child's head, limbs, and fat little tummy.

"There's your baby. I'm going to get some other information first, but I will be checking the gender. Do you want to know?"

Austin nodded to Katie who answered for them. "Yes. You need to let my husband know that this baby is a boy. He's been calling him a girl for the last twenty weeks."

The technician smiled. "So, I'm the one responsible for shattering someone's hopes today? That's always fun."

Austin shook his head. "No shattering hopes. Our only hope is that this little one is healthy. But we've definitely fallen on opposite sides of the fence in which sex we think we're having."

"Got it. If baby cooperates, I'll be happy to help you solve the mystery." The ultrasound technician didn't say much else as she adjusted the focus of the machine and clicked away on her keyboard taking various measurements.

AUSTIN GLANCED at Katie as he drove them home. She held the ultrasound pictures in her hand, but she wasn't looking at them. Her gaze was settled on the trees and houses passing by outside her window, but her attention seemed a million miles away. Not sure what was distracting her, Austin decided to let her keep to herself until they arrived home.

Her sigh as she set her purse on the table drew the question from his lips. "Are you okay?"

She turned to him, and he couldn't help seeing the doubt in her eyes. "I am. But I worry about you. Are you terribly disappointed?"

"Disappointed? Why would I be disappointed?"

"Because I was right. Because we're having a boy when you wanted a girl."

He grinned, hating the flash of anger he saw in her eyes when he did, but trusting his answer would alleviate both her fear that he was disappointed and what he interpreted as anger over her feeling he was laughing at her worry. "What I told the lady who did the ultrasound was true. Yes, for some unknown reason, I've simply thought our baby was going to be a girl. But it wasn't because I wanted a girl. I want a healthy, happy baby. That's all. I'm thrilled that we're having a boy."

Her eyes narrowed as she assessed him. "Are you really?"

He pulled her into his arms, roughing the hair on the top of her head with his stubbly chin. "Yes, really. I have been blessed with a sweet." He punctuated the word with a kiss on her temple. "Smart." He trailed his lips to the top of her cheek. "Giving." A series of butterfly kisses down her jawline. "Loving." Kisses back up the other side to whisper in her ear. "Incredibly sexy wife." He cupped his hand on the back of her head and brushed his lips across hers. She lifted her lips ever so slightly in response, but he didn't kiss her just yet. Without moving away from her even a fraction of an inch, he continued. "And now, she is going to give me a son. A healthy, happy, beautiful baby boy. And I couldn't be happier." He sealed his declaration with the kiss he'd been teasing.

After a few moments she pulled back from him. "How could I possibly believe you when you make such outrageous claims as having an incredibly sexy wife." She stepped away and patted her protruding stomach. "I mean, while I do make this work better than most, I'm not sure I'm headed for the catwalk any time soon."

Austin removed her hand before replacing it with his own, fingers splayed, allowing him to touch more of her abdomen than she had been. "This? This is what you're thinking keeps you from being sexy?" He moved his hand to her wrist and pulled her back to him. With his other hand, he brushed her auburn curls behind her ear and leaned in close to whisper. "I have a secret for you. The reason you have that little belly is because you're carrying my son. And as he grows, so will it. And here's the real secret. I find that super irresistible. Nothing that happens to your body will ever change the way I look at you. You are completely, undeniably sexy."

He traced a path of slow kisses down her bare neck. His arms came around her as he lifted her into them. "I believe I know just the way to prove exactly how desirable you are to me, now and always." She snuggled into his chest, kissing his jaw as he carried her to their bedroom.

KATIE WATCHED Austin pull his t-shirt over his head. When he caught her looking, one eyelid dropped in a flirtatious wink. Tucking her bottom lip between her teeth, she fought the smile. It would only encourage him to have her grinning back at him like a teenager in the middle of a crush. Of course, it wouldn't hurt for him to realize her crush on him had never gone away. From day one, even nursing a broken heart, she couldn't deny her attraction to him. Their friendship had grown before she had been free to acknowledge that attraction, but when she could, attraction and friendship exploded into love deeper and more quickly than she would have imagined possible. No, it wouldn't hurt to let him know she was still head over heels for him. She caught sight of her pregnant belly protruding under the bed sheet and let the smile come. No, it wouldn't hurt a thing, especially since he had just completely erased her doubts about her own attractiveness to him.

She patted the empty spot beside her. "Don't you want to snuggle a while?"

He combed his fingers through his mussed up hair. "You know I'd love to, but I'm already a little late in getting to the bakery. Lucy said she'd be happy to cover for me this morning while I went to the doctor's appointment with you, but at this point, it's been a really long appointment. I know I'm the owner, but I still don't want to take advantage of my employees. You know great employees like her are hard to find."

Austin hired Lucy after Katie's return to Bloomington to patch things up with Jacob left him broken and unmotivated to keep working his bakery on his own. He'd needed the help anyway, and he was right. Lucy was a hard worker. She wanted to learn the bakery business from top to bottom. She'd spent time with Austin in the kitchen, at the counter, and doing the office tasks of ordering and bookkeeping. She knew almost as much about By Sweet Design as he did. About to graduate from college with a restaurant management degree, Austin and Katie knew their time with her might be coming to an end soon. She'd applied to a cooking school near Chicago. If she was accepted, they'd need to find someone. They only hoped her replacement would be as dependable as she had been.

"Fine. Go relieve Lucy. And tell her thank you for me. I know she usually doesn't work on Mondays. I appreciate it. I need to call my parents and tell them they're getting a grandson. And don't forget to call yours sometime today too. They're as anxious as my parents to know."

He came to stand over her and leaned down to give her a quick peck on the lips. "Thank you. I'll put them on speaker and tell them on my way in to the bakery. And remember Lucy and Cole are going to take care of things on Saturday so we can spend the whole day together. Invite Erin over. Maybe Paul can even come down for the weekend. We'll make a day of it now that we know we're having a boy, and we'll get the nursery painted and set up. I'll see you after I close up shop."

A warm feeling spread through her as she watched him go. God had blessed her so much despite her failures. She could easily focus on all the time she'd left God out of her life or even the times she'd tried to make her sins right instead of letting Him make it right. Even after reconciling with God, she'd failed more times than not to handle things in a godly way. So much wasted time. So many people she loved hurt by her actions. Yet each time God forgave, and He had redeemed many of the situations blessing her beyond her wildest hopes. When she focused her heart on that, the gratitude she felt for God overwhelmed her.

Chapter Eighteen

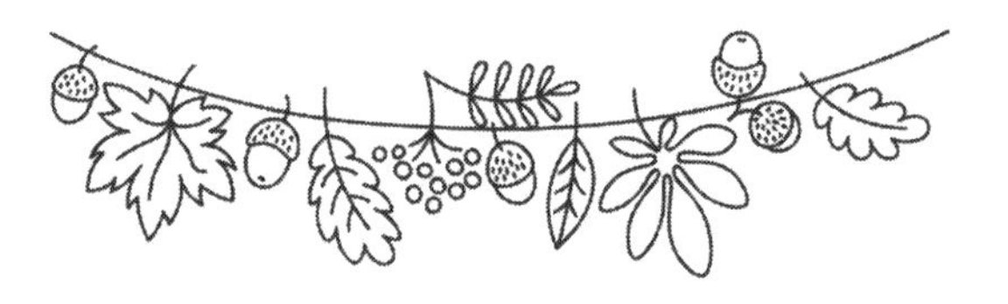

"I'm sorry Paul couldn't make it down this weekend."

Erin looked up at Katie from her place in the middle of the nursery floor, surrounded by wood pieces and hardware. "That's okay. Who needed him here anyway? We've totally got this."

Katie eyed the pieces dubiously. One page of directions resembling hieroglyphics and a screwdriver was supposed to turn this mess into a beautiful baby crib. "We may before this is all said and done."

Erin waved manicured fingers in her direction. "Pshaw, we don't need him. We are intelligent and capable women. That's why Austin trusted us to get this done while he runs to town to get the painting supplies. What color did you decide on anyway?"

"Hunter green with light green and yellow accents."

Erin raised her eyebrows. "That's a little bit non-traditional for you two."

"We want it to grow with him. Besides, the times when we've felt closest to God have been when we're enjoying His creation. We wanted to give our baby a space that brings the feeling of nature into his room."

The next few minutes passed in silence as Katie separated the lettered pieces and Erin studied the directions. "I think I've got it now. Where are the As and the Bs? I'm supposed to screw those together with the number nine screws."

Katie handed her the pieces she requested. "Not to change the subject, but how are things going with you and Paul?"

Erin lined up the pieces and began tightening the screws that held them together. Katie didn't miss the smile on her face. "Paul is amazing. I know people think dating long distance is hard, and in some ways it is. But I think having to spend time really talking to each other has helped our friendship grow in ways we could've been too distracted by dating to take advantage of if he was here. Yeah, it kind of stinks that we can't go out every Friday night, but we're both mature enough to handle that."

"How serious are you two?"

Erin shrugged as she reached for another screw. "We're serious enough to know we love each other and want to spend the rest of our lives together."

Katie's head shot up. "You're what? Did he propose?"

"Not yet. Simmer down. You know I'll call you first when he does. I'll be so excited I probably won't even wait until the date is over! We've talked about marriage, but it's not official yet. Paul's a romantic. He's going to plan something out of this world to ask me. He won't be content to ask me over the phone or anything like that."

"I wouldn't think so. When does he plan to get down here and pop the question?"

"Where are the Gs?"

Katie dutifully handed her the parts. "Well?"

"I can't say for sure about the proposing, but he is spending Thanksgiving down here. Wouldn't that be awesome? You and Austin looking forward to the baby, and me and Paul looking forward to getting married. That would make for a great Thanksgiving wouldn't it?"

Katie couldn't think of anything that sounded better. "Definitely."

Erin stood to secure the largest pieces of the puzzle making up the crib. "Where is that husband of yours? We've almost got this thing done, and he's not back with the paint."

Katie looked at her cell phone to check the time. "It's only been half an hour. Besides, I wouldn't put it past him to get distracted looking at the baby toys. Now that we know it's a boy, he's always bringing something little home for the baby."

AUSTIN STUFFED the plastic shopping bag under his jacket and lowered his head against the rain. He crossed the parking lot as swiftly as he could despite hearing his nephew's voice in his head telling him that he'd watched a myth dispelling show that proved you get less wet when you walk rather than run through the rain. It was counterintuitive. He would jog across the pavement, dodging puddles as he went. A jog was between a walk and a run. He'd only get mildly wet.

Opening the door to his truck, Austin tossed the bag onto the seat beside him. He couldn't help the hint of a smile that crossed his lips as he considered how Katie would react to his surprise. She loved rich, dark chocolate with almonds. He'd learned that early in their relationship. But now that she was pregnant, her infatuation with it had grown into an obsession. And she would ooh and aah over the stuffed sheep he'd picked out for the baby. It was fluffy and round like a ball with feet and eyes, giving it a comical look. But it was the softest stuffed animal he'd ever touched, and Austin knew it would be perfect for their son. Of course, Katie would say he was spoiling the baby before he was even born, but she wouldn't mean it. She loved preparing for their child as much as he did. He knew the girls were having a blast putting together the crib while he made a run to the store for the paint supplies he'd tucked away in the extended cab of his truck.

As he drove toward the intersection that would take him from the parking lot to the road, Austin couldn't help noticing the figure pacing around the trunk of one of the decorative trees the store had planted back when being green was the thing to do. Every parking lot sported at least one, not that it fooled anyone. But this particular tree would have provided meager protection from the weather if autumn hadn't left its limbs stripped of the leaves that could have served as nature's umbrella. Without their shelter, the man, whose head kept swiveling back and forth as if he were watching something move in the shadows, was getting soaked.

Still feeling the chill from his dash across the parking lot, Austin felt for the man. His threadbare jacket hung loose on his frame. And as tall as the man might have been, his hunched form shrunk him to an inconspicuous height. Austin watched him with curiosity. Most of the down-on-their-luck types in the area carried cardboard signs announcing their plights. This man didn't have a sign and didn't seem to want a handout.

The man looked up, making brief eye contact with Austin. Frustration rose as Austin recognized the man. "What's he gone and done now?"

Austin jerked the wheel to the right, lining the truck up with the curb. What was Jamie doing out of the rehab center? He'd just gone there to see him last week. The center hadn't been doing a lot of good for him, but when he fought it tooth and nail what could you expect? In the past they'd called Austin to talk him into staying. Jamie must have used up his good graces with his last attempt at leaving. Austin would call to find out what happened when he got home. First, he had to get Jamie somewhere dry and safe.

He rolled down his window. "Hey, Jamie. Whatcha doing out here in the rain?"

The young man mumbled something as he scratched his bare arms. Austin couldn't help noticing how red and irritated his scrawny appendages were. Like so many struggling with meth addiction, he'd scratched them raw.

"Get in the truck, Jamie. I'll take you someplace safe for the night."

Confused, anxious eyes stared at him but he made no move to the truck. More scratching. A quick look into the shadows behind him. Austin could only imagine what the young man's drug addled brain thought it saw before turning back to him.

"It's okay. I want to help. Get in, and I'll take you someplace safe." Austin hoped his tone was calm enough to persuade Jamie to get into the truck. He couldn't leave him in his current state.

Jamie slinked to the truck, turning at regular intervals to stare at empty spaces behind and beside him. His whole body shook uncontrollably. Austin wondered how long it had been since he'd had a decent meal. It broke Austin's heart to see anyone in this condition, but it seemed so much worse when it was a young man who hadn't even made it fully to adulthood yet. Not that you could see his youth any more. Meth had worked its demented magic on him turning him from a strong, athletically built teen into a scarecrow that had been left in both sun and rain for far too long without care. Jamie's hair had thinned more than a middle aged man's, sores plagued his skin, and broken teeth filled his mouth. It was only a matter of time before they became black from rot. Austin knew even with the rain, the temptation would be to keep the windows at least cracked. He'd been in close proximity to that mouth and knew in addition to ruined teeth, he'd be faced with the stench of the worst bad breath he'd ever smelled in the enclosed space of the cab of his truck.

"I can't. I can't go with you, Preacher." Jamie's words came quick and confused. "I can't. They'll know I went with you. They'll know, and they won't like it. They'll come after me. They're always watching me. They stay in the shadows, but they always see."

Austin looked at him, confused about what was happening. "Who won't like it, Jamie?"

"Won't like what? Are you here to take me somewhere?"

Austin shook his head, unsure of what Jamie was talking about. Trying to track the conversation was going to give him a headache. "Jamie, just get in the truck. I'll take you over to the homeless shelter. They'll give you something to eat and get you in out of the rain for the night."

Jamie opened the door with trembling hands. The shaking didn't ease as he sat in the seat. Austin watched as his eyes darted back and forth, like he was watching for something or someone. The shadow people who were always watching him? The scratching began again. Austin could see blisters oozing on his arms in addition to the raw places he'd scratched open. The sight was almost enough to turn his stomach.

Austin drove from the parking lot and headed toward the old run-down motel on the outer edge of the town that had been converted into a homeless shelter by a group of local churches. It wasn't an ideal plan, but it was the only plan he had. Austin had never seen Jamie this agitated before, and he prayed the shelter would be willing to take him in. Their rules were clear about housing those who were using, but maybe if Austin vouched for him they would make an exception. If not, he had no clue what he would do. He couldn't take him home, not with Katie and the baby. Katie. He made a mental note to text her about why he was running late as soon as he got to the shelter.

He looked at Jamie shaking and scratching beside him. "It's going to be alright. We're going to get you someplace safe."

Wide eyes turned to him. "No! No it's not alright! You can't make me go! The bugs are everywhere. They're everywhere! They put the bugs in me. They won't come out. They won't leave me alone. You can't take me to them! They'll know. They always know. You can't!"

KATIE BRUSHED her hand across the smooth wood of the crib railing as she glanced around the room. She could imagine what the room would look like once Austin filled the walls with color and the pictures of cute, baby forest animals they'd purchased. A satisfied sigh escaped her lips as her hand left the crib to rest on her protruding belly. The warmth of her touch inspired movement within.

"It won't be long now, Little One. Your daddy is going to make sure everything is perfect for you." Katie walked to the window. She smiled as she looked out across the green field to the woods that lay beyond it. She knew from her own explorations that these woods weren't home to a peaceful waterfall like the one near her childhood home, but they did contain a creek. Katie could almost see their child playing happily in the shallow water.

The chime of the front door bell pulled her out of her musings. She left the nursery, heading for the stairs. She didn't rush, knowing Erin was downstairs putting the tools they'd used back in the utility room. Rushing wasn't possible anyway. Katie had recently found her new girth had thrown her balance off. Rushing would only land her in a heap at the bottom of her stairs.

"Mrs. Blake? Katie Blake?"

"No, I'm . . ."

"I'm Katie Blake."

Katie spoke from behind Erin, but as Erin moved, Katie felt the breath rush from her lungs. A man in uniform stood outside her door. Something was wrong. Concern and regret was evident in his eyes as they took in her protruding belly. Katie reached a hand to grip the banister, steadying herself.

"Ma'am, I need to speak with you. Is there a place we could sit down?"

Katie wasn't trying to be inhospitable, but she felt rooted to her spot on the step. She shook her head. "Please. What's happened?"

The officer's eyes darted to Erin, still standing by the door. Katie watched her head dip in affirmation. The officer turned back to her. The resignation in his eyes told her it wasn't what he wanted, but he would deal with it.

"Ma'am, I'm sorry to be the bearer of this news. We don't have specifics yet, but sometime this afternoon your husband, Austin Blake, was involved in a stabbing."

Katie shook her head. "Is he…? Can I see him? Which hospital did you take him to?"

The young man's gaze fell momentarily before he made eye contact again. "No, ma'am. I'm sorry, but when we arrived on the scene, it was too late. There was nothing we could do. Your husband had lost too much blood. There was no way to save him."

Disbelief screamed in her mind. No. This man was wrong. Austin was fine. He would show up any moment, and the officer would realize he was mistaken. Austin couldn't be dead. She would have known, after all. She would have felt it if the man she loved had died. And a stabbing? How could Austin have been involved in a stabbing? It had to be a mistake. It had to.

Katie barely registered the officer's grip on her arm before he began leading her to the kitchen chair Erin had pulled out for her. She dropped into the chair, seeing none of the movement in the room. She didn't turn as he ordered Erin to get her something to drink. She barely registered it when Erin forced the glass of water into her hand.

Her head jerked up at the sound of her name, but she couldn't seem to focus on the man speaking to her. "What?"

He looked at her in pity. "Here, please, try to take a drink or two."

Shaky hands lifted the glass of water. She sipped it obediently. It helped to have something to focus on for a moment. Something other than the news that her husband was dead. But Austin couldn't be dead. She raised her eyes to the other occupants of the room. The man was discussing something with Erin that Katie couldn't quite make her mind pay attention to. Erin's tear stained face was etched with pain and fear. So, it was true. What the man said. Austin wasn't coming home. Austin was dead.

The man was speaking to her again. Why couldn't he just be quiet? She wanted him to leave, to leave her alone. If he would go away, then she would be able to wake up from this nightmare. That's what it had to be. Maybe she had gone upstairs for a nap. Pregnancy worries did strange things to a woman's dreams. If he would simply shut up, she could wake up and Austin would be there waiting.

"Ma'am. Please."

The voice was insistent. She glanced up at him without raising her head. It was apparently good enough to satisfy him. She needed to listen to what he was saying.

"Do you?"

Her voice was hoarse. "Do I what?"

"Do you have any questions for me before I leave?"

Why is my husband dead? Why is this happening? What am I supposed to tell our son? "No."

The officer looked relieved. "Well, then, I've left my card with your friend. If you need anything at all, my number is on it."

Katie nodded. Why did she feel so cold? And numb?

The officer spoke to Erin one last time before urging Katie to stand. She followed his directions without thought as to why he was asking her to do so. Gently he supported her as Erin led the way from the kitchen upstairs to her bedroom. He helped her lie down on the mattress while Erin retrieved a blanket from the closet.

They left the room, but she could hear their hushed voices in the hall. She turned her face and saw her wedding picture on the bedside table. Austin stood behind her with his arms wrapped around her waist. His smile was so full of love and promise. He promised forever. Forever had come too soon. The thought broke through her numbness, leaving her shattered and sobbing until exhaustion claimed her.

ERIN HAD STAYED strong for Katie from the moment she'd opened the door to find Officer Wright on the other side. Though just as blind-sided by the man's announcement, she'd kept her wits about her, asking all the necessary questions and getting all the information Katie would need as soon as she was able to process what was happening. Erin knew from Katie's reaction getting to that might take a while. She'd written most of it down on a notepad she'd found on the kitchen table before escorting him to the door.

Erin knew what she needed to do for Katie, but the gut-wrenching sobs coming from behind Katie's closed door were more than she could take. She sank into the living room recliner and allowed her emotions free rein as her own tears flowed. Austin had been more than a pastor over the years. He'd been her friend. He cared for everyone, and everyone cared for him in return. The idea that someone could hate him enough to murder him was beyond her comprehension. How did evil like that happen?

She wasn't the only one who'd lost someone today. Her best friend had lost the man she'd pledged her life to, the father of her unborn son. Katie's pain was so much deeper than her own, her loss more cutting. The weeping coming from beyond the closed door was testimony to the depth of Katie's loss. Her desire to be able to help her friend grieve and her complete inability to do so left Erin with a physical ache in her chest. There weren't words that would make this understandable or acceptable. There was only one thing she could do for Katie and that was to help shoulder her physical load. It would provide little solace, but there was nothing else to be done.

Erin swiped both hands under her eyes and went into the bathroom to splash cool water on her face. Katie needed her. She had to pull it together for her and her family. After drying her face with the hand towel beside the sink, Erin grasped the sides of the pedestal sink and stared at herself in the mirror. She could do this. She would do this. For Katie.

Her hands shook as she went to the living room and fished her cell phone out of her purse. Sharon and Cal were in her contacts. It was a good thing considering she couldn't have remembered their number at the moment if she'd wanted to. Her heart beat nearly drowned out the ring. Answer the phone. Please, don't answer it. The thoughts warred inside her.

"Hello."

Sharon. How could she tell the woman her son-in-law was dead? "Sharon." She cleared her throat afraid the shakiness would prevent her from being understood. "Sharon, is Cal with you?"

The elderly voice sounded wary. "Yes. Is something the matter? Is the baby okay?"

"The baby's fine. Please, just get Cal and put me on speaker phone. I need to speak with you both."

Erin heard rustling in the background. Sharon's voice called for Cal. More rustling and finally his calming voice came on the line. "We're here, Erin. What do you need?"

Tears rolled down her cheeks unchecked. "I'm only calling because Katie can't right now."

"What happened to Katie?" Panic laced Sharon's words.

"Hush and let her speak." The words might have seemed harsh if they'd come from someone other than Cal. He knew how to get through to Sharon in ways no one else could. "Go on, Erin."

Might as well put their minds at ease for a moment. "Katie's fine. The baby's fine. It's Austin. He's been stabbed."

"Oh, my word. Does Katie need us to take her to the hospital? Is he in Carbondale?"

"No, he's not in Carbondale. He . . ." Her voice broke as a sob robbed her of her ability to speak. "He didn't make it. Austin died before they could get him to the hospital. Please, I don't know what to do for Katie. She needs you."

"We'll be right there."

~

KATIE STOOD beside the open grave staring at the casket suspended above it. A large spray of flowers decorated it. Decorated a casket. Like a bunch of roses would make death more beautiful, more tolerable. It didn't. The pastor's message was exactly what Austin would want. It was a message of hope for those left behind. It was a call for those without hope to accept it while it was still offered. Austin's whole life had been about making sure others had a chance to hear those words and respond to the love in them. They were meant to bring peace. And though Katie believed them with everything inside her, peace hid. Her grief was too unexpected and her emotions still too raw.

"Katie, honey, it's time to head back to the church." Austin's mother spoke softly, touching her arm as she did.

Katie turned and looked into a face so much like Austin's the pain nearly crushed her. The only other time she'd met her husband's parents was at the wedding. They'd planned to come up for the birth of their grandson, a celebration of life, not the memorialization of a senseless death. It wasn't right. It wasn't supposed to be this way. She looked back to the casket unable to erase the picture of him lying in it lifeless the night before.

"I think I'm just going to go home."

"Sweetie, you need to take care of yourself. I know you don't feel like it, but why not come to the church and have a little something to eat?"

Katie fought the urge to roll her eyes. Casserole. The duct tape of the Baptist world. The cure-all for every ill. How many casseroles filled her tiny freezer at home? As soon as the word of

Austin's death became common knowledge, the parade of casseroles began. She had enough to last until Jesus' return.

She turned to tell her mother-in-law exactly what she thought of those casseroles, but the words caught in her throat. Austin's eyes stared back at her full of love and concern. And pain. She wasn't the only one hurting. Katie still carried her own baby inside her. She couldn't imagine losing that little one. Austin's mother had carried him just as she was carrying his son. She had raised him, comforted him, disciplined him. She'd watched him become a man. She'd had over thirty years to love Austin, and she said good-bye to him just as Katie had. Austin's mother might be the only one who understood her pain. For her, Katie would eat casserole.

Katie nodded. "Of course, I'll be along in just a minute."

Her mother-in-law nodded before going to join Austin's father and sister at the edge of the crowd of mourners. Austin's nephew was snuggled against his mother's leg. Family she barely knew because of the miles between them, but Austin had cherished his family. What would it be like for them without him there to bring them all together?

Erin and Paul worked against the crowd moving towards their cars. Katie noticed Erin's hand enclosed safely in Paul's as they walked in her direction. Katie knew it was more than affection grasping Erin's hand. It was the strength she needed to be able to get through the loss of her friend. Katie bit back her tears. She no longer had the chance to find those feelings in Austin's touch.

Erin freed her hand from Paul's and took Katie into her arms, pulling her down to her level. "I'm so sorry."

Katie wept on her shoulder, no one saying anything. When her tears finally ebbed, Katie sniffled and brushed her fingers under her eyes as if it could erase the evidence of her pain. "I guess we need to head over to the church."

A quizzical look from Erin reminded Katie that she'd already told Erin she planned to go home. "No, I'm still not in the mood to socialize, but my mother-in-law will send a search party if I'm not over there within a few minutes of her arrival."

"Honey, you don't have to do anything you . . ."

Katie held up her hand. "I know. But I think she needs me to be there. If I choke down a few bites of casserole and apple pie, she'll be convinced it's all going to be alright."

Erin opened her mouth, shutting it again without speaking. It was just as well. Katie didn't need yet another reminder that everything would eventually be alright. Her son, Austin's son, would come into the world without his father. Time would not make that alright. Nothing would.

"Have mom and dad already gone?" A change of subject would be good.

Erin nodded. "They wanted to stay, to bring you to the church. But your mom looked exhausted. Paul and I told them we'd make sure you got where you needed to go. I think they were headed over there for a little while anyway."

Of course, mom would never neglect to do what was expected no matter how tired she was. She would be first in the fellowship hall and the last one to leave. "Well, then let's get this over with."

Chapter Nineteen

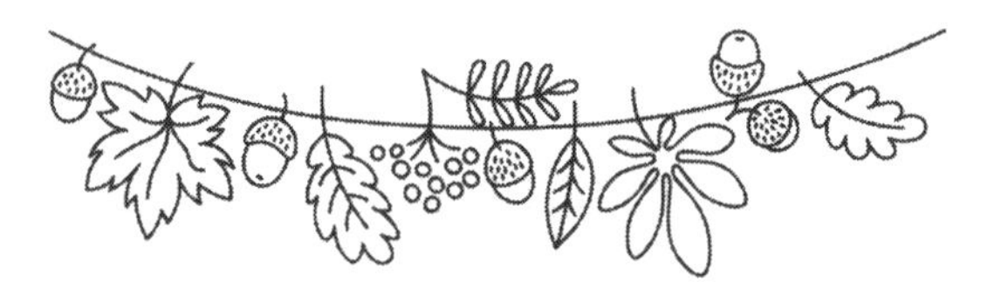

Katie held the cool metal in the palm of her hand. She stared at "Forever Love" etched in the brushed silver band that ran around the center of the ring like a ribbon. Forever hadn't lasted nearly long enough, mere months, not even years. She skimmed a finger over the smooth edge, blinking back tears. Maybe the ring should have been buried with Austin. Her parents were quick to express their concern that she wanted it. They thought it was too harsh a reminder, like she needed a physical reminder to remember her husband had died. But Austin didn't need it anymore. Death released him from his vows to her. Besides, it was asking too much of her to give it up. Hadn't she given up enough already?

She placed the ring in the cedar jewelry box her father had made for her in honor of her high school graduation. All her most precious treasures were kept safe inside. As she lowered the hinged lid, a gentle flutter drew her hand from the fragrant wood to rest briefly on her slightly rounded stomach. She'd made the right choice keeping Austin's ring. One day she could give it to their son to help him feel connected to the father he had been robbed of knowing.

Katie swallowed the ache in her throat. It wasn't fair. Every child should know their father. Every mother should have the man she loved beside her working with her to raise the child they'd created together. There was nothing about the situation that was right. But then, that was life.

Katie turned from the box hearing the creak of the front door. Only a handful of people would ever walk into her home without knocking and only since Austin's death would those few even consider it. Which one was it now?

"Katydid, you home?"

She wasn't surprised to hear her father's voice, but she'd half expected it to be her mom.

Her mom's voice called up the stairs. "I made an apple pie this morning, and we thought you might enjoy a piece."

Katie shook her head. So mom came too and brought the obligatory food offering. How else did a mother show her love in southern Illinois? It was always stuff them full and wash it down with a glass of iced sweet tea. She should be happy it was only pie. Her supply of casseroles was dwindling, but there were still a few stragglers in the freezer.

"I'm upstairs. I'll be right down."

By the time she hit the bottom stair, her mother had already cut and plated the pie. Katie couldn't help a small smile as she noticed the glasses of sweet tea beside each plate. She dutifully took a seat and cut into the flaky crust with her fork. Declining was not an option.

"I know you didn't come over just to bring me pie. What did you need?" She wasn't in the mood for beating around the bush. Better to get straight to the point.

Her parents shared a brief look before her dad explained. His voice was full of sympathetic understanding. "I know it's been less than a month, and I know you may not feel like it at this point, but please reconsider coming to Thanksgiving dinner at the church."

Though they always had a meal together on Thanksgiving Day,

Katie's family had always considered the church dinner as the real celebration. At home, it was only the three of them. At Orchard Hills Christian Church, it was the entire church family and then some. Katie's decision not to go had shaken her mother. It didn't help that she hadn't been able to make herself attend the worship services the last few weeks since Austin's death. She wasn't against church, and she missed her Sunday School class. But she just couldn't see the pulpit Austin had filled being filled by someone else.

She lifted her apple pie laden fork to her lips but paused short of taking the bite. "I'll think about it, if you guys promise not to rush me. I just need a little time to sort through everything."

Her mother's wrinkled hand patted her own. "Of course you do, dear. You've lost a lot and so soon after finding what you were looking for. It'll take time."

She felt a ghost of a smile. It was amazing how far her relationship with her mom had progressed. The smile faded as she remembered how Austin had a hand in helping that happen too. He had touched every area and relationship in her life. It would never be the same without him.

The trio ate their pie in silence. Her parents came to say their peace and having done so seemed content to let her keep her thoughts to herself. As each plate was finished, Katie watched her mother gather them, washing them in the sink before placing them in the drying rack.

Her dad stood, picking up her mother's purse and carrying it to where she stood by the sink. "I think it's time we got out of your hair and let you get some rest. Just let us know what you decide, Katydid."

She nodded. Before she could say anything, her phone started vibrating in her back pocket. She took it out to silence it, but the phone number flashing across the screen belonged to the officer who'd informed her of Austin's death. She slid her finger across the screen and turned from her parents.

"Hello. This is Katie."

"Mrs. Blake, this is Officer Wright. I don't know if you remember me, but . . ."

"I remember you. Is there something I can do for you today, Officer Wright?"

"Ma'am, I'm the officer assigned to your husband's case, and I need you to come down to the station. We've had some new developments I need to discuss with you."

Katie felt as if she'd been punched in the gut. "I'm free now, if you'd like to go ahead and tell me what's going on."

He hesitated. Katie's pulse throbbed in her neck.

"I'd love to, ma'am, but I can't. I would really appreciate it if you could come to the station to meet with me. I'm in until five today, and I work from eight until five every day this week."

"No sense in waiting. I'll be at the station in thirty minutes."

Katie hung up the phone. When she turned, her parents looked carved from marble. Neither spoke, but their pale, drawn faces asked the questions she knew she needed to answer. Too bad Officer Wright hadn't given her a few more answers during their conversation. "It looks like I'll be following you guys out. Apparently, I'm needed at the police station. The officer in charge of Austin's case said they need to discuss some things with me, and he said he can't simply tell me over the phone."

"We can come with you, if you like."

Company might be nice, but she had no idea what she was walking into. This whole ordeal had taken its toll on her, but she couldn't deny the strain it put on her parents. They loved Austin like a son. Would going with her be too much for them?

"I think I need to do this alone. But I'd appreciate it if you'd both spend some time praying for me. I'll call as soon as I know anything."

Her mother opened her mouth but shut it again as her father placed a hand on her shoulder. "We understand. We'll head on home and rest assured we'll be praying. If you need us, just ask. We'll be there before you can hang up the phone."

~

"OFFICER WRIGHT, I'm Katie Blake. You wanted to see me."

The man looked up from the files on his desk. He smiled, but it was tight. Born of training in the proper way to greet people instead of actual emotion. Katie tensed. She'd done fine on the drive over, spending her time in prayer. Now, her nerves were a jumbled mess taking their angst out on her stomach.

"Mrs. Blake, come in and have a seat please." He motioned a hand toward two equally uncomfortable looking options.

Katie did as she was told though her limbs felt stiff and awkward as she moved. "You said you had some developments in my husband's murder?"

If he was taken back by her directness, he hid it well. "We do. In fact, we have someone in custody, and I'd like to ask you about his relationship to your husband."

Relationship? Austin knew his murderer? Katie shut her eyes as a wave of nausea came over her. She concentrated on breathing. In. Out. In. Out. How could Austin's murderer have known him? Austin didn't have any enemies. A new wave threatened. In. Out. In. Out.

"Ma'am? Are you okay? Can I get you something? Water? A soda?"

Katie looked at the man across the desk. Worry creased the corners of his eyes. His muscles were tensed, primed to act the moment he gave the order. Giving the types of news he had to give was hard enough, she was sure. Giving it to a pregnant woman had to add to the strain. Katie offered what she hoped was a reassuring smile as she shook her head.

"I'm fine. I'm surprised is all. I never imagined my husband knew his killer. Austin never made an enemy in his life, much less someone who'd be mad enough to want to kill him."

He leaned back in his chair. "I'm sorry, Mrs. Blake. There is no easy way to deal with matters such as this."

Katie waved a hand. She hoped her inner shaking wasn't coming through in a way to discredit her words. "Don't worry about niceties. Just say what you have to say. I've always preferred ripping the bandage off quickly rather than little by little."

He regarded her for a moment before giving a slight nod of his head. "Right. We don't think the man we have in custody murdered your husband because he had an issue with him."

"My husband did not cavort around town with murderers. And innocent people aren't killed for no reason."

"But those reasons don't have to be about something that was said or done to them. They don't have to be about the victim as much as they're about the assailant."

Katie's head spun, but she wasn't sure if it was from the situation or the conversation. "I'm not sure I'm following what you're saying. So, a man my husband knew just decided to kill him even though my husband did nothing to him to incite him to that kind of action?"

"Mrs. Blake, do you recognize the name James Sawyer?"

James Sawyer? "Is that the man who killed Austin?"

"We believe it is, but before I can give you any more information I need to know what you know about him."

"James. I'm not sure, but I don't think I know a James Sawyer."

He pulled a picture from the folder in front of him and slid it across the desk. "Take a moment to look at this photo. Don't rush, but let me know if you've seen this man before."

Katie lifted the photo from the desk. She couldn't stifle the gasp that came with her immediate recognition. "Jamie? You're saying Jamie killed my husband?"

Another nod. "We believe so, but I need you to tell me how you and your husband know Jamie."

Katie stared at the picture, obviously taken at the station when he was arrested. The young man looked thinner and older than the last time she'd seen him at the church, but that wasn't surprising. "Austin first met Jamie through a program to feed those in need at our church. For whatever reason, Jamie took to Austin. He trusted him, and Austin tried to help him get cleaned up. I've only seen him a handful of times, but while he was in drug rehab Austin would visit him. He encouraged him, and the rehab counselors would call Austin to talk to him if they were having problems, which happened pretty frequently."

Katie watched Officer Wright continue writing on his notepad after she finished speaking. The silence gave her a moment to think. How did this happen? Why was Jamie even with Austin? He was supposed to be in rehab, wasn't he?

The pen stilled. "Why would Jamie attack my husband? He considered Austin a friend. What has he said about the attack?"

Officer Wright leaned back in his chair. "To be honest, his memory is fragmented. The nearest thing we've been able to piece together is that your husband picked him up off the street on his way home from the store. Jamie's fingerprints are in the truck, and we found the knife he used in a culvert. Prints and blood confirm it's the weapon. Given Jamie's state when we found him, we figure he was either high or in withdrawal when your husband found him. Meth does strange things to a person. It makes them paranoid. They see things that aren't there. They're scared. From what little we can get from Jamie and from watching how he's currently acting, we don't believe there was a fight between them or any other real incident to incite his violence. We believe Jamie acted out of whatever paranoid scenario his drug addled brain concocted."

Katie's head spun as she answered the rest of Officer Wright's questions. To think her husband was taken from her without any reason at all was almost more than she could understand. She was without the man she loved because he tried to help someone in trouble. He gave without hesitation, and it cost him his life.

People gave their lives for their faith every day, all over the world. Missionaries were slaughtered by guerillas. Those worshipping in underground churches were killed for refusing to leave their faith. Katie always felt for those people and their families, considering their sacrifices sad but noble and in some ways beautiful. But this wasn't a third world country or a ruthless dictatorship. Austin was only miles from home. He was trying to help in the only way he knew how. And it got him killed. That wasn't noble or beautiful. It was senseless and stupid.

Katie didn't remember exchanging the usual pleasantries with the officer before she left, but she knew she must have. At least, he didn't give her a questioning look or try to stop her retreat. She must have seemed at least somewhat normal and in control. It was a façade. She was far from normal, numb but not normal, and definitely not in control. Autopilot was more like it, and it was the only thing that got her safely home.

Dropping her purse on the entry way table, Katie trudged into the living room and sank into the sofa cushions. Using the hands free options on her phone, Katie had used the drive home to inform her parents, Austin's parents, and Erin of what she'd learned. Austin's parents would tell his sister. Erin would let Paul know, and it wouldn't take long for the news to spread to everyone else through the power of the little country church prayer chain.

Katie tilted her head back until it rested on the back of the sofa. She listened to the silence never having realized how loud it could be. A gentle roll in her growing stomach reminded her that the silence wouldn't last forever. Soon, her days would be filled with activity and noise. But what would chase away the silence that stalked her nights? Katie captured her bottom lip between her teeth as she willed herself not to give in to the tears yet again. She'd had nearly a month to adjust to this new reality however harsh. The time for sulking and wishing it different was done.

A knock on the door broke through her self-inflicted chastising. The door opened before she could make a move to answer it. Erin. Other than her parents, she was the only one at home enough to come in before the proper permission was given. This knowledge was confirmed with the voice that joined the door's creak in warning Katie of her visitor's approach.

"Knock, knock. I've come and brought much needed therapy with me!" Erin came around the doorway waving a plastic grocery bag in the air. She flopped down beside Katie and plopped the bag onto the coffee table before pulling out the contents. "I wasn't sure what mood you'd be in, so I got a little of everything. Double chocolate truffle gelato, a horrendously over-priced but oh-so-worth-it chocolate bar, a mixed bag of crunchy, salty, cheesy chip goodness, and a bottle of the best raspberry lemonade on the market. Where should we start?"

Katie eyed the food spread across the table. She wasn't really hungry, but then again, when had being hungry ever determined whether or not she ate something. "I'll grab us a couple of spoons. That gelato is calling my name."

In minutes the two of them sat next to each other on the sofa like teenage girls with their feet propped up on the coffee table, spooning out the contents of the tub of gelato sitting between them from opposite ends. The influx of sugar energized the baby who began to kick his approval.

Katie dropped her spoon into the container and grabbed Erin's hand to place it on her stomach as the baby kicked again. Erin's eyes were as wide as her smile. "That's so amazing. I've never really been around pregnant people before. Does he do that often?"

Katie shrugged. "Sometimes. When he first started to move, there would be days when I didn't feel him much at all. But now that he's bigger, he makes his presence known. There are times he's definitely more active, but he doesn't keep me up at night."

Erin laughed. "Well, I guess that's a good sign. He isn't a late night partier. Maybe that means he'll let you sleep when he gets here."

"I don't think that's how it works, but we'll pretend it's true for now. I can't imagine the sleepless nights continuing indefinitely."

Erin's mouth twisted as her brows drew together. "Still not sleeping?"

"It's hard." Katie avoided looking her friend in the eye by grabbing her spoon and scooping another cold, silky bite of gelato into her mouth.

"I can't even imagine. How are you doing with, well, I guess with finding out about Jamie and everything?"

Another scoop, too big to speak around but not large enough to cause brain freeze. Katie let it melt slowly while considering her answer. "I'm still processing it. All Austin did was try to help that kid, and he gets killed for it. It's not right. I don't understand how something like this can happen. This isn't Chicago. This is small town southern Illinois."

When Erin remained silent, Katie continued. "Of course, I know it's never right when someone gets killed, and things like this don't only happen in big cities. It just seems, I don't know, evil. I mean, all murder is evil. But to kill someone who's given so much time and energy to help you beat the demons that end up being the reason you kill him? That seems especially evil."

Erin nodded. "It really does. And I'm sure it will take time to get to the place where you can forgive Jamie."

Katie shook her head. "That's the strange part. I was mad at him. When Officer Wright told me what happened, I was furious. But Jamie wouldn't have done this if it hadn't been for his addiction. He was high, or he was needing to be. They aren't sure about that. His statements haven't been all that coherent. But whichever the case, I'm not even sure Jamie realized what he was doing or why. And I listened to Austin enough to realize how deeply rooted Jamie's addictions are. Every time I'd get frustrated with his inability to stay clean, Austin would remind me that one of the hardest things about recovery for a lot of addicts was returning to the same mess they came out of. It was a recipe for failure. The only positive he had in his life was Austin. Don't misunderstand me, what Jamie did should have consequences. And I'm not going to be the one championing for his second chance, but I can't find it in myself to hold onto hatred for him."

Erin leaned back against the sofa, her mouth dropping open. "Wow. I thought I'd come over here to cheer you up and encourage you, but here you sit encouraging and challenging me. I haven't been so forgiving. When I think of all you've lost because of this, I want Jamie to pay for the pain he's caused."

"I'm not sure it's forgiving as much as understanding and accepting. Nothing is going to change what happened. I could wish it didn't, but that doesn't do anyone any good."

Erin picked up the gelato and headed for the kitchen. Katie heard the doors to the freezer and one of the cabinets open and shut. She closed her eyes, resting her head against the back of the sofa. Despite her pronouncement, her spirit felt unsettled. But she believed every word she'd told Erin. Now she had to continually remind herself of that fact.

ERIN POURED two glasses of rosy raspberry lemonade as she considered Katie's words. She couldn't imagine what her friend was going through, but here she was trying to nonetheless. And what Katie was feeling simply didn't make sense to her. Austin hadn't even been gone a month. It didn't seem right that Katie would be able to get close to acceptance of the situation. It was too soon, especially acceptance after finding out Austin was murdered by someone he knew and cared for. How did one instill acceptance into a shattered heart? Erin had no idea, but from the looks of things Katie did.

Erin carried the glasses into the living room. Katie lifted her head from the back of the couch. It was a brief glance as Katie took her glass and only a flicker in her eyes, but Erin saw it. Katie wasn't as settled in her new circumstances as she wanted everyone to believe. There was anger and hurt and disbelief in that look but not acceptance. Did Katie even realize it?

Erin sat, careful to keep her lemonade from sloshing onto the furniture. "So, what's next?"

"Next? You mean with the case?"

Erin licked the tangy liquid from her lip. "Yeah with the case, but with everything else too."

"I don't really know. I mean, from what Officer Wright was saying, Austin's case is all but closed. With Jamie's confession and the evidence against him, they don't think the public defender will try to argue not guilty. The sentencing is the only thing up in the air at this point."

"What do you want to happen?"

"To be honest, I'm not sure. Jamie's been offered help time and again. It hasn't done any good. As much as I hate the idea of a life wasted in prison, maybe punishment is the best answer. At the very least, it could keep him away from what's messed him up in the first place and keep him from being able to hurt anyone else at the same time."

Erin took a long drink. "How many times was he in and out of rehab?"

She did a quick mental count. "I think he was in and out at least four times. And that doesn't include all the times he wanted to leave that Austin encouraged him to stay."

"Why do you think it didn't take?"

Katie shrugged as she finished off her lemonade. "From what I understand, an addict has to want to change. Even when they do, the addiction is so wired into their brains that it makes it difficult. If they get it under control but return to a negative environment like Jamie had, it triggers the desire again. There are a lot of factors that go into an addict's recovery. Jamie didn't have anyone but Austin, and he didn't have an overwhelming desire to stay clean."

Katie stood, taking Erin's now empty glass from her hand. Erin followed her into the kitchen. Katie set the glasses on the top rack of the dishwasher before leaning with her back against the counter top, arms crossed around her middle. The stance would normally make her appear solid and unshakeable, but with all that had transpired Erin couldn't help but sense fragility under the surface. How long could Katie go without breaking into pieces?

Chapter Twenty

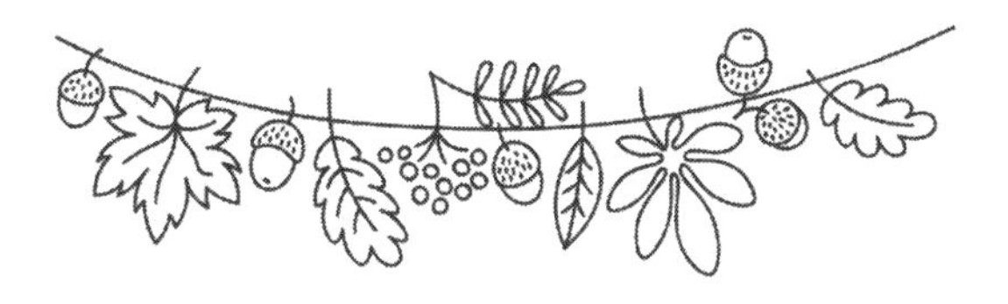

Katie dusted her hands on her jeans as she dropped the last box of Christmas decorations into their storage place in the garage. She'd survived the onslaught of holidays from Thanksgiving to the New Year, and now, with January nearing its end, life could get back to what passed for her new normal. Of course, Valentine's Day would bring some pitying looks. It was to be expected. She'd suffered through the same looks during the Thanksgiving meal at the church and the Sunday school children's Christmas program. If she hadn't needed to convince her parents all was once again right in the world, she wouldn't have gone to the Thanksgiving meal. But with Jamie sentenced to life in prison the week before, they needed the extra assurance.

And the twins were so sweet, leaving a hand colored invitation to the program with the bakery employees. She hadn't stepped foot in By Sweet Design since Austin died, but she spoke regularly with Lucy, who'd taken on managing the store. When Lucy gave her the invitation at one of their weekly meetings, it tugged at her heart. She missed all her Sunday school kids, but Tommy and Jake held a special place in her heart. While she couldn't face regular Sunday attendance at Austin's church, she couldn't say no to their innocent plea for her to watch their program. And it was worth it to see their smiling faces and have their little arms try to wrap around her ever growing belly as they hugged her.

It wouldn't be long until she'd feel her own child's arms around her. Only seven short weeks to go. Thanks to Paul and Erin, along with her mom and dad, the nursery was ready for her son's arrival. Even Austin's parents had come up for a weekend with his sister to help prepare the room. Finishing up what she and Austin had started together had been their Christmas gift to her. They'd even found an artistic side to Erin as she hand painted baby forest animals on the light switch cover to match the ones in the pictures Austin had purchased for the walls.

It was a bittersweet memory for Katie's first holiday season without Austin. Her loss was deep, but there were still blessings to be enjoyed. She'd reminded herself of that almost hourly to get through it, but she'd made it. Whether it felt true or not, God was good. Every well-meaning believer she'd come across echoed the sentiment. It said it right there in scripture so it must be true. Katie spent a lot of time reiterating that thought in her mind as well.

With all the decorations put in their storage space for the year enough work had been done for the day. Katie found her phone and punched in the number she knew by heart. It was time to take care of business, literally.

"By Sweet Design. This is Lucy."

"Hey, Lucy. It's Katie. I know we aren't set to meet until next week, but I was hoping you'd have a little time to speak with me today."

"Sure thing. Alex can handle things while we talk. Where should we meet?"

Katie took in a deep breath before plunging headfirst into what could be a disastrous decision. "I thought I'd come by the bakery. We can talk in the office."

Silence. Katie knew she'd shocked Austin's manager, no, her manager into speechlessness. "Lucy?"

"Ummm, yeah, sure. I'll see you when you get here."

If she didn't know how capable the young woman was, her stammering might have led Katie to believe there was something amiss at the bakery. But over the last several months, Lucy had proven herself time and again, shouldering the load of the business almost single-handedly.

Katie hung up and headed for the door. She'd avoided this talk and the bakery for long enough. Her son was due soon, and she needed to get things in order before he arrived. This was the final step to getting that accomplished.

Lucy looked a bit like a skittish colt as they took their places across from each other in the office. She'd never been nervous around Katie before, but then again, how often had Katie walked through those doors since Austin's death? It had to make an impression on Lucy and leave her wondering what was wrong. The young woman's mind had to be swimming with a million scenarios for what could possibly bring her to the bakery now.

Katie did her best to smile reassuringly. "You've done a wonderful job taking care of things around here."

Her shoulders softened. "Thank you. This place means a lot to me. I can't imagine being anywhere else."

Katie sensed the question in the statement. "I'm glad to hear you say that. I need to make some changes, but I'm going to need your help to put them into place."

"Whatever you need, bo . . . Katie."

Katie looked away briefly as she took control of her emotions. Boss. In all the months Austin had been gone, Lucy had never come close to slipping up and calling her boss. Boss was Austin. Boss would forever be Austin. It was more than a title. It was the way employer and employee had related to each other. Katie didn't want that title. She never had.

"I'm not a baker. And though I've had my own business in the past, this one was Austin's dream. It was a wonderful dream for him, and I've got a lot of amazing memories tied to this place. But running a bakery has never been my dream. I think it's time to let it go."

"You're selling By Sweet Design?"

The high pitch bore witness to the anxiety causing her eyes to grow round. Hearing the words out loud was almost enough to change her mind on the spot. Could she really give up Austin's pride and joy? How would her life change with this decision? And did those changes even matter in the scope of all the changes she'd experienced in recent months?

Katie swallowed past the lump in her throat. "Yes, Lucy. It's time for me to get out of the bakery business. I don't have the heart for it. I never did. As much as I love this place, my feelings for it are centered around Austin. But he isn't here anymore. You are, and I have a proposition for you."

An hour later, Katie left the bakery more lighthearted than she'd been in months. As hard as it was to let go, she was doing the right thing for herself, the bakery, and Lucy. Lucy loved By Sweet Design, and she would care for it as well as Austin had. As young as she was, Katie understood she couldn't buy it outright, but after their meeting with the lawyer next week, all of that would be taken care of. Lucy would run the bakery her way and make payments to Katie with the express purpose of buying it over time. If Lucy ever decided she wanted out of the deal, her payments would be considered rent and Katie would retain ownership to sell it to someone else. Through the contract for deed arrangement, the young woman would gain an opportunity she otherwise couldn't afford, and Katie would not have the weight of the bakery on her shoulders any more. It was the perfect plan.

Katie's phone rang as she climbed behind the wheel of her jeep. She buckled her seatbelt and put the vehicle in drive, carefully keeping her foot on the brake, before swiping to answer. "This is Katie."

The voice on the other end was near frantic and almost drowned out by a siren that was too close for comfort and voices she didn't recognize. Katie glanced at the caller id. Finally, she heard a familiar voice. "Dad, I can't hear you. Where are you?"

The background noise was suddenly silenced. "Katie, I need you. We need you. We're pulling up to the hospital now."

Her heart pounded as her pulse raced. "We? We who? What's going on, Dad?"

Katie could almost feel the ache as the words were ripped out of her father's throat. "It's your mother. They don't know what happened. It's bad, Katydid. Can you come?"

Chapter Twenty-One

Erin wove her way through the tables to meet Paul in his booth near the back of the restaurant. She'd told him her order when she called to tell him she was running late, and her drink was waiting for her on the table. It wasn't that long ago that she'd sat in the same booth with both Paul and Katie on the day Katie moved back from Bloomington. That was a great day. Her best friend returned home with her faith renewed, and Erin got to meet her soul mate though she didn't know it at the time.

She slid onto the vinyl seat across from Paul. His hand immediately reached for hers. With his right thumb, he caressed the back of her hand. With his left, he toyed with the diamond ring on her finger.

"I'm surprised you're wearing your ring. Didn't you stop by the hospital to check on Katie?"

Erin nodded and freed her left hand from his grasp. She held it up for inspection. "Yeah I did. I keep the ring box in my purse. I took it off when I got there, but this baby went right back in its place as soon as I left Katie's side."

Paul's brows lowered and his lips dropped into a slight frown momentarily before he schooled them into a more neutral expression.

"Are you upset that I haven't told her about your proposal yet?"

Paul retrieved her hand and brought it to his lips. "No. Of course, I wish we could share our news with her, but I understand why you feel like you can't right now. How is Sharon doing today?"

"It's been two weeks, and she doesn't seem to be improving. The stroke took her ability to speak, but I get the idea she still understands everything going on around her. I just wish she'd start getting better."

"I know you don't want to hear this, and I'm not saying we shouldn't keep praying for healing. But what if she's not going to get better? Strokes do some pretty serious stuff to people. Even those who regain all their abilities often still suffer residual effects."

Erin looked out the window as she fought an onslaught of tears. She watched a bird pecking at a long since forgotten French fry. "She's got to get better. I'm not sure Katie can handle much more, not so soon after Austin."

"I thought she was doing pretty well handling all that. Last time I spoke to her on the phone, she seemed to have come to terms with everything."

Erin squeezed his hands as she looked back at him. "That's part of the problem. She says all the right things, and I know she believes them in her head. But I get the sense that there's something off. She's accepted everything like a champ. But, I don't know. I just feel like there's still something broken underneath it all."

"Are you borrowing trouble? Maybe everything is good."

Erin considered his words in silence as the waitress brought their food. Could she be projecting her own feelings onto Katie?

Paul let go of her hands. "Would you like me to pray over the food?"

"Please."

Paul bowed his head. Erin followed suit. Even with everything else going on, she couldn't help feeling blessed as she listened to her fiancé praying. He never hesitated or changed his prayers just because they were in public. He spoke from the heart, and she loved him for it.

"Father God, thank you for this time I have with Erin. Thank you for bringing her into my life and letting her stay in it as my soon to be wife. You have blessed us both with a love that grew from a strong base of friendship, and we don't want to take that for granted. Be with Katie and her family. Strengthen them for whatever lies ahead. We ask for healing for Sharon. Touch her and give the doctors insight and wisdom. Let Cal and Katie feel your peace during this time. And, Lord, bless this food and those who prepared and served it. Let it provide us with the nourishment we need to do your will. In Jesus' name, amen."

"Amen."

PAUL WATCHED Erin dip a mozzarella stick into the small bowl of marinara sauce before gently placing it between her teeth and stretching the cheese as far as she could across the table. He grinned. One minute she could be wise and insightful, and the next she was as playful and impulsive as a child. Marriage to this woman was never going to be dull.

"Hewe." She instructed between clenched teeth as she passed the breaded cheese to him.

He dutifully took the cheese stick from her hand and continued to slowly stretch it across the table beyond what she could reach. He could never figure out what it was about mozzarella sticks that turned her into a five year old, but she'd completed the same ritual every time she ate them from the day they met. He had no doubt that it would continue until the day she died.

When the cheese finally gave way, Erin caught it in her hand and wove it back into her mouth. "That's the sign of a superb mozzarella stick. Of course, they're always good here, but that one was beyond. I've not been able to get one to stretch that far in ages."

Paul shook his head. "I'm not sure I understand why you don't just eat them."

His beautiful fiancé shrugged as she pushed a stray lock of blonde hair behind her ear. "Because it isn't as fun to do it that way. It's boring and ordinary."

A twinkle sparked in her light blue eyes and she threw her arms wide open. "Who wants to be ordinary when you can be extraordinary?"

At least she hadn't yelled it like she was declaring it from a mountaintop. Only their waitress seemed to notice, and she only giggled and kept on walking. Erin definitely moved him out of his comfort zone in public, but it was part of why she was good for him. "My dear, no one could ever confuse you with being just ordinary. You shine too brightly for that."

Long, straight hair fell over her shoulder as she regarded him with tilted head. "Have I told you that I love you more than anything, Mr. Wilson?"

"I can always hear it again, soon-to-be Mrs. Wilson. And speaking of soon-to-be brides, have you thought about when our wedding should take place?"

Erin speared the cherry in her limeade with her straw. "I'm not sure. We both agree on a short engagement period and that the wedding should be held here since your family doesn't live in Bloomington. But I want Katie to be my matron of honor, and I haven't even told her about our engagement yet."

"You could change that at any time."

Her eyebrows rose to an impossible height. "We've talked about that too. And I thought we were in agreement."

Paul tried to look contrite. "We did. We do. But I can't tell you there's not a selfish part of me that wants to tell her anyway so we can get this wedding underway."

Erin moved her empty plate to the edge of the table for the waitress before reaching across to take Paul's hand. "I know. I'm torn about it too. Believe it or not, it's incredibly difficult for me to keep something this exciting to myself."

Paul rolled his eyes. "I have no problem believing that at all. You tend to enjoy sharing exciting news, and our upcoming marriage has to top that list."

"I know, right? I can't believe I've lasted this long, and it's only been a couple of days. It's only because of what she's going through that I haven't spilled the beans yet. I don't really know how long I can do this. But I think we should go ahead and plan the wedding. Katie's mom will either get better or they'll adjust to this new way of life. Either way, when it happens, we'll share our news with Katie, and she'll be happy to know we've already begun working on the plans for our big day."

Paul laughed. When Erin was excited she talked a mile a minute. He wasn't sure he caught every word she said, but he understood enough to realize she wanted to begin planning and catch Katie up later. "So, if we're going ahead with plans, we need to pick a date."

Erin rested her elbows on the table and her chin on her fists. "Hmmm. It's February now. How about the end of August? That will give us just a little over six months. That's plenty of time to plan the wedding and arrange to move my life to Bloomington."

"I think that will give my family time to make arrangements to be here. Is there a particular date you'd like to shoot for?"

"The twenty-fifth is a Saturday. We could have a Saturday morning wedding and then be off on our honeymoon by early afternoon?"

"Saturday, August twenty-fifth at 10 am. Sounds like a plan to me. Now we just need to tell the matron of honor."

It was Erin's turn to roll her eyes. "I will. I will. I just need to wait until the time is right. Katie's got a lot on her plate right now. And I don't know that she can handle another, even if it is a good thing."

Chapter Twenty-Two

It was too soon for Katie Blake to be standing next to another freshly dug grave. Yet, here she was. The faces surrounding her were different this time, but the pitying looks and the sadness in their eyes were the same. Others wrapped their arms around their bodies for warmth, but Katie's arms were held straight against her sides. The frigid breeze didn't feel cold at all compared to the emptiness spreading through her body. She closed her eyes, swallowing the knot of emotion lodged in her throat. Watching them lower the casket into the hard earth was too much. A tear squeezed free and coursed down her cheek. She took a deep steadying breath.

A light touch to her arm drew Katie's attention from the gaping hole. Her father nodded toward the grave that housed her mother's body. Katie dutifully stepped forward to let a handful of powdery dirt flow through her fingers. It landed like heavy raindrops on a roof, but instead of comfort, the sound of the dirt coming to rest on the wood below signaled finality, at least this side of eternity.

Mourners slowly made their way to waiting cars. Tired, red rimmed eyes watched Katie. Her father touched her arm once again. Katie knew her tight lipped smile looked empty and forced.

How could it be anything else at a time like this? "You go ahead, Dad. Mr. Johnson will give you a ride to the church and back home. I may meet you there."

Her father's brow lowered. "Are you sure, Katydid? You should come get something to eat. I know the church ladies will have the fellowship hall packed with food."

Katie shook her head. "I'm not really hungry." Besides, the previous months had taught her an important lesson. When disaster struck her freezer would miraculously fill with enough casseroles to survive a zombie apocalypse. She wouldn't go hungry if she didn't make it to the church. "You go on ahead."

Her father looked doubtfully at her before shuffling off in the direction of the remaining cars. Katie waited until only her jeep remained in the lot before moving from her mother's grave. She didn't have to think about how to work her way through the maze of stone. She knew exactly where she wanted, no, needed to be and how to get there. As her fingers brushed over the rough gray granite, her tears began in earnest. Too soon. *God, why does it have to be so soon?*

When the initial stroke sent her mother to the hospital, Katie remained hopeful. She'd said her good-byes without belief that she would need to hold onto them. God wouldn't take her mother. He couldn't take her mother, not following so closely after Austin's death. God wouldn't be that demanding. Secure in her belief, Katie prayed and stood as the wall of strength that held up her dad until the end.

Three weeks and five days. That's how long her mother had remained in the hospital. In that time, Katie had witnessed fear and worry and ultimately peace passing through her mother's eyes, though her brain could never get her mouth to voice her thoughts. Katie stayed by her mother's side across from her father who held vigil on the opposite side, rarely loosening his hold on his wife's hand. In the end, she had known she was loved. When Katie had whispered those words to her mother, she saw recognition and love returned in her eyes as clearly as if the words had been spoken.

Not even the doctors had expected the second massive stroke. The blare of hospital machines sounded their warning too late in the night while they slept fitfully in the uncomfortable chairs beside her bed. Shooed out by hustling nurses and doctors, father and daughter held onto each other in the hallway waiting for news. They didn't wait long. Sharon McGowan had passed into eternity in minutes, and it wasn't right.

Katie dropped to her knees, her hand tracing a path down the polished front of the headstone. Her fingers caught on the etched out letters. She saw those letters in her dreams nearly every night for the first few months after he died. Austin Blake, Beloved Husband and Friend. She'd believed the worst was behind her after his murderer's arrest and conviction had finally allowed her to try to find a new normal for her life. The dreams had ended, but the pain had yet to subside.

Katie had claimed all the right verses of scripture. She'd prayed "Your will be done" and refused to let herself be angry. God could do what God wanted. He was, after all, God. What good would it do to argue with the Maker of the universe? She'd done everything but return to church. She'd believed it was because returning to her husband's church would be too hard. Was that true? Or was there something else lurking in her heart keeping her from fellowship and worship with other believers?

Her ragged breaths woke the little one. She laid her hand on her protruding belly as the child within tumbled and turned. Fresh waves of grief rolled over Katie as once again, she faced the reality that her precious child would never know his father. The anguish heightened with the realization that now he would never know his grandma either. When would her suffering be enough? How could she hope to stand up under the weight of it until it was through?

As she sat on the cold ground, it seemed she had tapped into a bottomless pit of pain. It outlasted her tears, and it outlasted her strength. Katie's head fell forward to rest on the gravestone, and she sat in silence with her grief incapable of recognizing anything else.

The hand on her shoulder should have startled Katie, but it barely pushed back the fog shrouding her heart and mind. She looked up to find Erin hovering above with concern in her eyes. "Katie, honey, it's time to come home. Your dad is worried sick."

Katie looked beyond Erin to find the sun dipping low in the sky. How long had she been there? It must have been a couple hours at least. As she tried to move, the stiffness in her muscles testified to the passing time. Without having to be asked, Erin extended both arms and grasped Katie's, pulling her up.

"Are you all right? Do you need me to drive you home?"

Katie started to shake her head, but a sharp pain in her abdomen cut off her movement. She exhaled deeply until the pain subsided. It wasn't the first pain of the day. They'd begun as soon as she'd crawled out of bed. Several passed in the time she'd been at the grave, but Katie had ignored them in deference to the emotional pain she was feeling.

Erin grimaced, and Katie realized she still held her arms, her grip unintentionally turning into a vise throughout the contraction. "Sorry," she mumbled. "Maybe it wouldn't be such a bad idea for you to drive."

"I think you're right. I'll tell Paul to follow behind us in my car. You take your time." Erin trotted off to the parking lot where Paul waited next to Erin's little yellow VW bug.

Katie carefully made her way down to her jeep. Each step worked out some of the stiffness in her joints, but it did nothing to ease the pressure in her stomach. Erin waited by the open passenger door to receive the keys from Katie before climbing in on the driver's side. Katie rested her hand on the door to heave her body up into the seat when another pain hit. She froze, panting through it. When it eased, she climbed into her seat and shut the door. Neither woman spoke as Erin drove toward Katie's house, but when another contraction hit, Erin pulled into a random driveway before backing out in the opposite direction.

Katie opened her mouth to question, but Erin cut her off. "Don't even start with me, Katie Blake. I am not in the mood. You've had three contractions in the last twenty minutes. You're going to the hospital."

"It can't be labor. I'm only 37 weeks. It's too early. It's got to be those Braxton-hicks things." The idea of returning to the hospital, no matter how good the reason for going, was not appealing.

"It can be that all it wants, but we're going to hear it from a doctor's mouth. We're going to the hospital."

While it was not in her original plan, Katie was relieved they were heading that direction when the next contraction hit. Maybe seeing a doctor to get some peace of mind wasn't a bad idea after all.

"Can I get you anything?"

Katie saw the concern etched on her father's weathered face. A twinge of guilt assailed her. He was in mourning for his wife. He'd barely left the hospital. He shouldn't be back. Erin was here with her, currently brushing Katie's hair away from her face. Her dad should be home resting, but he wasn't. He was sitting by her side. Katie only hoped he wasn't afraid of what this outcome might be. She wished there was a way to reassure him.

"Can you get me some ice chips from the nurses' station?"

He nodded and left the room only moments before another pain gripped her. In the last nine hours, the contractions stayed regular enough to keep her in the hospital but not powerful enough to bring her child into the world. She was progressing but progress was slow. The doctor's last visit ended with the welcome news that she was dilated to an eight. The end was in sight, but Katie was getting tired. She'd forgone an epidural, opting instead for IV pain medication. There was something about a needle in the back that made the giant band of pain squeezing her abdomen more tolerable. One last breath and it subsided.

Katie laid her head back onto the pillow and turned to Erin. "How has he seemed to you?" Funny how conversations continued between contractions without missing a beat.

Erin picked up the thread of thought. "Okay, I guess. He's tired. But I don't think he's stressing it too much. You've got to remember this is a very different situation. Even in his grief I think he can see that."

"Maybe you're right. He . . ."

Awkward silence reigned as the subject of their discussion came back into the room. Hopefully he didn't hear them discussing him as he came down the hall. But even if he did, he'd have known they were only concerned for him. He couldn't be upset at that. Katie watched him rub his arms before stretching them out with a yawn.

Katie frowned. "Dad? Where's the ice chips?"

"The what?"

"The ice chips. You were going to go to the nurses' station and get a cup of ice chips for me."

He rubbed his cheek. "Oh. I guess I was. Must have gotten distracted on the way. I'll go get them for you now. Be back in a minute."

He left the room, but true to his word came back quicker than Katie would've given him credit for. The doctor followed close behind. Not wanting to be in the room while Katie's progress was checked, her dad headed out of the room again after setting the cup on the movable tray.

Erin nodded towards the door. "I think I'm going to join your dad and maybe call Paul to give him an update. I'll be back."

Katie nodded her understanding. She hadn't wanted her dad in the room when the doctor came to check her, but she'd let Erin stay. After the first check, Erin had decided she didn't really want that honor. From then on when the doctor came in, the two of them went out. Katie understood Erin's hesitancy to stay, but she couldn't ignore the loneliness those few minutes would bring each time. Austin should be by her side. Or at the very least, her mother should have filled his place. Neither was here for her, just as neither would ever be here for her son.

"I know it's uncomfortable, but it will be over soon. It's not quite time for more pain medicine though. Can you hold out a little longer?"

The doctor's voice broke her out of her reverie. Katie looked to the foot end of the bed and found compassion in her doctor's expression. Pain medicine? The pain wasn't any worse than it had been. Why would she need more?

"Yes, I can go longer. The pains are bad but not unbearable."

Confused eyes looked back at her, but Dr. Taylor gave no clue as to why. "You're progressing nicely. You've dilated to nine. It shouldn't be long now. If you need anything, just buzz the nurse."

It wasn't until the doctor left the room, and Katie rubbed her cheeks as she yawned that she felt the telltale moisture of a few silent tears. They must have escaped when she was missing Austin and her mother. No wonder the doctor was confused. Crying generally meant pain. How was she to know these tears had nothing to do with her contractions and everything to do with the heart? If only this little one would make his appearance so she could go home, away from questioning eyes.

KATIE BORE down one more time. It felt as if someone was trying to split her down the middle, but she pushed past it knowing it was the only way she'd find relief. And the relief was immediate as her son's shoulders opened the way for the rest of him to quickly follow them into the doctor's waiting hands.

"He's a beautiful boy," Dr. Taylor stated as she passed the squirming infant to the nearest nurse.

It seemed like only moments passed before her son was placed on her chest. The first skin to skin contact and what everyone said was her first chance to bond with him. What they didn't understand was she'd been bonded to him for the last nine months. The devastation and loss had been his too, and it brought them together long before feeling him against her. But this bonding was different. It was a sweet moment that pushed the pain to the background, allowing only joy between mother and son.

Fingers reached out to touch the silky dark hair, and Katie looked up to see the awe in Erin's face. Despite her hesitancy to remain in the room when the doctor checked her progress, once it was time to push, Erin had not left her side. Her voice was soft. "He's so tiny and perfect."

Contentment drew a smile from Katie. While the doctor and nurses made sure everything was in order with the birth and took care of her, she was happy to cuddle her tiny son. Erin grinned beside her watching mother and son until the nurses scooped him up with the promise they would return him as quickly as possible.

"I've never seen anything like that." Erin's voice was the quietest Katie had ever heard it. "You were amazing. I only hope I'm as much of a rock star when it's my turn."

Something in her voice caught Katie's attention. "Could your time be coming soon? Have things progressed with you and Paul?"

Erin bit her lip. "We didn't want to say anything. You've been going through so much lately, and it didn't seem right."

"Did Paul propose? Are you getting married?"

A giant smile covered Erin's face as she nodded. "He asked me a couple weeks ago, and I said yes."

Katie's mouth dropped open in disbelief. Erin was horrible at keeping secrets. "A couple weeks? Why didn't you tell me?"

"Well, your mom was in the hospital. She wasn't improving,

and we didn't want to take the focus from what you were dealing with."

Katie took her friend's hand. "I don't care what I'm dealing with or not. I'm completely happy for you two. I understand, but I would've wanted to know even then. Promise me in the future you'll spill big news like that the moment it happens."

Erin laughed. "Yes. From now on you'll be the first to know anything that happens. If I find a good shoe sale, I'll call. If I win a million dollars, I'll call."

"If you get pregnant . . ."

"I'll tell you before I even share the news with Paul."

"That's what I'm talking about. So, where's the ring?"

Erin's cheeks pinked as she pulled a small felt box out of her purse. "I wasn't wearing it because I hadn't told you yet."

"Well, put it on, girl, and let me see it."

Erin slipped the band on her finger and held out her hand to Katie. She could feel the joy radiating from her friend. The oval cut diamond was surrounded by a dozen tiny chocolate diamonds set in rose gold giving it an old look. The look fit everything about Erin.

"Remind me to tell Paul he knocked it out of the park with this one."

Erin pulled her hand back and stared at the ring. "I know. I didn't even help him out. We hadn't talked rings at all. Marriage, yes, but in that 'when we get married' way, not the specific 'let's get married' way. Know what I mean? Of course you do. But then, when he came down the weekend after Valentine's Day, he took me out to dinner and surprised me with a proposal after dessert. It was so romantic, like I was in a movie or something. It was better than I could've imagined it, and I wanted to tell you so badly. I knew you'd be happy for me, but I just couldn't tell you. You were dealing with so much. Do you forgive me?"

It never failed to amaze Katie the way Erin could relate a complete story with only one breath to get her through the telling.

Truthfully, she couldn't be happier for her friend. Erin had stood beside her through all the good and bad over the years, and Paul was more than a former employee. He'd become a friend and spiritual support when she'd needed it most. To see them together was wonderful.

"There's nothing to forgive. I get why you didn't tell me, and I appreciate it. Just don't ever try something like that again. You and Paul are great for each other, and your news makes this day even better."

Katie dismissed the tightness in her throat. It was her exhaustion and elation working together against her. There was no reason for disappointment with this kind of news. Before she could investigate it any further, the nurse slipped into the room, pushing her son's bassinet in front of her. After checking the bracelets on both their wrists, she lifted the sleeping infant into his mother's arms. Katie snuggled him close and kissed the top of his head.

"Why don't I get your dad out of the waiting room? I texted Paul when the baby got here, but they'll both want to come meet him, if that's okay with you? Oh, and I got a text from Austin's parents. They're on their way now. They said his sister can't make it in until the weekend, but they should be here by tonight."

Katie didn't look away from the baby. "Thank you, Erin. I don't know what I would've done without you today. Go ahead and get my dad and Paul. I know dad will be chomping at the bit wanting to meet his grandson."

With the door shut and a few minutes of silence, Katie prayed quietly. "Father God, thank you for bringing my son into the world safely. He's the most perfect thing I've ever seen, and I ask that you help me be the mother to him that he needs."

She would have continued had the door not opened to admit her father, Paul, and Erin. They oohed and aahed over the infant before her father claimed him, moving to the rocking chair in the corner of the room. Katie loved watching him hold her son close, whispering in his ear about how beautiful he was and how wonderful it was to have him with them. Their heartache would still be with them, but her son's arrival was a bright spot to help them cling to hope of better days.

Paul pulled a chair close to the side of her bed. "If no one else is going to ask, I'm just going ahead. What are you naming your son?"

Katie didn't stop looking at Paul, but she felt the moment her father's eyes left the baby to find her. "Samuel Austin Blake."

She turned in time to see her father wipe a tear from his cheek. She was sure choosing to name the baby after Austin was not a surprise to anyone, but deciding to honor her father by using his middle name was something none of them had discussed. But Katie could not have chosen a better name. Calvin Samuel McGowan had always been her rock, and now, he would play a large role in her son's life too. Without a father of his own, Samuel Austin would need a strong male role model to show him how to be a godly man.

Her father looked down at his namesake. "A fine name, for a fine boy."

Chapter Twenty-Three

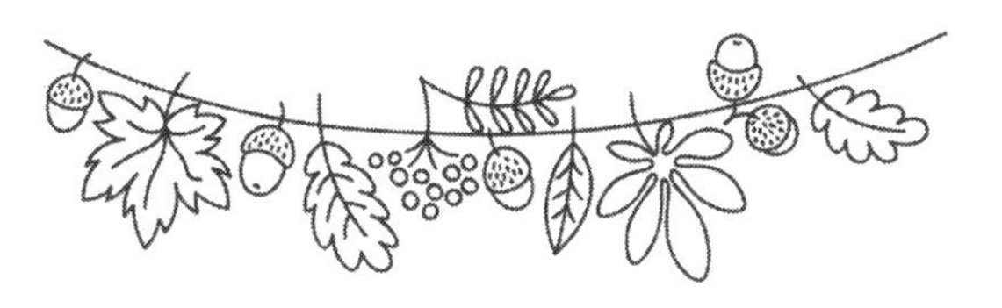

Katie stumbled from her bed, slowly making her way across the dark room. Eerie green light gave the corner an otherworldly glow. The sound that accompanied the monitor's lights brought her crashing back down to earth. Why did babies eat so little and so often? If only they'd eat a decent sized meal, they wouldn't have to wake up sleep deprived parents in the middle of the night.

The first two weeks hadn't been as bad. Her in-laws had stayed the first few days before returning home. After that Erin stayed with her, helping her through the day and even waking up once in a while to take a middle of the night shift. But now that she was on her own, Katie's fatigue was growing with every feeding. She navigated the hall to the kitchen with her eyes barely raised above slits. Refusing to force them to open further, she fumbled through preparing a bottle and headed to Sammy's room.

She shushed the tiny infant, lifting him from the crib as she did so. "Mommy's here, sweet little Sammy. I've got a bottle for your tummy, and then we can all go back to sleep."

She didn't even try to stifle her yawn as she lowered herself into the rocking chair and gave her son his bottle. The quiet lullaby she sang him did nothing to put him to sleep, but it worked wonders on Katie. She jerked her head up as the bottle started to slip from her fingers.

Enough lullabies. If she continued, she would never make it through the feeding. And she had to feed Sammy. He couldn't do for himself. He was totally dependent on her. Her alone. There wasn't anyone to provide backup for the midnight feedings. There wouldn't be anyone she could count on when he got cranky teething or the first time a stomach bug rampaged through their home. It was all her, all the time.

A sudden gasp brought Katie's attention to the fact that she'd been holding her breath while trying desperately to hold her emotions in check. It also made the calming infant in her arms startle awake. His quiet cries of helplessness mocked her feeling of helplessness. She couldn't be helpless. It was a luxury she couldn't afford. Her son needed her, and he needed her to be strong.

"Shhh. Mommy's got you. Hush now and go back to sleep." She pulled the empty bottle from his mouth and set him on her shoulder, coaxing a soft burp from him before laying him back in the cradle of her arms. As she rocked him and stroked his cheek, Sammy's eyes grew heavy. When she was certain he would stay asleep, she placed him in his crib. It was time to find her bed before the next feeding. It would come long before she was ready.

She considered the bottle in her hand but decided against returning it to the kitchen. There were other clean bottles to fill for the next round. Right now, sleep was the most important thing. She made her way down the hall, her bare feet chilled by the cool wood floor. She wasn't prepared when she stepped onto the long area rug, and it slid under her feet. With fatigue stealing her ability to react, Katie fell back.

Her scream of pain broke the silence of the night. Hot pain shot through her shoulder as it connected with the unyielding corner of a small chest against the wall behind her. Katie panted through the worst of the pain before deciding to move. Gingerly she shifted and the pain spiked. Katie bit her bottom lip to stave off another scream. It wouldn't do to wake Sammy if she couldn't get to him to soothe him. The coolness of the night and her pain double teamed her, leaving her shaking uncontrollably. Tears flowed unchecked.

Rustling from her son's bedroom woke Katie where she'd finally fallen into fitful sleep on the floor. Her intent had been to get to her bed. Her reality had turned out quite differently when the pain prevented her moving. It was the perfect metaphor for the direction her life was going. Metaphor? She must really be exhausted to think in literary terms about her life.

Sammy had ceased his restlessness, oblivious to the predicament his mother found herself in. However, Katie knew she could no longer stay on the floor. He would wake soon and need her. Keeping her shoulder as stable as she could in her position, Katie pulled her abdominal muscles tight and lifted her torso. She'd never given much thought to sit-ups. That would be the first thing she'd change after she got out of this mess. Heat seared her abdominal muscles as she forced them to pull her weight so soon after their trauma of giving birth.

Whether it was pain or lightheadedness causing it Katie couldn't tell, but a wave of nausea overtook her as her body reawakened to the reality of her injury. She swallowed hard to fight the urge to vomit. She could only imagine what the heaving movement would do to her pain levels. Sitting with her knees bent up in front of her Katie scooted across the floor until her back was against the wall. The pressure heightened the intensity of her pain, but she figured this was the lesser of two evils in trying to get up from the floor. Leaning as much of her weight into her unhurt shoulder as she could she pushed up with her feet and slid herself up the wall until she was standing. She exhaled the breath she'd held through the ordeal.

Holding her arm tightly against her side, she went to the kitchen. She retrieved ibuprofen from the cabinet and worked the lid with one hand until she finally got it open. She swallowed three pills with a drink of water before deciding to make up Sammy's next bottle. His morning feeding time was getting close, and she wasn't sure how much she wanted to move. Before making her way back to his room, she snatched an ice pack from the freezer. Laying it on the back of the rocking chair she lowered herself into the chair and back onto the numbing coldness of the pack. Maybe if she stayed perfectly still she could get a little more rest before Sammy woke.

"KATIE, why aren't you answering your phone?" Erin's voice carried through the house as the front door opened and closed.

Katie put her finger to her lips as Erin came into the nursery. Trying not to wince too much, Katie rose from the chair and placed Sammy back in his crib. He'd risen like she'd expected and eaten quickly before falling right back to sleep. Thank goodness he wasn't at the stay up and play stage yet.

Erin followed her in silence until they were in the kitchen. "No offense, but you look awful."

Katie's mouth twisted in a sarcastic frown. "Don't sugar coat it. I wouldn't know what to do with a healthy self-esteem that comes from having friendly friends."

Erin shook her head. "Oh stop it. You know what I mean." She punctuated her words with a playful smack across Katie's shoulder.

Erin's face went white as Katie howled in pain. "What in the world happened to you? I barely touched you."

Katie pressed her hand to the front of her shoulder. "I fell. I couldn't move most of the night the pain was so bad. It's not any better this morning."

"Hold still. I'm going to take a look at it."

"I don't need you to baby me. I'm going to be fine."

Erin looked like a warrior with her hands on her hips facing off with Katie. "I didn't ask. I'm going to take a look at that shoulder. You can deal with it, or you can try to fight me. But I guarantee with your level of pain, I will win. I may be small, but I'm tenacious."

Katie braced herself as Erin lifted the back of her shirt. Even the movement of the material around the injured area caused intense pain to pulse through it. Erin was gentle, careful to avoid touching her shoulder. "This looks bad Katie. I'm going to call Gigi B to come watch Sammy. You and I are going to the doctor."

Katie opened her mouth to argue but shut it again as another wave of nausea struck. "Fine. Call my dad too. Let him know what's going on."

"You go get changed if you want to and can. I'll get the calls made."

"I THINK we need to talk about this whether you're ready or not."

Katie glared at her father from the hospital bed. She was ready to be done with hospitals for a while, but that was the only thing she was ready for at the moment. "There's nothing to discuss."

"I think there is. I've got a house that's much too big for an old man like me to putter around in all by myself. You could use another set of hands helping out. It's the perfect arrangement."

She could feel her lips tighten into a firm line. "Daddy, I'm not having this conversation. Austin provided us with a nice home. I don't need to give that up and come running home. I fell. It could have happened anywhere, to anyone. It doesn't mean I need to move back home."

"I'm not saying you can't take care of yourself."

"That's sure what it sounds like."

"Fine. We'll talk about it later. I'm going after a cup of coffee."

Katie watched her father stalk from the room. He moved with

surprising ease for a man as old as he was. What he said made sense on paper, but Katie could handle things on her own.

"You know he's just trying to help." Erin's voice was soft from the corner where she sat.

"I don't need this from you too." She hoped the irritation came through more than the fatigue. That would only strengthen the opposing argument.

Erin scooted the chair close to Katie's side. There were tears in her eyes as she spoke. "You can ask for help, you know? It's not you against the world."

Katie fought the hot fury that ignited in her chest. She closed her eyes and took a deep breath. She didn't want to push Erin away, but this conversation had to end. God had given her this road to walk. It's the way things were, and she had to be okay with that. If everyone would just leave her be, she could accept it.

"I'm aware of that. Can we skip the speeches and just focus on getting me out of here and back to my son please?"

Erin's eyes reflected regret. Her closed lipped smile was forced as she nodded. "Sure. Whatever you need."

Relief shot through Katie as her dad walked back into the room. A nurse came with him, and Katie hoped she was there with answers that would allow her to go home.

The nurse looked only at her father. "Here you go, Mr. McGowan. I told you I'd have you back to your daughter's room in no time."

Katie looked to her father as the nurse retreated from the room. So, no answers, but Katie had a few more questions now.

Her father looked at her and shrugged. "This place is like a maze. Every room and hallway looks the same. Got myself turned around."

Katie pushed away the unease his explanation brought. She had enough to worry about with the pain her shoulder was causing her. Bruised and sore or possibly a fracture. The x-rays they were waiting on would decide her fate for the next several weeks. She prayed it wasn't a fracture and her pain would lessen considerably in the next day or so. It would be difficult to manage a baby with her arm in a sling.

Since there was no danger and Erin was driving, her father had headed back home after the first hour but not before issuing a mandate that she call if she needed anything. After Katie's earlier outburst, the girls had talked little and kept the subjects superficial. This left a lot of silence to fill, and Katie passed most of it dozing or staring at the ceiling. She was counting the ceiling tiles for the umpteenth time when the doctor finally made his way back to her room.

"I've checked out the x-rays, and they look good. No breaks or fractures. Try to ice and rest your shoulder the next few days. Take ibuprofen when you need it. And don't avoid using that arm completely. It could lock up on you if you don't use it at all. Then we'd have to get into physical therapy, and that's time I know you don't have as a new mom. I'll send the nurse in with your paperwork, and we'll get you home to your son."

Katie smiled. Finally, she was going home.

Chapter Twenty-Four

"Well, what's the verdict?"

If the ride home hadn't jostled her shoulder until she felt she would scream, Katie would have had the energy to smile at the way Gigi B got the question out before she'd actually made it inside the door. As it was, she crossed the living room and made a beeline for the kitchen. When she came back into the room with an ice pack draped over her shoulder, Erin and Gigi B were discussing the doctor's diagnosis and recommendations.

Gigi B reached over to pat her knee. "Praise Jesus it's not worse than some bruises and sore muscles. You'll be right as rain in no time."

Katie forced a smile. She didn't trust herself to say anything. She was too tired to keep rein on her emotions, and maintaining the proper attitude was becoming harder with each sleepless night.

Before anyone could comment further, Sammy's cry came over the baby monitor. A quick glance at the clock told her it was time for a feeding. Katie rose and went into the kitchen to prepare a bottle. Gigi B had been busy while she was gone. Every bottle in the house was washed and paired up with a nipple and ring. Katie found this wasn't as much a blessing as she'd hoped when she tried to get one loosened to add the water and formula powder. She might as well be a baby herself with the weakness in her arm. Every time she grasped the bottle and went to unscrew the top, stabbing pain shot through her shoulder. Finally, it gave way and the unexpected movement caused Katie to drop her arm. She cringed as her hand smacked a glass on the drying mat knocking it to the floor. Gigi B and Erin came running into the room at the sound of glass shattering on the wood floor.

"Land sakes, girlie! What's going on in here?"

Katie stood panting by the sink, refusing to turn and face them or answer Gigi B's question. If she could simply get the stupid bottle made and her child fed, it would all be fine. She popped the top off the jug of bottled water she kept by the sink and poured it into the bottle. From the corner of her eye, Katie could see Erin moving to the pantry to retrieve the broom and dustpan. She watched her begin sweeping the broken shards into a pile.

"Don't."

Confusion filled her voice. "What? Don't sweep?"

She didn't mean for her voice to go flat, but she was exhausted. "Leave it. I'll get it later."

"Why would I do that? You feed Sammy, and I'll clean up in here."

Katie turned to glare at her. "I said leave it. I'll get it later. I can take care of my child and my mess."

Gigi B reached a hand out to Katie's good arm. "Of course you can. You're a capable woman. But there's nothing wrong with asking for or accepting help. You don't have to do everything alone."

Fire exploded in Katie's chest as tears burned her eyes. "Tell God that! If He wanted me to have help so badly why did He decide this was the time to take my husband from me? Obviously I'm supposed to do it myself!"

Katie stalked from the room refusing to look at either woman. She paused briefly at the doorway to Sammy's room. Below, she heard the front door close and knew she'd been left alone with her son and her anger. She sniffed and wiped her eyes while taking a calming breath. She didn't want her hostility to mar the time she had with her son. Though it still boiled under the surface, Katie felt calm enough to go in to Sammy. It took creative maneuvering and caused her pain to intensify, but she managed to lift the infant from his crib to feed him.

Holding him usually worked like magic on her frayed emotions, but this time she'd broken a dam she'd kept fortified since Austin's death. She'd known there was no place for anger so she sealed it away where it couldn't harm her or push God away from her. She had enough issues without adding disappointing God to the mix. A broken glass and ill-timed words had finally worked their way into the cracks in the dam she'd erected, freeing everything that lay behind it to burst out with unexpected force. Now she couldn't even find solace with her precious Sammy. While she should have been basking in their love for each other, she was wrestling with questions and feelings she knew she shouldn't even have much less give time to.

Katie felt sick when she realized she was glad the baby went back to sleep immediately after his feeding. It shouldn't be this way. If only she'd been able to keep all of this at bay a little longer. She laid him in his crib and went to rinse the bottle and loosen the tops of the others so another fiasco like this one wouldn't take place.

She started when she walked into the kitchen and realized she wasn't alone. When she'd heard the front door close, she'd assumed both women had left. She wouldn't have blamed them, and part of her had known relief at what she thought was their hasty retreat. Gigi B proved her wrong as she sat at the kitchen table with her hands folded in front of her. Great. The last thing she wanted was to get into a discussion about her bad attitude.

Katie decided the best course of action was to head it off at the pass. "I'm sorry, Gigi B. I shouldn't have spoken to you that way, and I know my attitude was wrong. What happened, happened. I can't hold that against God."

She watched as Gigi B regarded her in silence. Her perfectly penciled brows lowered as her lips pursed. Katie couldn't figure out if she was angry or disappointed. She wasn't entirely sure she cared. As much as she chafed at the idea of having to go through life alone, she found herself wishing for solitude at this particular moment.

"Sit down, Katie."

Her tone left no room for argument. Even for someone as headstrong as Katie, proper raising kept her from arguing with her elder. She pulled out a chair and sat.

"I wasn't asking for an apology. I didn't need one. But I've got some things to say, and you're going to listen. You've got to put a stop to this nonsense."

Katie bristled but fought to keep her tone even and respectful. "I know. I didn't mean to lose my cool. I'm tired is all."

Gigi B's hand raised as she shook her head. "You misunderstand me. Erin's spoke of nothing but how well you're taking things. She's been impressed and challenged by your ability to accept first Austin's death and now the passing of your mother with such strength and faith. I've seen it myself. But I'm here to tell you, it's a lie. I think when you knocked over that glass you were honest for the first time in months. You're angry, and you need to stop pretending you're not."

Katie twisted a stray curl around her finger as she considered what Gigi B said. She'd seen through Katie, discovered she was nothing more than a fake. She sucked in her lip to keep it from shaking and closed her eyes against tears. It would be futile to try convincing her she was wrong. The elderly woman was too wise to fall for smoke and mirrors. But would she let everyone else in on the secret? Could Katie keep up the pretense of being a faithful follower, accepting of her lot?

"You're right. I'm a hypocrite. I claim to love God. I tell

everyone how okay I am with all of this, but it's a lie. My faith isn't real after all."

A finger pointed in her direction. "You stop right there. That isn't what I'm saying at all. You seem bound and determined to misunderstand every word coming out of my mouth today. I'm not sure we're even speaking the same language at this point. I'm not calling you a hypocrite or questioning your faith. I'm saying you're angry, and you need to give it vent."

"But that's what I said. I am angry. I'm angry at God, and I was trying so hard to pretend I wasn't. But it's true. I can't believe God would let this happen, and now that it's out, everyone's going to know my faith wasn't strong enough. I'm nothing more than a kid play acting at having faith."

"Why on earth would you think that?"

Katie rolled her eyes. "Because it's true. If I had faith, do you think I'd be angry at God?"

Gigi B put her hand under her chin, tapping one finger on her lips. She looked toward the ceiling as she thought. She was matter of fact when she spoke. "I think it takes a great deal of faith to be angry with God."

"That makes absolutely no sense."

"I beg to differ. It makes perfect sense. If you didn't have faith, you wouldn't be upset with Him. But you believe something so strongly about God that this seeming inconsistency makes you angry and confused. You believe God is good and loving and faithful. You believe He honors those who seek to honor and serve Him. You believe He wants good things for His children. So when life throws you some of the worst curve balls it can, the facts you believe about God don't seem to match up with your current reality. How could a loving God take a man from you that wanted nothing more than to love and serve Him? When people don't act in ways that line up with what we believe about them anger is often the result. We feel betrayed by the one we love. The one just happens to be God this time. So, yes, I refuse to believe your faith is a lie. Your anger is all the proof I need to know it's real."

Katie scoffed at her suggestion. "Say you're right. Maybe my faith is real. But does it matter? Right now I'm struggling to want anything to do with God. So I'm sure the feeling is mutual. If He is who you say I believe He is, then He knows without a doubt that I'm furious with Him."

Katie seethed as a grin spread across Gigi B's face. How could she smile at a time like this? Didn't she realize how serious this situation was? Even if she was right and Katie's faith wasn't in jeopardy, there was still the problem of her anger at God. He wasn't likely to take that in stride. The creation mouthing off to the Creator? It was a recipe for disaster.

"How small do you think God is?"

Katie knew momentary confusion at the unexpected change in topic. Where was Gigi B heading? "What?"

Gigi B tilted her head in much the same way a parent would do while waiting for a child to answer when the answer was already clear. Katie let the patronizing action slip by. Let her have her say, and she'll go away.

"How small do you think God is?"

"What does that have to do with anything?"

"Is God too small and too weak to handle your negative thoughts and feelings? I don't think so. God doesn't ask us to run around with smiles plastered on our faces even as our house burns down around us. He doesn't ask us to play pretend. He offers peace in the trial. He shows us how we can find contentment, but acceptance of a situation and liking it are two very different things. And God knows how our emotions work. He made them. He knows the grieving process. When Lazarus died Jesus cried. He knew God would bring him back minutes in the future, but Jesus hurt for his friends. He didn't smile and tell everyone to get over it. He didn't chide Martha when her pain came to the forefront and she told Jesus if He'd only been there sooner her brother wouldn't have died. He values honesty too much, and hurt was the honest emotion. My God is big enough to handle your hurt, anger, or anything else you can throw at Him. Maybe it's time you started being honest with Him."

Katie stared at the table top as Gigi B stood with a quiet, "I'll leave you to think about what I said."

The front door closed quietly leaving her alone with her thoughts. Was she wrong for vocalizing words of faith when she didn't really feel them? Gigi B was right. She knew deep inside beyond the hurt her faith was real. The beliefs she expressed were true. But by holding those beliefs like a banner in front of the emotions she was feeling, by pretending those feelings weren't important or worse that they didn't exist was she being dishonest with God?

Katie fidgeted in the wooden kitchen chair. Her legs itched to walk the familiar paths to her waterfall or the cliff she shared with Austin. She did her best thinking when she could get out in nature. But there was a baby to think about, and like it or not she was alone. She couldn't go traipsing around the woods and leave her son to fend for himself. Yet she needed to move. She needed the solace and clarity that nature brought, the closeness it made her feel toward her Creator. The desire was overwhelming.

She hesitated only a moment before picking up the cordless baby monitor and snatching her jacket from the hook by the back door. She knew the monitor's range should reach the back porch, and if she turned it up all the way she could at least move about the back yard. It was better than nothing. She placed the monitor on the wide banister. The chime of tiny bells floated on the breeze. She ran her fingers under the cool metal of the wind chimes creating a momentary frenzy of ringing before they settled back into the relaxing tones brought out by the air swirling through them. She walked down the flagstone path to the flower garden near the back edge of the yard. It was too early for flowers, but soon a rainbow of colors would surround the large rocks that edged the small garden pond Austin put in when they moved into the house. The pond and the spout that circulated the water through it in an endless cycle were dry having been emptied for the winter months. Austin would have refilled it by this time, but she hadn't had the energy or desire until now. With her eyes closed, Katie could almost hear the gentle splash of the water running over the rocks. Austin had given her a private waterfall to enjoy in place of the one she'd grown up with. It was a precious gift and one that made her ache to have him close once again.

"Why?" She cried into the empty air without thought to who might see or hear her. "Why did you have to take him? He was a good man. I needed him. We needed him. It took so long to find him, and then you snatched him away without warning. How is that good? What could even begin to make that good?"

A large rock at the edge of the pond served as her altar as Katie fell to her knees beside it. The cold stone chilled her but she didn't care. When she'd received news of Austin's death and of her mother's death, she'd allowed herself tears of grief. The tears she shed now were born of anger and frustration. They were tears she'd denied for fear they would drive God away. They couldn't be denied any more as they tore through her chest. Between gasping breaths she vented her true feelings.

"How could you do this? I love you. Austin loved you. My mother loved you. How could you betray me like this? It isn't right. Austin was willing to do everything you asked of him, and still You demanded more. You took everything from him when he would have given it to You freely. And You didn't stop with taking it from him. No, you took it from me too when you took his life. But not even that was enough. You had to take my mother too. It wasn't that long ago that I wanted nothing to do with her. You know that. You know we'd only recently worked out our relationship. Why couldn't we have more time? Why couldn't You at least give me that?"

She pounded the fist of her good arm against the rock. Contact with an immovable object jarred her, sending shock waves across her shoulder and into her injured arm. The pain fueled her tirade. "Is this how you love? By taking everything someone could love from them? Austin and I loved you together. We served you together. And now what? I'm just supposed to keep serving you and loving you all on my own when I've seen what it's like to serve you with the man I love? It's too much. It hurts too much. You've asked too much!"

Katie laid her head down on the arm still stretched out on the rock. "I can't do this, God. How am I supposed to do this? Please. How do I keep going without them?"

Stillness surrounded her. Even the breeze stilled, refusing to intrude on her solitude. Her tears were spent in her angry monologue, and she felt hollowed out. She'd skipped straight from denial to bargaining in her journey of grief. She'd stayed in that place, being everything she thought God wanted her to be, and now she realized what her heart had known all along. It was futile. God hadn't agreed to the bargain.

Opening herself up to the anger she'd kept at bay and being honest with herself and God exhausted her. It left her defenseless. What if God didn't accept her anger? Honestly, she was too tired of faking it and fighting it to care. Real was the only thing she had left to be. She wouldn't go back. She couldn't. She didn't want to fight anymore. Anyway, God wasn't fighting back. What was the point in a one sided battle? What was left for her?

Surrender.

It wasn't the answer she wanted. The tiny spark of will left inside fought against it. Surrender meant loss. It meant opening up to the possibility of more pain, more heartbreak. She considered the possibility that God could somehow mend her brokenness. But what if the path ahead held only more devastation? What if instead of beauty for ashes she found only one storm after another until the end? She'd believed in the healing. She experienced it when she allowed God to move her past her anxieties to marry Austin. She moved forward in faith. She hoped, and she found happiness. That life was gone forever. Was there no hope for anything better?

Surrender.

But would it get better? Would surrender finally bring the beauty for her ashes?

Surrender.

Even if . . .

Even then. Surrender.

He was offering no promise of restoration. There was no guarantee of better days ahead. God offered her neither of these. She knew it as surely as she knew the rock under her head existed. Surrender to "even if" left no room for bargaining. It meant no matter what. It meant God could allow the bad to keep piling on. But where would that leave her? In the fire? Alone?

Katie sat up from the stone as she saw the image of a fiery furnace in her mind. In scripture three young men were thrown into the flames, but Katie saw only herself. She could feel the intense heat on her skin. It was enough to blister and burn without mercy. She searched franticly for a way of escape. It was an empty hope. There was no exit from the fire. The walls were solid without a vent within reach. Could she claw her way out?

Surrender.

It was then Katie realized something fear had disguised. She was standing in the middle of flames that should have destroyed her on contact. She stood, and she could find no sign of the fire anywhere on her person. Not even her clothes were scorched. Why?

Surrender.

She turned in the direction of the voice. A figure stood in the fire with her. She couldn't see His face through the smoke. He was more like a shadow to look at, but it didn't matter. She knew who He was, and He was there with her. He was the reason she stood in the flames without so much as a burn. She didn't need taken away from the flames as long as He was there with her. With flames surrounding her, feeling the heat on her skin, she knew peace. The fire could not destroy her. He was her hope.

A hearty cry sounded through the monitor on the porch railing, pulling Katie from the picture in her mind. As it faded, Katie wished she could hold onto it a little longer. It hadn't erased her anger. Her circumstances were still unfair. But she knew without a doubt what she needed to do. The only question was whether or not she was ready to do it.

Chapter Twenty-Five

Katie felt her throat tighten as her stomach churned. She was beginning to think the bowl of cereal she'd had for breakfast was not her best idea. When Erin suggested she join her and Gigi B at their church, it seemed like a good idea. She needed a place to worship where memories of Austin didn't lurk around every corner. Faith Chapel's sanctuary was closer to the size of the church she'd briefly attended in Bloomington than her home church, but it was far smaller than some of the big churches in Carbondale. She'd never had a desire to attend one of those churches where she could easily get lost, but right now, the thought wasn't unappealing.

Standing in a room of strangers cradling Sammy in her good arm, her other safely contained in a sling, Katie felt the urge to run. Why did she agree to meet Erin instead of coming with her? People glanced her way from where they stood in groups talking. A few even nodded in her direction. She tried to smile in return, hoping the result didn't resemble a grimace.

"Good morning. I'm glad you could join us today. I'm Pastor Thomas Vincent, but most folks just call me Pastor Thomas."

Katie gave the man her attention. He seemed pleasant enough.

A little older than her but not elderly by any stretch of the imagination. Maybe mid-forties? He wore khakis and a button up shirt with the top button undone where a tie would have taken up residence if he'd wanted to look less casual. As he extended his hand, Katie looked from it to Sammy and then her injured arm and back to him. He had the grace to blush as he pulled his arm back to his side.

He cleared his throat. "Sorry about that. Hazard of having a job where greeting those who come through the door is as natural as breathing. I didn't mean to offend."

Feeling more at ease, Katie smiled. "I know you don't know me, Pastor Thomas, but I can assure you I'm not easily offended."

"And you are?"

"Katie! You made it."

Katie watched Erin nearly run down the center aisle to meet her. She refused to look anywhere except at Erin and the pastor as she handed Sammy over to her best friend. She could only imagine the looks the scene would have inspired in the people milling around. How could she have even entertained the notion of slipping in without making a scene and slipping out just as quietly? She knew better than that where Erin was concerned.

"Pastor Thomas, this is my friend Katie."

"So I gathered."

"And this gorgeous little man is Sammy. Well, don't just stand there. Gigi B is in the fellowship hall making coffee for her Sunday school class. She'd absolutely kill me if we didn't go see her before service starts. She's going to be so excited to see you. I didn't tell her you were coming in case you changed your mind, but she loves surprises. And she's definitely going to love this one. Come on. We don't have much time."

Katie pushed her discomfort aside and stifled a giggle as Erin finished her speech and started back up the aisle without even waiting to see if she followed. A quick look at Pastor Thomas' twinkling eyes told her he not only understood her friend's personality but found it enjoyable. "I'd better head that way, or I may never get my son back. It was nice meeting you."

He nodded his head toward her. "And it's good to finally meet Erin's best friend. I've heard so much about you. Please know you've been in my prayers."

The thought brought more peace than she would've expected. "Thank you."

Katie moved in the direction she saw Erin go. When she might have gotten lost, Gigi B's voice could be heard cooing at Sammy. She followed the sound into the fellowship hall. Sammy smiled and flapped his arms excitedly from his perch in Erin's arms. His attention was focused on Gigi B, and Katie couldn't blame him. Katie tended to be a flunky when it came to fashion. She wore what was comfortable without much thought to whether or not it was in line with current fashion trends. Gigi B was the exact opposite. Her slightly fitted, long coral top coordinated perfectly with her turquoise knee length vest since it was accented with the same coral color. Her light gray slacks were fitted, and her turquoise platform sandals finished off the look. Most women her age couldn't have pulled off the look. They would have been chided for trying to dress younger than their more mature years demanded. But Gigi B was not most women. Katie was having a difficult time determining whether Sammy was enthralled by her voice or by the kaleidoscope of color.

"Maybe I should be offended. Here I am visiting your church, and you only have time for my son."

Blue eyes flicked up from Sammy to her. "Tsk, tsk. You know better than that, child. You've never been far from my thoughts and prayers. Now get yourself over here and give me a hug."

Not usually one for public displays of affection, Katie couldn't say no. She crossed the room and stepped into the woman's embrace returning it wholeheartedly. "I was afraid you'd be upset with me."

Gigi B waved a hand in the air. "You didn't need to fret about something as silly as that. You were hurting. You can't take to heart the words of someone in as much pain and denial as you were in. But we're past that now, right?"

Katie shrugged. "I'm getting there. I can't say my anger has dissolved completely, but most of the time I'm able to put it in perspective."

"And what perspective is that?"

"No matter what fire life brings into my life, God is there with me. My circumstances don't determine my hope."

Gigi B reached a slender finger to boop the end of Sammy's nose. Her sing-song voice was meant for him, but her words were solely for Katie. "Well, then, where does your mommy find her hope?"

"My hope is in trusting the promises of scripture and knowing that God is right there beside me in the good and the bad. He doesn't have to take it away. He can show me how to live in it."

Gigi B took Sammy from Erin before reaching out to grasp Katie's hand with a squeeze. "It sounds like you're well on your way."

Katie motioned to the sanctuary. "I don't know how far down the path I am yet, but I figured the best place to start was getting back in God's presence again. I mean in this way. I know He's always with me, but there's something special about a church family."

"And we're so happy to have you come join ours. Erin mentioned your hesitance to go back to your own church. I can only imagine how hard that would be. Let Faith Chapel be your adopted home as long as you need."

The melody of the worship team's first song filtered into the fellowship hall. Katie's nerves were still a little raw, but underneath the unease that came with the unknown was a peace she hadn't felt in several months. She took her son into her arms. "Thank you, Gigi B, for everything."

ERIN PASSED the ceramic platter piled high with chicken to Katie who picked through it with her fork until she found a breast piece and passed the chicken on to her father. It was sweet of Gigi B to think of inviting him to Sunday dinner even though he'd not attended church with them that morning. He didn't have any desire to leave the church he'd spent the last fifty some odd years in.

"Katie," he'd said the night before. "It's hard to face the memories there, but strangely enough I find peace in them too. My Sharon and I spent many years serving together in that church. Staying there brings back that feeling, and I feel close to her memory there."

She'd understood, though she couldn't pretend it worked that way for her. Even though the wall she'd put between her and God was breaking, what she'd said all along was true. Services there weren't the same without Austin behind the pulpit, and she didn't think her emotions could take that disappointment yet. Maybe they never would. But if that was the case, God would take her where she needed to go. It might be Faith Chapel. Time would tell.

Erin questioned Katie as she passed her a bowl of mashed potatoes. "What did you think of our services?"

She scooped the creamy side onto her plate. "It wasn't that different from Orchard Hills, with the exception of adding a guitar to the piano during worship. But it was enough of a change to make a difference."

Erin nodded knowingly.

"I think I'd like to go back, if you don't mind. It's time to make some changes in my life."

Her father paused with a forkful of green beans halfway to his mouth. "Changes? Other than leaving the church, what changes are you thinking of making?"

"There's a lot I've been holding onto. I sold the bakery, but that was more out of necessity. I simply didn't have the heart or time to run it in a way that would honor Austin. But I've not done anything with most of his other things. It's time to clean out the closets and put his truck up for sale. I'm not going to be using it any time soon. It's a waste to keep up insurance and registration on it."

Gigi B shifted Sammy where he was resting on her shoulder before reaching for her glass of sweet tea. "I know you're a do it yourself kind of girl, and I can relate. But if you'd like help with the cleaning, all you need to do is ask."

"You're right. I do tend to take care of things myself, but I think that's another thing that might need changing. I didn't fight having help when it was Austin doing the helping. But he's gone. There's nothing wrong with accepting help from others. It might even make this difficult task a little easier. So, what do you all say? My place Tuesday afternoon? I'll even feed you. Taco soup maybe? It's a family favorite."

Katie watched all three heads nod in agreement. "Great. And later on, I'll know who I can call to help me pack up and move."

Her father looked to her in confusion. "And where are you moving to? This is the first I've heard of this. You're not heading back to Bloomington are you?"

Erin grabbed her hand in excitement. "That would be amazing! When Paul and I get married, we'll be living up there. It would be sweet to have a friend there. And I wouldn't have to suffer from Sammy withdrawals."

Katie laughed as she removed Erin's hand from her own. "Don't jump to conclusions. As much as Sammy and I are going to miss you, I am not moving to Bloomington. I've done that, and it's not for me. This is home. You and Paul will have a wonderful life there, and when you come visit, we'll be waiting for you." She turned to her dad. "You talked about me and Sammy moving in with you a while back. I wasn't ready to hear it then, but I am now. If the offer's not still on the table, I understand. But I can't deny I've been thinking about it more and more. I want to know what you think of the idea." She included the others at the table in her look. "I want to know what you all think of the idea."

Erin pretended to pout. "Well, it's not Bloomington, but I guess I think it's a great idea anyway."

Gigi B leaned back in her chair watching her silently as she considered the move. "I'm not sure it's my place to say. But you've both lost so much in the last few months. I can't think of anything better for you than to have the family you have left together under one roof."

Katie noticed her dad had been quiet. His fork was laid beside his plate and not even his drink had been lifted since she started talking about a move. Maybe he had changed his mind. In the last few weeks, he could have adjusted to his new solitary life, found that he liked it. If that was the case, she'd have to respect his feelings. "Dad?"

A smile lit up his face. "I say, welcome home Katydid."

Katie flew from her chair to wrap her arm around his neck. "Thank you, Daddy. It'll be good to be home."

The chatter around the table through the remainder of the meal centered on plans to pack up her current home and get it ready to go on the market. No one pushed her to do anything in a specific time frame understanding it had to be on her terms. She appreciated their input and their willingness to allow her to lead the process. It would make things easier as they packed up her things in addition to Austin's on Tuesday.

"Hey, Erin, you're . . ." Katie stopped mid-sentence as she opened her front door to Nathan. "You're not Erin."

"Not last I checked." He tipped his cowboy hat in her direction and grinned. "Nathan Phillips, mover extraordinaire at your service."

Katie looked past him to her driveway. His truck complete with hauling trailer sat next to Austin's in her driveway. Where were Erin and the others and why was Nathan standing at her front door with an expectant look on his face?

"Are you gonna let me in? Gigi B saw me in town yesterday, and she mentioned you were moving. Said you could use an extra hand and possibly even my truck and trailer."

"I believe what I said was, we could use some young muscled arms like yours to help carry the heavy stuff."

Nathan turned as the woman in question spoke from behind him. "Well, good morning, Gigi B. Let me take that from you."

He lifted several empty boxes from her arms and moved aside to let her pass. She swatted his arm. "That is not the heavy lifting I was speaking of. I may be old but I'm perfectly capable of carrying a bunch of boxes with nothing in them but air."

"Yes, ma'am. I know you are, but just because you can doesn't mean you should. My mama raised me better than that."

Katie swallowed hard. It sounded so much like what Austin had told her the first time he'd opened a car door for her. How could a memory be sweet and still hold such a sting?

Gigi B squeezed his cheeks in her hand. "Such a sweet boy. She did raise you right, didn't she?"

"She tried her hardest." He followed her through the door and looked around before settling his gaze on Katie. "Where would you like these?"

Katie pulled her mind from her memories. She supposed she should be happy for the extra help. There were limits to what she and Erin would be able to handle. Paul was in Bloomington, and her elderly father and Gigi B weren't going to be much help with the furniture or heavy boxes. She was just caught off guard by his sudden appearance.

His relaxed expression turned into a frown before she realized she hadn't answered his question. "Why don't you put them on the island in the kitchen. I've got the packing tape and markers in there too. It might work best to keep everything together."

Nathan stacked them where she directed and returned to the living room. Erin and her father walked in the door without bothering to knock.

"Hey, Nathan. How's it going?"

Katie couldn't help noticing that Erin didn't seem surprised to find Nathan there. She watched her father shake his hand. He took it in stride as well. Was she the only one Gigi B failed to tell?

Gigi B must have gauged her thoughts. "Didn't mean to spring him on you like that. I knew we'd need more help, and I figured you might be hesitant to ask. When I saw him yesterday, I thought he was exactly who we needed to get this job done. With your independent streak, I wasn't sure you'd accept his help. So, I didn't ask. Forgive me?"

Katie knew she was right. She would've made excuses. Asking for help was still a struggle, but it was one she knew she needed to get over if she wasn't going to leave a foothold for her anger to grow again. And truth be told, Gigi B was right. Things would go a lot quicker and smoother with his help inside and his truck and trailer outside.

"There's nothing to forgive."

"Great. Then what do you say we get started. There's a lot to do today."

Erin nudged up against her side. "Where do we begin, boss?"

Katie rolled her eyes. "Let's start in here. We'll need kitchen stuff to eat later, but I can do without a TV or a sofa without a lot of trouble."

Her father looked around the room. "What are you keeping? What do you need at your new place?"

Katie frowned before laughing it off. "Dad, you should know better than anyone what I need since I'm moving in with you."

He chuckled, but it was uneasy to her ears. "True. Wasn't thinking about it is all. We have all the living room furniture we need. My sofa and tables are in good shape, though maybe not your style. Your television is better than mine though. Might want to keep that."

Katie nodded in agreement. "Great. Let's leave the things we want to get rid of and only pack the things that are moving with me. I've not quite figured out what to do with the extra things yet."

Erin chimed in with an idea. "What about a yard sale?"

Katie considered it. Yard sales were common in the area but not usually until summer and fall. Besides, she wasn't sure she could handle selling off Austin's things one by one. Even the thought of passing off her precious memories to strangers for a quarter each hurt enough to take her breath away. Actually doing it would be worse.

"I'd rather not. That's a lot of hassle."

Gigi B toyed with a throw pillow on the couch. "What about storing it for a time?"

Katie shook her head. "No. I need to get it done and over with. I don't want it hanging over my head indefinitely."

Her attention was caught when Nathan shifted his weight from one denim clad leg to the other and looked anywhere but at her. When he finally made eye contact she spoke before he could look away again. "Do you have an idea?"

He ran a hand through his short ash brown hair giving it a haphazard look. "This is a family matter. I'm not sure I even fall in the friend category anymore. Any ideas I have aren't important. Y'all need to decide this without my input."

Gigi B touched a hand to his arm. "You are most certainly a friend. Why else would you give up your day when I told you I needed you and your muscles to help on moving day? Now what idea is swimming around in that handsome head of yours?"

Katie chuckled. Gigi B's forthrightness was amazing to watch. Katie couldn't begin to imagine the feathers she could ruffle in the wrong situation. But it seemed to work this time. When she noticed Nathan's silent plea for permission from across the room, she nodded.

"There's a youth group at my church. They go on a mission trip each summer, and they have to work together raising the funds to go. One of their fundraisers is a yard sale. They're always looking for donations, especially of items like furniture. They'd come get anything you want taken, and after the sale, they take anything they have left to the thrift store. Except for clothes. They try to take good clothing that's left to the homeless shelters in the area."

Katie was certain Austin would have wanted his things to help others spread the gospel. It was especially fitting to have it benefiting a youth group. He was passionate about ministering to area teenagers, and he would have done anything to help them reach their goals. "Okay."

"You sure?"

"Yeah. Austin would have wanted it this way."

Nathan tipped his head in her direction as he fished his phone out of his back pocket. "Well, then, while you guys get started in here, I'll step outside for a minute to work out the details with the youth leader."

Katie watched the door shut behind him before giving instructions to the others in the room on what needed kept and what would be left for donation in the living room. Seeing they had everything under control, Katie rethought her decision about waiting to tackle the kitchen. She knew better than anyone, except maybe her father, what kind of kitchenware awaited her at her parents' home. She should be the one to sort through all of her things and figure out what should be taken to replace her mother's worn out items. She'd start with the cabinet full of bakeware. Of all the things in the kitchen, this one would be most difficult. She didn't bake often, but Austin kept a supply of professional pans to use at home. It always amazed her that the baking he did for By Sweet Design didn't discourage him from his own personal baking. Those pans would definitely be better than the flimsy, ancient pans her mother kept.

The carefully balanced stack of muffin pans and cookie sheets clattered to the wood floor as Katie turned to find Nathan standing behind her. Her hand flew to her chest as she caught her breath. How did he manage to sneak up behind her wearing cowboy boots? She must have been deep into her own little world.

"I'm sorry. I didn't mean to startle you." His sheepish smile told her more than his words. He may not have meant to, but that didn't mean he didn't enjoy scaring her silly.

She gathered up the scattered pans and held them up to him. "It's okay. I guess I was focused on the task at hand. Can you put these on the table with the others while I sort through the rest of this cabinet?"

He took them from her, and she returned to the task. She found a couple of cake and bread pans to take before pulling out a contraption she doubted she'd ever seen and was sure she would never use. She fidgeted with the buckle on the side which loosened it enough that the bottom dropped out. "Ooops. I'm not sure what it is, but I think I've just rendered it unusable."

"It's a springform pan."

Her mouth dropped open as she turned to Nathan. He'd taken it on himself to pack the things she pulled from the cabinet instead of piling them on her table. It would save her the work later. She was thankful for that but as his cheeks reddened, she wondered if she'd hurt his feelings with her surprise.

He shrugged nonchalantly. "What? I know stuff."

As much as she didn't want him embarrassed, she couldn't help questioning him. "And what is it for, Mr. Smartypants?"

"Did Austin ever make you a cheesecake?"

Turtle cheesecake was her favorite. He'd made it to celebrate the day they'd found out about Sammy. She nodded.

"He probably made it with this pan. You can use it for other things too, but that one's pretty popular. I take it since you didn't even know what it is, you probably don't want to keep it?"

She ran a finger over the buckle. She couldn't explain her sentimental need, but the pan would move with her. She held up the pieces to him. "No, I'm going to take it. Maybe one day I'll learn to make cheesecake. By the way, what did the youth group say?"

He reassembled the pan before placing it in the box. "I can't believe I forgot to tell you. That's the whole reason I came in here in the first place."

"You were too busy enjoying startling me to remember, I guess."

A crooked grin. "Could be. But anyway, they said they'd love to take the donation. I figure with all of us working today, we should be able to get you moved out in record time. But just in case, I told them to wait until Saturday. That will give them a week to get things sorted and priced before the sale. Can you be here to let them in on Saturday?"

"As far as I know I don't have plans."

"Great. I'll confirm it with them after we're done here."

She closed the cabinet and used the counter top to help pull her to standing. Now that the pots and pans were sorted through, the rest would be quick and easy. Her commercial series mixer and food processor would go, but the rest of the appliances could stay.

"I only have a few cups and mugs I care to take. Mom's dishes and silverware are old, but they're in good shape. So, all of that can stay for the youth group."

"What about this and the other knick knack items?"

Katie considered the coffee themed items they'd chosen to decorate the room with. It was their way of paying tribute to the day they met and weaving it into their life together, but none of it held enough sentimental value on its own to make the move with her. "We'll leave all of it."

She turned to see Nathan holding a small wooden ornament that hung on the window. She watched him run his thumb over the tree design wood-burned onto the flat, round disc of wood. "Except that. That does not stay."

She reached over and removed it from its place of honor.

Austin had hung it from the kitchen window in his apartment after she gave it to him for Christmas the year they met. It was a reminder of not only their favorite spot at Giant City State Park but also the path they'd taken to finally find each other. It kept its place in the kitchen when they'd married, and it would hang in her mother's kitchen when she moved. She carefully wrapped it in a kitchen towel and placed it on top of the other items in the box.

"I'm sorry."

Nathan still stood by the window. His eyes were full of understanding and compassion. Katie had to look away. How many more times would she get choked up during this process? And what about Saturday? How much harder would it be to see the last of their memories carried out?

"It's okay."

His voice was soft and smooth. "No, it's not okay. I wasn't able to make it to Austin's funeral, but I was at your mother's service. I wanted to tell you then how sorry I was for your losses. But when I got the opportunity, you were visiting another grave. I'm guessing it was Austin's, and you looked like all you wanted was privacy. I should have found you later or come by to check on you or something. I'm sorry I didn't say it before now, but I am sorry for all you've had to go through."

She could argue that other than their brief conversation during the Bread of Life meal they hadn't seen each other in years. She could remind him that he barely knew Austin and that though his sister had been her best friend growing up, he hadn't spent any time to speak of with her family in the past. She could explain all the reasons why he shouldn't feel bad about not having reached out sooner, but in the end, did it really matter? He only wanted to express empathy with her situation. "Thank you."

"If there's ever anything I can do to help you, please let me know."

Could she ask it of him? He offered. Was it sincere or simply what one said at times like this? She decided braving the topic was the only way to know for sure. "There is one thing you could do for me, if it's not too much trouble."

"Name it."

She sealed up the box with packing tape and wrote "kitchen" in block letters on the outside. "If I gave you the key to the house could you come by on Saturday and let the youth group in? I don't think my emotions can handle it. Teens will be teens while they get the job done, and I'm not in a place where I can laugh and play while emptying my home of everything we dreamed of."

He lifted the box from the table. "It's no problem. I'll take care of everything."

She didn't see any signs of reservation or regret over offering, but that didn't mean anything. "If you can't or don't want to, I understand. Please, don't feel like you have to do this. I can see if someone else can. I only figured you would know the youth group and stuff. So, it might be a little easier for you. But it's okay if you don't want to. I won't be upset or anything. How could I be after everything you're doing?"

He set the box back on the table before turning to grasp Katie's upper arms. He waited until she looked him in the eye before speaking. "Breathe, Katie. If I didn't want to do this for you, I wouldn't have agreed. If I thought it was too much, I'd let you know. I understand why you'd want someone else to handle this job, and I'm happy to do it."

He waited until she nodded her understanding before dropping his hold on her arms. Picking the box back up from the table, he carried it to the living room where he stacked another on top before carrying them both out the front door to his truck. When the door shut behind him, Katie finally felt freed from the spot where she stood. He was right. She was being silly, but she was sure it was only because the move was bringing out so many bittersweet memories.

She quickly did a final sweep of the kitchen before determining she'd packed away everything she wanted to take. Joining the others in the living room, she found that trio had successfully completed their task. At the rate they were going, she might be moved out by the end of the day. The thought left her unable to join in the easy conversation around the table while the group ate a quick lunch. It was a relief to get back to work on her room, the office, and the bathrooms.

Sammy's room was left until everything else was packed. Everything in it would make the move with them. While Katie left everyone else to get his things loaded on the trailer, she took Nathan to the garage and tool shed.

She placed her hand on a dusty cardboard box. "I'd like to take these three boxes. I know my dad has Christmas decorations, but for now, I'd like to keep my own too. But his shop is fully furnished. That means everything else in here and in the tool shed can stay for the youth group. I want you to look through everything though."

"Why?"

Katie shrugged. "I'm not a tool person. You may see something you know I shouldn't live without. You'd also know if something is of great enough worth that I shouldn't leave it for a yard sale. I'm leaving almost all of my furniture for the youth, but I'd like to take anything you think would sell for more individually. I'll take care of selling those items myself. I'm going to use the money from them and Austin's truck to start a savings account for Sammy's future. I think Austin would want that. Do you think that's selfish of me?"

He shook his head. "Absolutely not. You don't have to give any of this to the youth group, but you are. These are your things and Austin's. I may not have known him well, but I know he'd want his son taken care of. I think you're doing exactly what he'd want. I'll tell you what. I'll pull all the things for the youth group out of the shed, and I'll move all the things for you to sell out of the garage. Those will go in the shed, and the youth group items will come in here. Saturday, the youth group will know they can clean out the house and garage, but the shed isn't to be touched. How's that sound?"

It sounded like a heavy load being taken from her shoulders. "Thank you. That sounds perfect. I'll leave you to it and go help Erin move the nursery furniture to the trailer."

He was already carrying the Christmas decorations to the truck when she made her way across the yard to find Erin. With only the nursery left and Nathan tackling the outdoor items, Katie and Sammy would be on their way to their new home in no time. It would even give them a few days to adjust at her dad's house and make sure there wasn't anything they missed before the youth group cleaned out everything on Saturday. The house would be ready for a realtor to look at by Monday morning.

Things were moving quicker than she'd imagined possible, but maybe that was good. There hadn't been time to let memories goad her into questioning her decision. She'd felt their bitter sweetness throughout the day, but the feeling had passed quickly each time in the flurry of activity. And despite the things she'd miss, Katie knew she was making the right choice.

She reached the top of the stairs and entered her son's room. The walls were already stripped bare and all but the furniture boxed up ready to move out. Her dad rocked Sammy while feeding him a bottle. Gigi B and Erin chatted easily as they watched him. Katie couldn't help smiling at the cozy scene. She hated to break it up, but there was work to be done.

"Break time's over, Erin. Time for you and me to move this furniture to the trailer. Sammy and I have a new home to get to."

Chapter Twenty-Six

Katie stood staring out the window of the bedroom she'd grown up in. The trees had lost their early spring blossoms in favor of the green leaves of summer, though real summer weather had yet to begin. With the upheaval in her life, Katie had completely missed the arrival of spring. Now, with April ended and May beginning, it seemed like she could take it in for the first time in ages. She ached to take her first walk to the waterfall, but it wouldn't be today.

Boxes stood against the wall waiting to be unpacked. Everyone had stayed long enough to help unload her things from the trucks, but after that they'd made themselves scarce. Katie couldn't blame them. They'd worked hard all day to get her and Sammy moved in with her dad. And they'd done it in record time. As soon as they left, Katie divided the boxes between the rooms, but other than exchanging the old bedsheets for the ones she'd brought with her, setting up Sammy's crib, and hanging Austin's ornament on the kitchen window downstairs she'd decided the rest of the unpacking could happen later.

Everything was happening so quickly. She was moved out of her home in a day. The truck was listed for sale in the paper.

Saturday the home she'd shared with Austin would be empty and ready to put on the market. It was a lot of change. It should have unnerved her, but Katie had known only peace throughout the process. It had been a melancholy task, but even in the sadness she knew the peace that came from knowing she was following God's will for her life. It was time to move forward, and God was beside her helping her do just that.

Her dad's voice preceded him into her room. "How are you settling in, Katydid?"

"I'm doing fine. How about you? Do you feel like your space has been invaded?"

He shook his head. "Absolutely not. You and Sammy are right where you should be. We're family, and family should stick together. Besides, now I'll get to see my grandson whenever I want. What could be better than that?"

As if on cue, Sammy began to cry from the room across the hall. Katie raised an eyebrow. "You might rethink that statement before it's all said and done."

"Never. Babies cry. It's what they do. Why don't you let me tend little Sammy, and you go take a walk. After all the spring rain, the creek should be flowing and the waterfall should be filling up the pool below without any problems."

"I didn't move in here so you could babysit."

He shooed her away with his hands. "Don't be silly. I want this time with the baby. He needs to know his grandpa. And unless I'm misreading my girl, she could use some time to think in her favorite spot. Now get on out of here." He winked at her before moving down the hall to get Sammy.

Katie heard soft words coming from her father though she couldn't make out exactly what he said. Whatever it was worked like a charm if Sammy's cooing back was an indicator. She smiled. Her dad knew her so well, and he was graciously giving her this time alone. It was a gift of love especially after the hard day's work he'd put in helping her move, but because of that work she couldn't take him up on his offer.

She had no desire to interrupt their time together. Her dad's gentle laugh was sweet to hear. There had been precious little to laugh about in recent weeks. Maybe this move would be a start to healing, not only for her but for him as well. Katie headed down the stairs but rather than heading out the door and down to the waterfall, she made her way into the kitchen.

Opening the freezer, Katie pushed past the remaining casseroles to find a package of hamburgers. It would be easier to stick a casserole in the oven, but she wouldn't do that. She and her dad had eaten enough mourning food to last the rest of their lives. It was time for them to live again. Hamburgers weren't fancy, but it would be better than an edible reminder of what they'd lost.

Katie set the burgers on the counter and went to light the grill. While it heated up she found a bag of chips and got the pickles from the refrigerator. There weren't any buns that she could find, but they could eat their burgers on bread this time. She needed to go through the cabinets and make a shopping list, but that would wait until tomorrow.

With the burgers on the grill, Katie decided to make the most of the time by unpacking her kitchen boxes. Pots and pans were quickly put in their new spots until only the small kitchen towels remained. As she folded the last towel into the drawer under the sink, she couldn't help looking at the wooden ornament hanging from the window. She brushed her fingers over the trees burned onto the flat surface. She coughed to clear the tightness from her throat and turned from the ornament. Maybe one day when she looked at that small wooden disk the bitter would melt away leaving only the sweet memories to keep her company. Until then, she determined to treasure every painful glance. After all, those memories were all she had left.

Her father's footsteps coming down the stairs broke into her reverie. Katie fished a long-handled spatula from the drawer next to the stove and went to check the burgers. It wouldn't do to char her dad's first non-casserole meal in months.

"I've got the table set up whenever the burgers are ready. I'm just going to put little Sammy in the bassinet in the living room while we eat."

Katie's heart plummeted when she looked to the table and saw three place settings. How many times in the past few weeks had her father's old habits left him with an empty plate next to his own as he ate his meals? Without a word Katie removed the extra setting, placing each piece where they belonged before taking her seat. If her dad noticed the missing plate when he came to the table he chose not to comment.

He sat at the head of the table and immediately bowed his head. Katie barely had time to lower her own before his prayer began. Katie smiled. It was good to be able to hear her dad praying again. She'd missed his confident voice going to God like a friend on their behalf.

If she were being honest, she had reservations about this move. She'd be silly not to. It was a big step for her and Sammy. She didn't doubt it was the right decision and that God directed her to it, but it was still a lot of change in a short amount of time. However, sitting at the kitchen table where she'd eaten so many meals growing up, listening to her dad pray as he'd done each night of her childhood, Katie couldn't deny the warm feeling of contentment spreading through her. It was different than she'd expected, but life was moving forward.

Chapter Twenty-Seven

Katie grasped her side as pain knifed through it. She took a deep breath to calm her laughter, but one look at her best friend sent her into a new fit. “Stop. If you want to have a matron of honor beside you at your wedding, please stop.”

Erin batted her eyes in feigned innocence. “I’m only trying to find the best look for you for the ceremony. You know it has to be perfect.”

Katie snatched the hanger from Erin’s hand and held it in front of her. Fitted until the mermaid style flared out dramatically at the knee, Katie couldn’t help feeling the skirt’s bottom would be twice as wide as she was. Big white flowers accented the front of the waist in a pseudo belt that made no sense with the dress’ overall design. The sweetheart neckline was the only attractive thing about the dress, but it was ruined by a line of sequins that covered the top three inches in what looked to be paying homage to the mermaid scale pillows that were recently popular. And the color? Katie was sure it wasn’t listed this way on the tag, but she’d seen that color green before. Too bad it was in Sammy’s diaper.

Erin brushed a hand over the sequins changing a strip of them from light green to a darker color. “But look. You can change your style to match your mood. Isn’t that genius?”

Katie returned the dress to the rack. “If my mood ever matches either of those colors, please send me to see a counselor. And that’s saying something because green is usually one of my better colors.”

Erin’s face lit with a smug smile and twinkling eyes. She was pleased with herself about something. The whole scene was familiar. She shook her head as she realized why.

“You are determined to see me in an ugly dress, aren’t you? Don’t deny it. You tried to dress me like a fluffy, big bowed marshmallow for my own wedding. Now you’re trying to give your own an under the sea flair. Well, I won’t have it.”

A pretend pout pursed Erin’s lips. “Fine. If you’re going to be difficult, we’ll just keep looking. I can’t believe how hard you are to shop for. We found my dress in ten minutes.”

Katie glanced at the gown hanging by the check-out counter at the front of the store. It was perfect for Erin. “Of course, you’ve conveniently forgotten that we picked out your dress style a year ago when we were picking out mine. That does make it a little easier.”

Erin waved her hand in dismissal. “Excuses. Excuses. I think I’m easier to shop for because I love to shop. You, however, eschew all things girlie, including shopping which makes it much more difficult to please you.”

Katie rolled her eyes. “Did you really just use the word ‘eschew’? Who does that in everyday conversation?”

“I do. It’s a perfectly acceptable word. In fact, more people should use it. Now, let’s keep looking.”

Katie turned back to the racks and pushed the discarded dress to the side. Most of the gowns were fine, but they weren’t her style. Even if they were her style, they weren’t Erin’s style. Her wedding dress was definitely on the quirky side, and they had to find a bridesmaid dress that could match the mood set by the bride's dress.

A squeal from across the store stole her attention from the dresses in front of her. "This is it! This is perfect for you!"

As Katie joined her, Erin held a royal purple dress up for inspection. "Look at this one. The purple will look gorgeous with your auburn hair, and the style matches my dress perfectly. Don't you think so?"

While not a style she would generally pick, Katie had to admit it was exactly the one they needed for the wedding. Just like Erin's dress, this one had a sweetheart neckline. Instead of the sheer polka-dotted lace that created a top on the bride's dress and three-quarter length sleeves, Katie's dress had halter style straps that tied behind the neck. The delicately polka-dotted lace overlaying Erin's entire dress was referenced through the white polka-dots scattered throughout the royal purple dress. A black satin ribbon tied around the waist before the skirt flared out until it stopped right below the knee. A tiny strip of the black ruffled tulle petticoat peeked out from under the hem of the skirt giving fullness to it. The dress was a more casual, colorful representation of Erin's dress.

Katie took the dress from her. "I have to admit, as much as it pains me. You are right. I don't think we'll find another dress that fits the style of yours more perfectly. But what will Paul say about the nod to the fifties coming out so clearly in your wedding? Is he okay with that?"

"One of our first dates was at Sonny's Fifties Café. I think he understands my fascination. Besides, we picked the perfect suit for him. It's a light gray fitted suit with a vest. A royal purple tie and pocket square to match your dress color will look absolutely amazing."

"Then let's get this thing tried on and mark dress shopping off our list."

With the dresses left at the store for minor alterations, Katie and Erin made quick work of finding shoes to match. Suede wedge pumps with a thin ankle strap in black for Katie and white for Erin were safely nestled in the boxes hanging in bags from their wrists as they navigated the parking lot to Erin's car. Clothing for Erin's big day was taken care of down to Erin's veil and the single flower that would be bobby pinned in Katie's hair.

Though they'd accomplished much in getting items marked off the list of wedding needs, Katie knew Erin well enough to judge she was ready for a break. The two of them would recharge with a snack and then dive back into shopping until nothing else remained on their list.

As Erin pulled away from the mall and headed west, Katie's stomach clinched. Traditionally, Erin and Katie would stop in at By Sweet Design during their outings. Lucy did a marvelous job with the bakery now that she owned it. Katie heard from the regulars that while they missed Austin, the atmosphere and food were not suffering with Lucy in charge. But Katie didn't know how she would handle the onslaught of memories as she tried to drink her frozen mocha.

The band tightening around her chest loosened as Erin passed the turn off to the bakery without slowing down. She looked to her friend who kept her eyes on the road as she spoke. "I know it's not a frozen mocha, but Sonny's makes a mean chocolate malt. I thought maybe we'd try something different today."

Katie forced a smile. "Sounds good to me."

Thank you, Lord, for an understanding friend. I don't have to say anything at all, and she's watching out for me. Katie's silent prayer was heartfelt as she looked out the passenger window to hide her fight against the tears that threatened. It had only been a little over a year since she and Erin had done the shopping for her own wedding. She could still remember every detail of that day, and the memory brought an ache with it. But this excursion wasn't about her. It was about Erin and Paul and their special day. If Katie could only keep her mind focused on that, she could make it through the rest of the day.

Her self-inflicted pep talk continued until Erin pulled into the parking lot at Sonny's. Go time. Katie forced her thoughts back to Erin and found thoughts of her two best friends getting married was enough to make her smile genuine as they chose stools at the soda fountain instead of one of the booths.

Erin held up two fingers to the guy behind the counter. "Two chocolate malts, please."

"I'd love to get a juke box for the reception. Do you think they rent those?"

Katie turned to the corner where Erin was looking. The colorful neon and upbeat music would definitely make a statement at the reception. "I don't even know where you could ask about something like that. I'm not sure it's a widely requested item at the local event rental place."

"You're probably right. It would be cool though to have instead of a D.J. Have I shown you a picture of the centerpieces for the tables at the reception?"

Before she could answer, the waiter brought their malts. She nodded her thanks to him as she set it down on the napkin in front of her. "No. I don't think so."

Erin pulled out her phone and scrolled through her photos until she found the one she wanted. "Don't you think these are perfect?"

An old-fashioned soda glass, similar to the ones their malts were served in, sat in the middle of a vinyl record. Each glass was filled with a small bouquet of red carnations with two purple straws tucked inside. Erin reached across to the screen and swiped to the next picture. Red labeled glass soda bottles with purple ribbons and a note that said "Thank you for sharing in our special day" sat in rows for guests to take home.

"Just one question for you."

"What's that?"

"Is all the music at your reception going to be from the fifties? I don't even know how to do the twist."

Katie didn't hold back her smile as Erin laughed. "I'm sure we can work something out. Seriously though, I've got several of the oldies on the playlist, but there's plenty of new stuff too. I'm not prejudiced against a good song no matter what year it came from."

"That's good to know. It sounds like you're getting things worked out for the perfect start to your and Paul's new life together."

Erin closed her eyes and shook her head with her fingers massaging her temples. "Brain freeze. Wow that's painful."

Katie waited patiently for her friend's pain to pass. "Sorry about that. I hate it when that happens. Anyway, things are falling into place for the wedding and reception. I can't believe it's only two months away. Paul took a load of my things up to Bloomington with him on his way home after his last trip down. In just a couple months, life is changing in a big way."

Katie frowned. "I'm going to miss you so much. But I wish you and Paul all the best, even if he is taking my best friend away from me."

Erin nudged her shoulder with her own. "You're not getting rid of me. There are things called cell phones and we can facetime and we'll be down to see my family at holidays and you can always come to visit us and do you really think we'll be able to stay away from Sammy? We are his godparents after all."

Katie slid the malt glass away from Erin as she laughed. "I think you've had more than enough sugar for the day. You may need to go easy and eat something of substance."

Erin snatched it back defensively. "I am not on a sugar high. I just don't want you to feel deserted. It's the only hard part of Paul and me getting married. I don't like to think of you being down here on your own."

"I'm not alone. Dad and I will keep each other company, though he's not nearly as much fun to get manicures with."

"How's that going, by the way? You being back at your dad's house?"

Katie shrugged as she finished taking a drink of her malt. "I'm adjusting. I know it was the right move, and it will be good for Sammy to have a man in his life as he gets older."

Katie looked away from Erin's questioning gaze. "But?"

"But what?"

"I know you, Katie. There's something bothering you. What is it?"

Katie wound a strand of hair around her finger as she thought about how to answer. Honestly, she hadn't given words to the niggling doubts she'd been having. She wasn't even convinced they should be labeled doubts. "I'm not really sure. Maybe it's nothing."

"That would be good for sure. But in case it's not nothing, what's going on? Are you feeling like your dad doesn't want you there as much as he thought he would?"

"No. It's nothing like that. Dad's thrilled to have us there. And we're getting into a pretty comfortable routine. He's great with Sammy, and I think Sammy helps him not feel as lonely without mom."

"Then what's the issue?"

"Something just seems off about him. I noticed it a little bit before we moved in but dismissed it. He'd forget things or get things mixed up. Nothing big. Stupid stuff that really didn't matter. And I only saw it during stressful times like when mom was in the hospital or after Austin was killed. It didn't seem like a big deal. Of course his mind wasn't focused on the little details during those times."

"But he's still doing it?"

"Not often, but yeah. Little stuff like going for something and coming back without it or looking for something he hasn't had in years or forgetting someone's name that he's known forever. But I'm sure it's nothing."

"I'm sure you're right. But if you need me remember I'll only be a phone call away."

Katie snorted. "A phone call and four hours. A lot of help

you'll be, but I can't begrudge you a happy ending with your prince. I just hope Paul realizes what a gift he's getting."

Erin picked up her purse and went to the register to pay her bill. "If you think about it, you might remind him of that. With all the wedding details, I think he may be forgetting."

Katie led the way, holding the door for Erin. "It's a man thing. He'll remember just as soon as he sees you walking down the aisle. And if, for some reason, he ever forgets, just give me a call. I'll set him straight in a heartbeat. But I have a feeling Paul's not the type to take a gift like you for granted."

Erin's cheeks pinked. "I think you're right. He's pretty special. And in just a few weeks, he'll be mine for the rest of our lives. Now, let's get back to it. If we want that day to be the special start for our life together, you and I have got more shopping to do."

Katie groaned as she dropped into the passenger seat. If shopping meant special, Erin's wedding would be the most special day anyone had ever seen.

Chapter Twenty-Eight

Katie stood at the front of the church and scanned the audience until she spotted her dad. She'd thought he was going to sit near the back with Sammy, but it looked like Gigi B had intervened. He sat next to her in the rows reserved for the family of the bride. Katie smiled. At least he didn't have to sit alone or try to wrestle her squirmy six month old son by himself. Gigi B would make sure they were both well taken care of.

As the bridal march played, Katie's attention was drawn to the back of the church along with everyone else's. The guests rose from their seats as Erin and her father started down the aisle. Erin's eyes shone as she looked at the stage or more specifically the man waiting for her at the front of the church. Katie stole a glance at Paul who stood only a few feet from her watching his bride.

Erin's vision for the wedding was spot on. Paul looked his handsomest in the tailored dove gray suit with royal purple tie. It complemented the style of the rest of the wedding party flawlessly. As Erin's father placed her hand in Paul's and took his seat, Katie noticed Paul's blue eyes sparkling with more than happiness. She couldn't see Erin's face, but she could almost guarantee she'd find tears brimming there too.

Katie was surprised to find she wasn't struggling with the same inclination. Off and on as the wedding day approached, her feelings had been a roller coaster. She was ecstatic for her friends. The brief time she'd known as a married woman had been one of the sweetest chapters of her life. Living and serving side by side with the man she loved had been better than anything she'd ever imagined. It was only made happier by the news of Sammy's pending arrival. Now, her best friends were going to know the same joy she'd known.

That was the blessing of the wedding, but it was also the doorway to the sadness she'd been fighting the last few weeks. Her own wedding hadn't been that long ago. Her happy dream had turned into a nightmare all too quickly. She'd recently had to fight to keep Erin and Paul's happy moments from shining a light on her own devastation.

At times, she was sure Erin had known of her struggle, but neither mentioned it. It wasn't fair to them to have the cloud of her loss darkening their happiest day. So, Katie had kept it to herself and pushed her feelings to the back of her mind, only letting the pain surface again when she lay alone in her bed each night.

But today was a day to, once again, focus on the happy side of things. God had blessed her with two amazing friends who'd stood beside her through her worst and celebrated with her in the best times. And God had chosen to bless them with a love that was full of life and solidly based on their faith in Him. Though it meant losing a friend to the distance between Carbondale and Bloomington, she couldn't begrudge them their love.

She watched them pick up their individual taper candles to light the pillar candle standing between them. *Lord, let their love for each other and for You always keep them working together as one. They are so different in personality and style. Don't let them lose who they are, but work in them to make their differences complement each other as they face the ups and downs of life together. Amen.*

"I'M NOT A SPEECH PERSON." Katie announced her deficit as she stood nervously in front of the crowd gathered for the reception. She fought the urge to sit down, ignoring the duties of the matron of honor. A glance at Erin's upturned face smiling at her gave her the courage to continue. "But if anyone deserves a speech in their honor, it's Erin. It's hard to believe but when I came back to Carbondale, I wasn't the easiest person to love. Erin did anyway without reservation or question. She befriended me when I needed one and moved me out of my comfort zone. She loves life and embraces who she is with abandon. That is an inspiration to me. Her example encourages me to accept the same in myself. She gets me to loosen up when I need to, but she's also stood beside me and held me up in my darkest times. She's been my best friend, a better one to me than I've been to her at times. And now, she gets to be that and more for someone new."

Katie included Paul in her gaze. "Paul, God blessed me with Erin when I needed her most. And though I know our friendship will last our lifetimes, it's going to change with this new adventure you and Erin are beginning. I know what it's like to have Erin in your corner. It's an amazing gift to have Erin as your cheerleader, confidant, and challenger. And it's a gift that you're getting to enjoy today and for the rest of your life. Knowing what it's like from experience, it would be easy to envy you. But I'd rather just be happy for you both. Treat my best friend well." She raised her glass of punch. "To Erin and Paul, may God bless your journey together using each of you to bring out the best in the other. Congratulations."

"YOUR SPEECH WAS WONDERFUL."

Gigi B's compliment pulled Katie from her thoughts as she

worked to pack up the reception decorations. "Thank you, but Erin deserved that and then some. She's an amazing Christian woman and a great friend. I couldn't be happier for her and Paul."

Gigi B's slender hand came to rest on her forearm stilling her cleaning. "I love my granddaughter more than you can imagine. I'm so proud of the woman she's become. But you do understand, don't you, that you've also been a great friend to her? She's what you'd call a social butterfly, but that doesn't mean she's had opportunity to collect teems of close friends. Her free spirit is a blessing and a curse. It draws people to her because she's fun and easy to be around. But often those same people who seek her out for the good times fail to see her worth in the difficult times. You've accepted both in her, and that has been a wonderful gift to her. When I look at her I see a loving, Christian woman, but I see the same thing when I look at you."

Katie busied herself with clearing the table as her cheeks heated. "I don't know about all that, but thank you."

The hand rested on her arm again. Gigi B waited to speak until Katie made eye contact. She did so reluctantly. "I know you don't. But I do. Today couldn't have been easy for you. I imagine the memories rode you hard. But you put that aside for your friend. This was supposed to be her happy day, and you let her shine without any reservations. Today you were the definition of a godly, selfless friend. Thank you for taking care of my girl."

Katie bit her lip. To argue or deflect would only create more discomfort as the conversation would continue. Besides, it really didn't matter if she accepted the words. Gigi B believed them to be true, and that's all that mattered. A gracious acceptance of her sentiment was Katie's only choice. "Thank you."

The change in Gigi B was instantaneous reminding Katie where Erin's personality got its start. All seriousness faded from her eyes replaced with exuberant joy for her granddaughter's wedding. "My, wasn't that a great party. I don't think I've had this much fun in ages. And everything was simply beautiful, especially my granddaughter."

Katie scanned what was left of the decorations scattered around the room. Her smile was full. "It was definitely all Erin. I don't think anyone could deny her touch in every part of the ceremony and reception. It was as unique as she is."

Gigi B gathered up a stack of vinyl records and placed them in a box. "You're right about that. When she was a little thing she'd spend the day with me. We'd put on records, a lot of the songs she played today, and we'd look through all my old photo albums from when her mama was just a little thing. She loved the clothes. She'd beg to go through my scarves and bandanas. I don't know why I never got rid of them, but I didn't. I kept them in an old candy box, and Erin loved to go through it. She'd try on different ones each time and spend the rest of the day with her hair up and a scarf tied to the side around her neck. Those are memories that I'll always treasure. Today was like getting to go back in time to those childhood visits. It warms this grandma's heart to know the days we spent together touched her in such a special way too."

"I can't deny you two share the same tastes in music and clothes. But you've shared more with her than just those superficial things. She changes people for the better. She can't help it. It's who she is, and I'm pretty sure she gets that from you too."

"Hmmm." Gigi B didn't argue or agree, but her silent smile before she moved to the next table told Katie she'd made her point.

Katie watched her for a moment before returning to the task of gathering up the flowers and sundae cups from the centerpieces. Gigi B had a point about her struggles through the planning and execution of the wedding. She had experienced ups and downs through the last few weeks. Sometimes she'd thought her heart might break all over again. But now, with her friends married and on their honeymoon, she couldn't think of one thing to be down about. It was a beautiful day, and she felt blessed that the happy couple had given her the opportunity to be part of it.

Chapter Twenty-Nine

Katie stared out Sammy's bedroom window while he played on the colorful, musical play mat her dad brought home for him after his last trip to the store. The leaves on the trees beyond the barn yard were still green, but that wouldn't last much longer. Within a month the quickly dropping temperatures and shorter days would cause the riot of fall color she loved. The whole landscape would change with the arrival of autumn.

Things were always changing. It amazed her. How could everything in life change so drastically in such a short amount of time? It was almost too much to take in. A sigh escaped without warning.

She started at her dad's voice from the doorway. "Katydid, you've been home almost five months. With getting settled and the wedding and everything little Sammy needs, you've run every moment since you got back. I see you staring out every window in this house, and you're looking at the same thing every time. I think it's high time you follow your heart where it's leading. I've got Sammy. You go on. Take a walk down that familiar path and take some time for yourself."

She shook her head. “I can’t go now. It’s almost time for me to get dinner started.”

“Nonsense. I may be getting older, but I’m still capable. I can handle seeing to our dinner while watching my grandson. You need to take care of yourself for once.”

Katie considered his offer. It was on the tip of her tongue to decline. She looked over her shoulder and out the window. It would be nice to finally get down to the waterfall. Maybe just this once she could put aside the things she should do for the one thing she needed to do for herself. She looked back to her dad. His eyes were full of expectancy.

Realization hit Katie. He wasn’t offering to be nice. This wasn’t one adult doing a favor to help out another adult. This was her father offering to take care of his little girl. He wanted more than anything to give her what she needed. For the first time she was able to see that desire through the lens of a parent’s heart. How could she say no to that type of love?

As she crossed the room, she kissed her fingers and brushed them across Sammy’s silky hair. “I’ll be back in a bit. You be good for your grandpa.”

She stopped in front of her dad. Though not often given to overt displays of affection, she wrapped him in a firm hug. “Thank you, Daddy. I love you.”

“Get on out of here. And don’t come back until you’ve had the time you need.”

He didn’t need to tell her twice. Katie left the room and made her way down the stairs, pausing only long enough to grab her jean jacket from the peg by the door before heading towards the tree line beyond the old pasture. Even with the trail more grown up than she remembered, Katie could have walked the path to the creek blindfolded.

She followed the creek as it sloped slowly downward. Though she wore a jacket, the cool air kept her from getting hot. Summer rains had swollen the creek so that the water bubbled over the rocky bed creating a peaceful gurgle as she walked along the edge. In minutes she reached the place where the bed fell sharply creating a small waterfall that pooled below. Katie sat on the flat rock at the top of the fall and pulled off her shoes and socks. It was too cool to dip her toes into the water, but she still didn't want to chance them getting wet.

She shut her eyes and let her senses take over. Cool air and tiny droplets of water swept over the bare skin of her feet. She could feel rays of sun hitting her cheeks as they fought their way through the canopy of leaves overhead. She breathed in the scent of water and earth. Silence wasn't really silent. The water spilling over the edge of the fall gently splashed into the still pool. Birds chirped in the background. Silence had given way to sounds of peace, and she allowed them to fill her spirit. Katie thought she'd found it when she moved back in with her dad, but in this moment she knew beyond a doubt she'd come back home.

She considered everything that brought her to this point. Her love and her loss. The joy of becoming a mother and the heartbreak of losing his father. The pleasure of watching her friends fall in love and the loneliness that came with having them move away. Every event had played a part in bringing her to this place and had helped shape her into the woman she was today.

She knew she'd never be able to say she enjoyed every part of her journey. There were parts she wouldn't wish on her worst enemies, but she could look back and see God with her in those fires and how God brought her through them in the end.

Even now, Katie didn't have the answers of what tomorrow would bring. There were no assurances that all was going to work out like a fairy tale now that she'd come through the fires. There were unanswered questions and worries she hadn't even voiced to herself, much less to God. But she didn't need to fear the unknown any more. She'd found the hope that would keep her through anything life would bring her way. She'd found it when she'd finally come to see that no matter what happened on her journey, God was right beside her loving her and strengthening her.

When had her heart changed so completely? She couldn't single out one individual event, but each step along the way had softened it. By the time God planted in her mind the vision of Himself standing with her in the fire, her heart was finally ready to receive the truth of God's message for her. With her surrender, she opened herself up for God to work in the circumstances. God never left her alone to face the challenges and His love never dimmed. But more than that, He was always working to grow beautiful things in her life and replace her ashes with something of beauty. This was the hope she could cling to no matter what she faced.

Katie pulled her feet up from the waterfall and used the outside of her socks to dry the mist from them before putting them on. She slipped her shoes back on and stood up from her place on the rock. She knew she would visit this spot again. And she knew she would find peace when she did, but it wasn't this place or nature itself that ushered it into her heart. The peace came because at the side of the waterfall with her feet dangling over the edge she sat quietly in God's presence. Maybe one day she would learn to do that wherever she was. For now, she was grateful God had given her the gift of this place.

"Thank you, Father, for everything. Thank you for being my hope." The praise slipped effortlessly from her lips with complete sincerity. She turned from the waterfall to make her way back to the path. It was time for Katie to go home.

Acknowledgments

I never want to fail to thank God for His blessings, not the least of which is being able to minister doing something I love to do. I pray I can bring Him glory and honor through this ministry.

Thank you to my husband, Andy, I'm blessed to walk through this life with you. You've been my cheerleader and encouraged me to grow. And even though you secretly wanted it for yourself, you gave me the empty room to use for writing when our son moved out. Thank you for that and everything you do to support me.

Thank you to my children, including the in-laws, for believing in and encouraging me. For those at home, thanks for your willingness to put up with "whatever you find in the kitchen" instead of home cooked meals when I'm up against deadlines. God blessed me greatly by giving me you.

Thank you to Kathy Cretsinger and the Mantle Rock Publishing team for this opportunity and working so hard to make Grasping Hope a reality. Your patience and dedication are appreciated. I'm proud to be one of the Mantle Rock family.

Last but not least, thank you to those who had a special hand in making this book what it is. To the Carbondale Christian Writer's Group, I can't explain what a blessing it is for you to edit, critique, and encourage me as I write. To Kelly B, thanks for being that voice in my head telling me to write and for letting me borrow Nathan. And to my own Gigi B, you are the best “aunt” a girl could have, and I couldn’t have asked for better inspiration for this character.

About the Author

Heather Greer grew up as a pastor's kid in rural southern Illinois and has been a pastor's wife for the past thirteen years. With various ministries playing a large role in her life from childhood through adulthood, she has experienced first-hand the ins and outs of faith in small churches from the Bible belt. It has also given her a passion to equip other believers with tools to help them understand and grow in their own relationships with God. When she isn't busy with ministry or writing, Heather enjoys baking and spending time with her husband, four children, and grandson.

Also by Heather Greer

Katie McGowan left her parents and their faith behind years ago. However, when faced with a devastating betrayal, Katie is ready to go back to Carbondale, Illinois to help her elderly parents despite their tempestuous relationship. Drained by the constant friction, Katie finds emotional support and encouragement in Austin. His practical, simple faith speaks to Katie, and she finds herself yearning for a new connection to God. As their friendship grows, so does the attraction between Katie and Austin. Before her fledgling faith and thoughts of romance have a chance to take root, Katie's cheating fiancé returns, remorseful and promising change. Can her tentative faith strengthen their past love? And if her heart breaks again, will Katie's journey to faith end before it has really begun?

Also from Mantle Rock Publishing

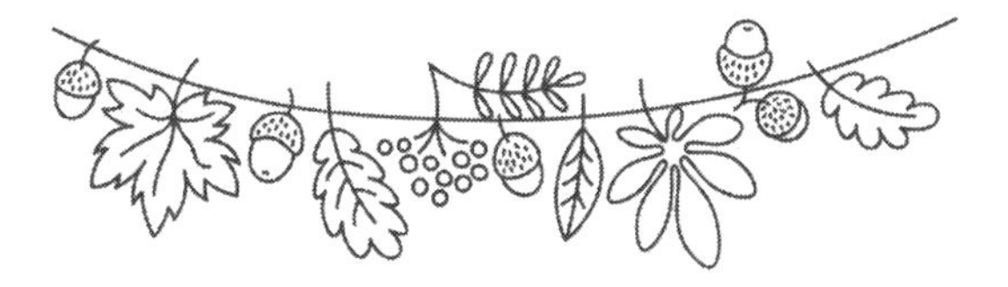

Cheryl Richardson doesn't know that her landlord who owns the other half of the duplex where she lives is plotting to build a bomb—but the FBI does. In order to discover what her landlord is planning to blow up, agent Steve Gableman moves next door to get closer to Cheryl to learn what she knows, namely the target and motive, so they can stop it. But when Steve involves himself in every area of her life, including her dog, will Cheryl be the one to explode?

The Other Neighbor by Gail Sattler.

~

First-year Special Education teacher Charly Livingston demonstrates God's love on the outside but is resentful that God allowed back-to-back tragedies in her family.

Rance Butler is a top-notch medical intern. He's on his way to the top, and when he meets Charly, he knows things will only get better. When he discovers family secrets and a dying father he never knew, his easy, carefree life seems to disintegrate.

Even in the idyllic ocean breezes and South Carolina sunshine, contentment turns to bitterness and confusion except for God's amazing grace.

Carolina Grace, the third book in the Southern Breeze Series by Regina Rudd Merrick.